# POWDER BURNS

AN ORPHIC ASSASSIN NOVEL

## SAM LUNA

*For the Paramount Movie Club*
*My first readers*

Powder Burns
An Orphic Assassin Novel

Sam Luna

I told them to fix their hearts or die.

— *David Lynch*

# PROLOGUE

*Los Angeles, California; Present Day*

Damien waited for the third chime from the doorbell before opening his front door—his left hand on the knob, right on the nine-millimeter pistol tucked behind his back. The man on the other side was graying, bookish, and smiling.

Damien relaxed his finger off the trigger and smiled in return.

"Hi there," said the man.

"Hello," Damien replied.

"This your property, sir?"

Damien nodded.

"You're not a renter then. You own this house?"

"Yes," Damien said. "Something the matter?"

"No. Well, I hope not anyway. I'm a biologist with the park service. Max Berke."

Max dug into his front shirt pocket and produced his business card, glossy in the late-afternoon light.

Damien read it over. "One second." He stepped behind his door, placed the weapon in the umbrella stand, then walked back out to the porch. "What can I do for you, Mr. Berke?" he asked, closing the door behind him.

"Call me Max. Sorry, I didn't ask your name."

"Damien."

"This is going to sound a bit strange, Damien," Max said. "You'll have to bear with me."

"All right."

"Part of what I do with the park service is animal tracking. I monitor several species in the Los Angeles area. Coyote packs, for example. One of the animals my team tracks is a cougar. A mountain lion known as C-33. She roams the area right over there, in Griffith Park." Max pointed southeast. "Not far from these hills."

"Sure," Damien replied. "The Hollywood sign photo, right?"

"Yes! Exactly. Yes. That's her. One of our motion cameras caught C-33 as she walked right in front of the Hollywood sign. So you're familiar with her."

Damien smiled. "It's a fantastic photo."

"Well, thanks. We were thrilled with it. It did a lot to publicize our conservation efforts."

"I'll bet."

"About this time last year, we darted C-33 with a tranquilizer and fitted her with a collar. A radio collar."

"Wow."

"Every few months since then, we catch up with her and tranquilize her again, and we remove the collar," Max said. "Has a little gray box on it, with a microprocessor inside. Takes about sixty readings a week, mapping out her coordinates."

"That's interesting," Damien said.

"We think so," Max said, laughing. "So this last reading, we discovered something very unexpected. C-33 has been leaving the confines of Griffith Park, her usual territory, and has moved into this area here in the Hollywood Hills."

"Really?"

"Oh, yeah. Even more amazing is that she keeps returning to the same spot over and over. Almost every night for the last couple of months, in fact."

Damien crossed his arms and nodded, his green eyes wide with curiosity. "Where does she go?"

"Right here." Max pointed to Damien's porch. "And when I say right here, I mean *right here*."

Damien followed Max's finger to the porch. "Seriously?"

Max nodded. "I'm completely serious. This animal returns to your house again and again."

"My house."

"Yes."

"You're kidding me."

"Nope."

Damien looked up and down the length of the expansive front deck. "Oh, my goodness."

"I'm not here to alarm you," Max said, "but the park service would be remiss if you weren't made aware. Mountain lions tend to avoid humans, but for some reason this animal has found something that benefits her survival on your property."

"I don't know what to say," Damien replied. "That's incredible."

"Like I said, I'm not here to scare you. I just want to figure out why this lion might be attracted to your home."

"Okay," Damien said.

"Do you keep any type of small farm animals? Chickens or the like?"

"No."

"Dogs? Cats?"

"I travel for work," Damien said. "I don't have any pets."

"Well, that eliminates that then. What about a grill? Cook meat outdoors frequently? A barbecue in your back-yard, maybe?"

"Don't eat meat," Damien said. "Vegetarian."

Max resisted the urge to roll his eyes. Of course the handsome, lean, muscular man standing on the porch of his Spanish colonial revival was a vegetarian. He probably jogged five miles every morning before downing his kale-smoothie breakfast. Thinking of the half-eaten fast-food hamburger on his truck's dashboard down Damien's winding driveway, he forced a smile.

"So I'll cross meat off the list," he said. "What about crit-ters? Raccoons, skunks...they a problem for you?"

"I smell skunks in the winter sometimes, at night," Damien replied. "I usually leave the windows open."

"But you haven't found *dead* animals?" Max asked. "All torn up? Skunk heads, raccoon heads? That kind of thing?"

Damien shook his head.

"Gotcha," Max said.

Max took in the view of Los Angeles from Damien's porch. The ever-present layer of brown summer smog floated above the city as twilight approached.

"Like I said, these animals usually don't want to be around humans," Max continued. "They avoid us. How often do you travel for work?"

"Most of the year," Damien said. "I'm rarely home."

"Well, there you go," Max replied. "It's entirely possible C-33 has found herself a quiet spot to hide out." He stepped down the deck stairs, peering over the railing. "What's under the house?"

Damien shrugged. "Nothing really."

"Any way to easily access it?"

"I don't think so."

"I already know the answer to this, but I'm gonna ask anyway. You haven't heard any crazy sounds at night, right? Screeching or roaring? Giant cat sounds?"

"No."

"The females make certain noises when they're in heat. You would know it if you heard it. Makes your skin crawl."

"God, no. Never heard anything like that."

"Yeah. Figured," Max said, blousing his button-down shirt over his gut as he stepped back up to the porch. "No scratching, growling..."

"Definitely not."

"Yeah. Okay."

Max again removed his card from his pocket and handed it to Damien. "Here's my number."

"Do I need to move?" Damien asked, taking it. "Or get a hotel room?"

"No. That's not necessary. But I'm going to alert this area's animal welfare office of the situation. If for any reason you see or hear anything related to this lion, call me. Anytime. And the park service will send folks out."

"I'm kinda freaked out. Truly."

"The complete opposite of my intention," Max said. "Look, C-33 isn't out here to harm you or anyone else. She's just a lion being a lion. Be careful, sure, but there's no need to panic. She's more scared of you than you are of her."

"Yeah?"

"Yeah."

"Okay," Damien said. "Thanks for the information."

"Thank *you*," Max said, shaking Damien's hand. "Be in touch, okay?"

"I will, Max. My goodness."

Max chuckled. "You've had a mountain lion right under

your nose for the last few months and had no idea. I guarantee you she wants to keep it that way."

Max headed to his SUV. When he reached it, he opened
the door, turned back to Damien, and gave him a salute.

Damien waved in return.

When Max pulled out of his driveway, Damien went
back inside.

---

Damien stopped at his stove and lifted the lid off a pot of
soaking pinto beans. He'd left the nine-millimeter in the
umbrella stand and walked through his living room, empty
of furniture but for the couch he used for sitting and reading, a hobby he rarely had time to enjoy. He passed his
packed bookshelves and headed to the bedroom at the end
of the hallway.

As he opened the door, C-33 raised her head from her
paws, exposing giant yellow incisors with a yawn. Damien
sat on the bed and the lion rolled onto her back, allowing
him to scratch her belly.

As he ran his fingers underneath her radio collar, the
lion's eyes closed into slits, her ears flat against her head
with pleasure. The force of her purring made his hand
vibrate.

*I have to go.*
*Where?*
*You know. Work.*
*Be careful.*
*I will.*
*Promise?*
*Yes. I promise.*
*Okay.*

Damien rose from the bed, eyeing his overnight bag, which he'd already packed for his trip to Manhattan. He went back to the kitchen and his dinner of beans.

That night, the lion lay by Damien's side as he fell asleep. When he started snoring, she left, slipping out the open bedroom window to hunt.

---

Damien checked in with the lobby desk and was shown to the elevator banks, where he informed the security guard he was headed to the fifty-second floor. The guard held the elevator doors, pressed the appropriate button, and twisted a key into a slot.

"Straight up, no waiting," the guard said.

"Many thanks," Damien replied.

He arranged his bag over his shoulder as the elevator ascended.

---

"Mr. Anderson. Hi. Can I get you a water or coffee?"

Damien shook his head and pulled out his parking ticket. "Call me John. And I'm good, thanks. Can I get you to stamp this?"

Damien slid his parking-garage ticket across to the young receptionist, who already had her validation stamp ready. Damien had taken the subway here, but had visited the ticket kiosk on his way up nonetheless. He figured it might buy him a few hours of confusion during the upcoming NYPD response.

The receptionist introduced herself as Julie, offered him a seat in the lobby, then disappeared. He didn't pick up any of the papers or magazines off the coffee table, financial trades he had no interest in beyond his recent research, in which he was now expert.

Ten minutes later, Julie returned. "Mr. Griggs is ready. Right this way."

Damien collected his bag and followed her down a long hall toward the suite.

---

Andrew Griggs appeared exactly as he had on the cover of *Time* magazine: blue suit, red tie, gray hair dyed black and slicked flat against his scalp.

"Hey there!"

Damien pumped his hand, and Andrew pointed to the guest chair in front of his desk.

"Sit, John, please."

"Nice furniture," Damien said, taking his seat.

"I'm an antique nut," Andrew replied. "Well, you've probably already heard all about it. How was your trip?"

"No issues. They didn't drag me off the plane anyway."

Andrew chuckled. "Right? What the hell has happened to air travel in this country?"

"I think you'd probably do okay," Damien said. "You own two private jets."

"Hey, I still put my pants on one leg at a time like every other guy. Did Julie offer you something to drink?"

"Yes, I'm fine," Damien said. "Great office, by the way. Fantastic view."

"Keeps the rain off our heads," Andrew said with a shrug. "Nothing? Water? Coffee? Whiskey?"

"I'm set, sir. Thanks."

Andrew slapped his laptop shut and slid it to the edge of

his desk. "All right, John. Let's hear it. Where should we start?'

"We'll start at the beginning, I suppose, and work our way from there," Damien replied. "But what I really want to talk about today is why you want to write your autobiography. What you want to say about your life and how I might bring that story into being."

"Wow. Yeah. Well, there it is," Andrew said, leaning back in his leather chair. "I dunno. Something for my grandkids to read, I guess. Set the record straight."

"The record," Damien repeated. "Meaning your involvement in reckless lending and shady securities dealings."

Andrew's eyes went wide. "Alleged involvement," he said. "And yeah, that record. You don't waste any time, do you?"

"If I'm going to ghostwrite your autobiography, we have to lay it out on the table, warts and all," Damien said. "The fact is your banks offered exotic mortgages to people who had little to no chance of repaying them. You were one of the architects of the housing bust. You destroyed the financial futures of tens of thousands of people. Decimated pension plans. You're a criminal and a fraud."

Andrew's face twisted into a shocked, tight smile. "Wow," he finally said. "How do you really feel?"

"I feel you're a world-class violator," Damien replied. "And my name's not John. It's Damien. Damien Attica."

Andrew's face fell. "Excuse me?"

"No, Andrew," Damien replied. "I don't think I will."

He rose from his seat and removed an industrial-size window punch from his shoulder bag. Andrew wheeled around in his chair as Damien approached the office's floor-to-ceiling window, brought the tool to the pane of glass, and pulled the lever.

The glass shattered. Damien dropped the window punch and turned around. He then snatched Andrew out of his chair by the throat and crotch, hoisting him over his head like a barbell.

Andrew tried to cry out but was unable to, as his windpipe was sealed shut. Damien tossed him out the window.

He waited until the screaming faded, then peered down just as Andrew's body exploded onto Pearl Street, fifty-two stories below.

Damien pulled out his phone and opened the camera app, then flipped the angle so his own face filled the screen.

His eyes were black.

"Change," Damien whispered. "Change."

His green irises slowly reappeared as a police siren echoed. There was no time to wait. He removed a pair of sunglasses from his pocket and put them on, an unfortunate but necessary accessory that might draw attention on an overcast day.

Damien slipped out of the office and down the corridor past Julie, who was scribbling notes as she listened in on a conference call. He gave her a little wave, and she waved back, making a point to check the time. Her boss had cleared an hour for this appointment, which had only ended up taking a few minutes.

Damien raced down the building's inner stairwells to the lobby before slipping out the revolving doors and pushing through the gawkers converging around what remained of Andrew Griggs.

He returned to his Los Angeles home hoping to find C-33 waiting for him on the couch, but it was empty. He then ate what was left of the beans and went to bed.

The next morning, Damien half listened to cable news while getting dressed. The murder of the infamous Wall Street banker was dominating the headlines. The aerial footage of the glassless office window, juxtaposed by a white sheet over Andrew Griggs's body fifty-two stories below, sat in a box in the upper-left-hand corner of the screen as the pundits debated whether the incident was terrorist related. The current thinking was that it wasn't.

"It stands to reason the man had many enemies," the morning host opined.

Damien stood up from his bed and grabbed his keys from the bureau.

Traffic on Wilshire was particularly bad, even for rush hour. He crawled along in his red Mustang convertible, dreading this morning's appointment.

He arrived at the waiting room five minutes late and pushed the call button on the wall underneath a bronze placard that read:

PAST-LIFE REGRESSION HYPNOTHERAPY
PARTNERS OF LOS ANGELES

A minute went by, and he anxiously shifted in his seat.

Just over a year had passed since Damien's first session in this place. He had picked it at random off a list generated from a search engine query: *expert on dreams that might be a past life in Los Angeles.* The top result went straight to voice-mail. The second answered on the first ring.

The woman on the other end was kind and didn't interrupt his monologue, only listened. Damien told of childhood night terrors and waking up stuck to his sheets, drenched in sweat. Of dreams in places that felt more real than those he visited on a daily basis, and people he could still hear and even smell upon waking. She said *yes* and *uh huh* and scribbled down notes. When he finished she told him to come in the next morning at nine, if he could make it. He could, and he did.

The first sessions were awkward and fruitless. Damien had a great deal of difficulty submitting to hypnosis at first, but in time realized it was less a parlor trick and more a simple agreement. If he were willing to suspend disbelief and open himself to suggestion, she would reward him with insight that gave shape to his nightmares. Once this bargain was struck, progress was made.

Over time the dreams became stories, told and retold with little discrepancy between sessions. His sleep improved. He had kept faithful appointments ever since.

The door finally opened, and his hypnotherapist Angela waved him inside with a smile.

"How are you?" she asked as they headed for the dark room at the end of the hall. Her long gray braided hair swung above a flowing hand-stitched skirt, the hippie throwback ensemble smelling of patchouli oil and incense.

"Can't complain," Damien said.

"Did you see the thing about that Wall Street guy getting thrown out of a building in New York?"

"Yeah."

"So crazy. Right?"

"Yeah."

She stepped to the side, allowing Damien to enter the room first. He sat in the same overstuffed chair he always did, underneath the framed hypnotherapy license displayed on the wall.

The light on the coffee table pulsed blue then green, red then yellow, blue then green.

"I want to hear about the cowboy today," Angela said, her tone light and soothing. "The outlaw. You were just starting to get some clarity with that."

The colors swirled within the light, the room's curtains drawn.

"Okay," he said.

"Watch the light. Relax. Take all the time you need. All the time in the world."

"Okay."

"Are you comfortable, Damien?"

"Yes."

"Good. Breathe in on a count of four."

Damien did so.

"And hold for a count of seven."

The room was quiet for seven seconds, save for the distant traffic on Wilshire.

"And slowly release on a count of eight," she instructed.

Damien did so.

"Breathe in on a count of four."

Damien's shoulders dropped.

"I want to hear more about the cowboy. Watch the light. And slowly release on a count of eight."

Damien did.

"Breathe in on a count of four. The outlaw. Hold for a count of seven. The cowboy. And slowly release on a count of eight. The outlaw. Breathe in on a count of four. Hold for a count of seven. Go into the light, Damien. And release on a count of eight. The cowboy. Breathe in on a count of four. Hold for a count of seven. And release on a count of eight. The outlaw. Breathe in on a count of four. Go into the light, Damien. Hold for a count of seven. And release on a count of eight. The cowboy. Breathe in on a count of four. Hold for a count of seven. And release on a count of eight. Go into the light, Damien. The outlaw. Breathe in on a count of four. Hold for a count of seven. And release on a count of eight. The outlaw…"

Damien went into the light.

# PART I

## CHINDI

## 1

_____

*Hades, Banks of Acheron*

He had crawled a thousand miles through hell by the time he reached the Pool of Memory, his throat slashed, his veins bloodless. Greeting him at the water's edge stood a demon, perched high above on a bone-white rock, her lips parted in a smile. She was the most beautiful and most terrifying thing he had ever seen.

"I am Damien of Attica," he said, rising to his feet.

At a sudden loss for what he was supposed to say next, he grasped the gold chain that dangled from his neck. His hands trembled as he removed it, fumbling with a small cylinder attached to the necklace. He opened it and pulled out a parchment, then unrolled it and read the words he'd transcribed in the temple the morning of his death.

"I am but mortal flesh, a child of the gods," he recited. "Take pity on me, and allow me to drink from the sacred water."

Finished with the requisite greeting, he replaced the parchment and put the necklace back on, his eyes cast on the scorched ground beneath his feet, unable to look the demon in her wide black eyes. He had an overwhelming fear that he would lose what little was left of his sanity if he did.

"Greetings, Orphic," she finally said, her voice low and soft. "Indeed we are well met." She unfurled a talon at the end of a long, thin finger and pointed to the clear liquid in the pool between them. "You may drink."

Damien fell to his knees and dipped his hand, the swollen tongue protruding from his mouth salivating at the promise of its thirst being quenched. He cupped the water and had nearly put it to his lips, when the demon again spoke.

"The gods have bestowed a gift upon you. A unique one, I think. I trust you will use it well. To do any less would be an insult to them. And to me."

Damien let the water pour out of his hand. Summoning his courage, he looked up to her, at the shining pulsating organs beneath her translucent skin. "I will do my best," he said.

"I should hope so," the demon replied.

He bowed his head respectfully and again dipped his hand.

"One last thing before you leave," she said.

Although Damien was mad with thirst, he stopped himself from drinking. He lifted his head, body going numb at the smile that had returned to the demon's face, revealing her mouthful of razor-sharp fangs.

"Whatever happens in this next life, there is one thing, one *rule* you must abide by," she said.

Damien swallowed dryly. "And what is that?" he asked.

The demon leaned forward, her dark eyes narrowing. "Don't bore me."

Damien brought the water to his lips and drank.

## 2

---

*Silver City, New Mexico Territory; October 1855*

Colonel Balazarus sat with a dead Steller's jay in his right hand, his left pushing a wad of cotton into the bird's hollowed-out body cavity with a pair of forceps. The knock at his door went unanswered until he had filled out the carcass's thorax to his satisfaction. Only then did he set the jay down, sweeping a loose piece of cotton off his desk and onto the floor.

"Enter."

The door swung open, and Jimmy poked his head inside, shotgun in hand.

"Dude's here to see you, Colonel."

"What dude?"

"Letter-on-the-blue-paper dude."

Acid flooded the colonel's stomach as the contents of the letter replayed in his mind. He had lost sleep over it, and although that alone would have been enough for him to vow retribution, it was the letter's condescending tone that had stoked his ire for the better part of the last three months. The only thing that had allowed him to fall asleep or finish a meal was the contemplation of what he would do to its author when he finally met him.

The colonel removed his army slouch hat from his head; the sweat that had broken out on his scalp was sufficient to smooth down what little hair was left. He heard Jimmy invite the man to stand up from the bench in the hallway and walk toward the office.

Another knock at his door and Balazarus straightened in his seat. "Enter."

The door opened and Jimmy shuffled in, carrying the shotgun. The man following closely behind him made the colonel burst into laughter.

He was a dandy, dressed comically in a colorful suit, a straw bowler hat atop his head. He was grinning, his well-kept teeth stretched across a gaunt face, eyes green and bright behind gold-rimmed glasses.

"Colonel Balazarus, so good of you to see me, sir," the dandy said. "May I sit?"

The colonel rolled his head and cracked his neck as Jimmy headed to a wooden stool in the corner. He grabbed it with his free hand and plunked it on the floor behind the dandy's knees.

"Much obliged." The dandy sat.

Jimmy took his post in the back corner of the room, holding the barrel of the shotgun across his left palm, his finger resting an inch above the trigger. The dandy cleared his throat then crossed his legs in a manner Jimmy had only seen women and young girls do.

"Colonel, I will be brief," the dandy said. "My name is Mr. Anderson. John McKenzie Anderson. I represent the interests of one George Llewelyn. He is your tenant on the acreage owned by Mr. Isaac Greeley's land trust north of Silver City."

Jimmy's eyes flicked from the back of the dandy's head to his boss, whose jaw muscles clenched and unclenched under his whiskered skin.

"As you are well aware, through various letters and subsequent telegrams, Mr. Llewelyn's daughter Josephina was violated in a most intimate way by your agent, Mr. Morrow, while collecting rent," the dandy continued. "Are you aware of this, sir?"

Balazarus leaned back in his chair, hitching his pants up around his belly and glancing across the room to Jimmy. "Is he speaking English?" He looked back at the dandy. "Are you speaking English?"

The dandy smiled. "Forgive my magniloquence. I will speak plainly," the dandy said. "He raped her. Are you aware of this?"

"I am aware," the colonel replied. "Also aware Morrow got shot and disemboweled two weeks ago in Tularosa."

The dandy doffed his hat, leaned forward, and carefully set it on the edge of the colonel's desk in the empty space between a large hunk of obsidian rock and a wooden carving of a duck. He resumed his upright position, both hands resting on his crossed knee. The dark hair on his crown stood up in wisps, enhancing his overall visual absurdity.

"The girl, who is my principal concern, has never recovered her faculties," the dandy continued. "She is currently under the care of the Sisters of the Good Shepherd outside of Santa Fe."

"Brief," the colonel croaked.

"I'm sorry?" replied the dandy, cupping his palm to his ear.

The colonel leaned forward, brow creased. "You said you'd be brief. And how about you speak English?"

"Yes," the dandy said. "Indeed."

He reached into the attaché next to the stool, taking the colonel's gunman by surprise. Jimmy raised his shotgun, aiming it square at the back of the dandy's head.

"Take your goddamn hand outta there 'fore I blast it off its wrist, shitbird," Jimmy barked.

The dandy raised an empty hand and sat upright. "No offense intended."

Jimmy stepped forward, the shotgun trained on the dandy, his free hand reaching down to pick up the case. He took it by the handle and backtracked to the corner of the room where he could inspect the contents. He fished inside the bag and pulled out a fistful of papers covered in scribbling he couldn't read.

"Just paper, Colonel."

The dandy raised both hands in supplication, looking between Jimmy and the colonel. "My sole intention," he said.

When Jimmy dropped the papers on the floor next to the stool, the dandy reached down and retrieved them. He licked his index finger, flipped through the stack, and stopped at one page.

"Mr. Llewelyn has found no satisfaction for the crime committed against his daughter with the county's sheriff, nor the local courts. Due I'm sure to Mr. Greeley's, shall we say, overwhelming influence on the community of Silver City, Colonel." The dandy looked up from the document for the colonel's reaction. Receiving none, he continued. "I am here to tell you that Mr. Llewelyn, my client, *will* be satisfied. And I will be the agent who brings about that satisfaction."

The dandy released the paper in such a way that a bit of breeze floated it across to the colonel, its short journey to the desk stopped by the dead bird.

"Fuck is that?" Colonel Balazarus asked.

"My client seeks compensatory damages in the amount of five hundred dollars," the dandy said. "This figure is the sum of his daughter's hospitalization, the income to the farm lost while she convalesced and during her current stay at the nunnery, and her transport via locomotive to Santa Fe."

The dandy removed his gold-rimmed glasses, dropped them into his suit's inner front pocket, and folded his hands on his lap.

Colonel Balazarus glanced at Jimmy, then back at the man across from him in his immaculately tailored suit, sitting as prim and proper as could be. And then he laughed.

"I'm sorry, Colonel. Is something funny?" asked the dandy.

"Yeah, something's funny," the colonel said, catching his breath. "That silly getup you're wearing, for starters. And these here papers, them's the punch line."

The colonel slammed his fist on the desk, the force of which made the dead Steller's jay pop up and onto the floor. No longer laughing, he glared at John McKenzie Anderson.

"You ever see a day's combat in your miserable life, you squirtified dandy fuck?" asked the colonel, spitting the words through clenched teeth.

"No," the dandy answered.

"Ever seen a man with a fresh pellet in his eyeball, metal still smokin' with gun heat? Writhin' around in the dirt, calling for his mama?"

The dandy adjusted the cufflink on his left shirtsleeve, a gesture Jimmy found to be unnaturally casual under the circumstances.

"No, sir," replied the dandy.

"You ever see a man get shot? Bleed out in your arms?

"No."

"Well, I have," said the colonel. "I seen all those things. They ain't things you forget."

Colonel Balazarus rose from his seat and planted his meaty hands on the oak desktop. His nostrils expanded with each word, as if he were a bull readying himself to charge across the room and pin the dandy to the wall with one of his horns.

"You get them papers off my desk and the fuck out of my office, and you'll leave with your balls. That's the best I have to offer. To you and your fucking *client*. You hear me?"

The room was quiet for a moment, the only sound a teamster-driven stagecoach outside the windows. Jimmy looked to the dandy, wholly baffled as to how he could be sitting there so calmly in the face of the colonel's threats. When the dandy rose to his feet, Jimmy's finger slipped back onto the trigger. Although there was seemingly no reason to be, he was surprised to find himself frightened by the man.

"Sir," the dandy said, his voice steady. "I am compelled to disclose to you that if you do not appear in Silver City to address these grievances, Mr. Llewelyn will have no choice but to employ the services of Damien Attica."

It was as if the air had been sucked out of the room.

"What...what'd you just say?" the colonel replied.

"Damien Attica, sir. He is here in the territory and has made my client's acquaintance. Mr. Attica is ready to take on this case, so to speak, if Mr. Llewelyn is left without recompense."

Colonel Balazarus sank back into his chair. "I'm going to let you live, Mister whatever your name is, for one reason and one reason only. And that's to tell your client he has one day to clear off my property. One day. Or I'll start burning things."

"Colonel—"

"Threaten me with some no-account assassin motherfucker? *Here*?"

The dandy held up a hand, stopping Balazarus' speech. "Colonel. Legend has it Mr. Attica can shoot the wings off a housefly at fifty paces, and that apparently is no exaggeration. I'm confident you're aware of that."

"I'm aware," the colonel said, "that I could spot Attica six miles outside of town, not that he wouldn't be dead ten seconds after he crossed my county line. Attica don't scare me."

"They say he's a master of disguise," the dandy said with a shrug.

The colonel maintained his dark expression. "They'll say anything to sell their fucking newspapers. And now you have my message. Better deliver it while my mind's inclined to let you live long enough to do so."

The dandy exhaled and removed a fob watch from his waistcoat before consulting the time. "Colonel," he said, retrieving his bowler hat off the desk. He reached down, picked up his attaché, and headed for the door. He was nearly through it when he stopped short, turning to the men as if he'd just remembered something he meant to say.

The dandy stepped back inside and pointed to the shotgun in Jimmy's hands. Jimmy stared at the dandy's finger, then up at his face, finding himself frozen to the floor at what he saw.

The dandy's green eyes had turned solid black.

"May I borrow this?" the dandy asked, and grabbed the shotgun.

With one strong move, he twisted it over in Jimmy's

hands so the barrel was pointed to the floor. As Jimmy tried to wrestle the weapon away, the shotgun went off. He screamed, staring down at the blood pooling around bits of bone that moments earlier had been his toes. The dandy then spun the shotgun and jammed the hot metal barrel under Jimmy's chin.

He lifted the lackey's wide, terrified eyes to his own, which were as black as the obsidian rock on the colonel's desk.

The second blast took the top of Jimmy's head off, ventilating his brains onto the wallpaper.

The dandy, now revealed as the assassin Damien Attica, expected to find the colonel at arms. Instead he found him frantically trying to squeeze his fat frame through the double-hung window behind his desk. Damien raised the shotgun in one hand, discharging the final shell into the colonel's buttocks.

"*Christ Jesus!*" Balazarus shouted, falling backward through the window and onto the floor. He rolled onto his stomach, face crimson, eyes bulging in their sockets. Smoke rose from the dark wet hole in the back of his pants, the fabric catching fire from the heat of the shotgun pellets.

The colonel slapped at the flames as Damien cracked the shotgun's cylinder open, ejecting the spent casings.

"Where are they?" he inquired, the tone of his voice as low and even as if he were asking for a glass of water.

His sweating face creased in agony, the colonel, who had managed to extinguish the flames, looked up at Damien. "Where is wh-what?" he stammered.

"Shells," Damien replied, as if there could be no other reasonable answer.

"Greeley's gonna fuckin' k-kill you, Attica. You're a dead man."

"Top drawer?" Damien asked, walking to the colonel's desk and pulling it open. A white box sat among the bits of pencil and paper. Damien flipped the top open, revealing twelve fresh red-topped shotgun shells.

"Top drawer."

He snapped the cylinder shut, then wedged his right foot under the colonel's hip before rolling him onto his back like a sack of grain. The colonel looked up at the dark-eyed man above him and gasped.

Damien raised the shotgun and fired a shell into Balazarus's crotch, sending the man's head against the floor with an eye-watering shriek. He then set the barrel on the colonel's right cheek and pulled the trigger.

He stepped back, studying the man to ensure his wounds were fatal. They were. The man's right eye and most of his nose were gone, a halo of blood seeping from under what was left of his skull. Satisfied, Damien looked back to Jimmy, an unwitting casualty in this portion of the contracted assignment. He too was undoubtedly deceased, the wall above his corpse liberally coated with the contents of his head. The job here was done.

Damien exited the office and headed into the wood paneled hallway. The lobby was decorated with taxidermy animal heads, dozens of glass eyes staring lifelessly. He glanced them over: a fox, a badger, a wild boar, and a magnificent elk's head. The colonel had killed them all by his own hand, had shot and stabbed them and slit their throats and caused them pain, fear, and agony. Replaying the scene from moments earlier in his head, Damien felt better.

He yanked off his bow tie—the better to breathe without it—and ripped his collar open. He pointed the barrel of the shotgun to the floor as he left through the recently departed colonel's front doors, hoping the crowd who had gathered outside would react less hysterically to a man emerging not fully at arms.

Half the town stood gathered on the raised wooden sidewalks, children protectively clasped against their mothers' skirts, a hundred wide eyes waiting to see what sort of gunman would emerge from the colonel's office. Damien made a beeline for his horse, a black Morgan colt acquired days earlier while he had executed Morrow.

A sparrow flew down from the sky, landing on his shoulder. More birds converged, fluttering from the woodsheds and barns and butcheries and all manner of structures lining the town's stinking thoroughfare. They all perched themselves along the road, singing.

He gently tugged on the Morgan's reins, carefully steering it among the congregation covering the path. The flock followed.

Damien didn't seek attention, and when it was given, it brought him the heat of embarrassment. So he lowered his head to the horn of the Morgan's saddle and rode that way out of town, the birdsongs heralding his departure.

---

He rode an hour's journey, returning to the previous evening's camp. It lay within a small grove of pines at the base of the Sacramento Mountains, their growth stunted by a season's lack of rain. He tied the Morgan to one such tree and inspected his campfire, poking at it with the end of a branch. He then spread out his bedroll under a canopy of shade the trees provided, lay on top, and kicked off his shoes.

Damien wiggled his toes, pushing blood back into the

extremities, and picked up a well-worn book, finding his page. It was a novel written by Walt Whitman, about a man named Franklin Evans and his journey out of alcoholism. Damien had read the book several times. After only a few pages, his eyes grew heavy, the book falling open onto his chest. In a matter of moments, he was deep asleep and, very soon after, dreaming.

# 3

---

*Attica Peninsula, Greece; the Month of Thargelion, 435 BC*

When Damien dreamed, it was of his first life, the one he had lived centuries earlier on the peninsula that had given him his name. In this day's memory dream he was twelve, seated on a cliffside rock bleached white by the sun, his feet splashing in the sea. That afternoon, the wine in which he dipped his barley bread wasn't diluted with water —the first time it had been served to him this way. Feeling giddy, he watched the sunlight play off the surface of the water.

"Damien."

Ignatia stood beside him, tall and lithe, hands clasped behind her cotton smock. She was the youngest music teacher at the Orphic temple and also the most patient and kind. Damien set his krater of wine on the sand.

"Drink your wine," she said.

Obediently he picked it back up and swallowed the remainder, the red liquid blooming warm in his chest. Ignatia sat next to him and pulled her smock up to her knees, the sea foam running between her toes. Her hazel eyes searched his for a moment before she spoke.

"Damien, it is time to talk about why you are here."

Not a week went by that Ignatia didn't bring up this subject, and he answered her the way he had every single time before. "I am here to learn about the gods."

Ignatia looked over the sea, the breeze sending her auburn hair into her eyes, which she brushed away. "I am going to show you something today. What I will show you is not meant for children's eyes. But then you're not like the other children, are you?"

Damien didn't know how to respond. His teacher walked back up the hill, and he followed.

---

When they entered the temple, Ignatia pulled Damien by the hand down the dark stone hallway. "We can't be late," she said, breaking into a run. "Come quickly."

Damien ran alongside her toward the Great Round Room. The doors were open, the interior dimly lit in a way he hadn't seen before. He squinted in the darkness as they entered. When his eyes adjusted, he stopped short at the sight before him.

There, in the center of the room, a large stone wheel lay on its side, brightly illuminated by a shaft of sunlight penetrating the dimness from a hole in the ceiling. Ignatia steered Damien to a spot on a bench in the last row, behind the Orphic monks. Their bowed heads were shaved bald, their eyes closed. They were dressed in smocks that had been dyed dark red with their own blood. Hoping for another glass of wine, Damien looked around the silent room.

One of the Orphics rose, his hands steepled in front of him. He stood like this for a moment then walked onto the slightly raised stage before the wheel. He raised his head, revealing a face made thin from ritualistic fasting, then cleared his throat. In a voice that hadn't been used in two years, he spoke.

"I am Markos," he said, struggling to form the words. "I am blessed by the gods."

"And also are we," Damien repeated with the rest of the group.

"I am a mortal sinner."

"And also are we."

"I am a seeker of communion with the gods."

"And also are we."

"I ask that my Initiator come forth," Markos said, then bowed his head.

A woman stood, her wrinkled face solemn. She made eye contact with every person, including Damien, whose skin goosefleshed when she did. Then the Initiator spoke in the great booming voice all the old monks in the temple possessed. "A soul reunites with its body ten times, chained to the wheel of reincarnation. Markos of Thasos seeks freedom from the grievous cycle. Today we send him on his quest."

The monk extracted a thin gold necklace from the pocket of her robe. She held it up to the light; a small gold scroll dangled from the chain.

Ignatia leaned over to Damien. "That is his *totenpass*," she whispered. "It will guide him through Hades."

As the Initiator secured the *totenpass* around Markos's neck, the other Orphics rose to their feet, lifting their bowed heads as one. Damien's heart pounded at the sight.

The Initiator held out her hands, and a second monk

rose, holding a long *kopis* by its hilt. He walked slowly toward the Initiator, who took the sword from him and raised it above her head, sunlight bouncing off the thick curved blade.

The Orphics filed out of their stone pews, surrounding Markos in two columns. Markos fell back into their arms, and as if governed by a single brain, they lifted him like a corpse, then laid him on the great stone wheel.

The Initiator addressed her next words to Ignatia. "Bring the child forth."

Ignatia herded Damien toward the Orphics and the wheel. It was large enough that every Orphic had his or her own place to stand around it. She placed Damien to the right side of Markos's face.

The young Orphic was tied to the wheel, bound at the wrists and ankles with thick rope, his body pulled taught into an X. Damien now saw the stone was intricately carved, with ten deep cups scooped out of the rock around the edges of the wheel's perimeter, all connected by grooves that radiated from underneath Markos's head like a pointed star.

Markos squinted into the sun beaming down on him from above, his chest rapidly rising and falling, light bouncing off his golden necklace. Damien jumped when a pair of hands rested on his shoulders. It was Ignatia, wearing a serious expression. The Initiator took her place at the top of the stone wheel, the blade held high above her head. After a moment's silence, she spoke.

"A river runs through Hades. The departed bathe in it, rinsing away all recollection of their existence on Earth," she told Markos. "Though your tongue is withered, do not dare drink from it. Seek instead the Pool of Memory. Seated atop a great stone is its sentinel. A demon. What will you tell her?"

Markos swallowed, his wide eyes traveling back to meet the Initiator's. "I will tell her," he began, his words coming in short, quick gasps, "that I am Markos of Thasos. I am but mortal flesh, a child of the gods. Take pity on me, and allow me to drink from the sacred water."

The Initiator held the edge of the *kopis* over Markos's throat. "We pray the infernal monarch hears your plea. Your thirst quenched, may you reincarnate and continue on the Grievous Cycle."

The Initiator drew the blade across Markos's neck.

Blood jetted up and out of the jagged wound the blade left behind. Damien screamed. Desperately he tried to twist himself free, but Ignatia held him firmly. Markos's eyes rolled back in his head.

Damien's legs gave out as the blood ran in ten thin rivers through the grooved channels that spiraled out to the edges of the wheel, filling the stone cups to the brim. Ignatia caught him as his knees buckled.

Markos went still, his dead eyes fixated on the square of light above. The cups on the wheel's edge overflowed, blood dripping onto the stone floor. Damien's head slumped forward as he drifted into unconsciousness, his terrified screams fading in his ears.

**4**

———

*Llewelyn Farm, New Mexico Territory; October 1855*

George Llewelyn stared at an army slouch hat on his kitchen table. The man he had heard about only in stories sat across from him, silent. The old farmer picked up the hat, turned it over in his hands, and put it back on the table.

"Balazarus," George said. "That's his topper, what that is."

"Yes, indeed," Damien replied. He pulled out a folded handkerchief from his vest and set it next to the hat. George opened it. Inside was a gold tooth, nestled in a bloodstain.

"Morrow," Damien said.

George's imagination stirred as he tried to picture the circumstances under which the incisor of the man who had raped his daughter had ended up in Damien Attica's vest pocket. He only wondered about these things but didn't ask.

He placed his hands on the table, steadying his arthritic limbs as he rose to his feet. After shuffling to the wood-burning stove in the corner, he pulled out a rusty tin can and shakily removed a wad of cash. He unfolded several large worn bills and laid them out before Damien on the table.

"You ain't gonna kill me now, are you, sir?" George asked.

Damien looked up from the cash. "No, I'm not going to kill you." He scooped up the money and headed for the door.

"Ain't you taking your gold?" George asked, holding up the tooth.

"That's your property now." Damien tipped his hat and walked into the midday sun.

He had just mounted his Morgan when the Llewelyns' farmhouse door clattered open and closed behind George. The old man limped toward him through the dirt.

"Mr. Attica! Sir!" Winded, George peered up at Damien. "Mr. Attica, sir. I meant no offense in there. Truly. You just hear stories. Rumors and such. God bless you, Mr. Attica. God bless your soul."

Damien tipped his hat, clicked his heels against his steed's flanks, and rode down the path that led away from the farm into the countryside.

———

Balazarus and Morrow were dead, killed at the hands of the assassin Damien Attica for the sum of fifty dollars, everything the farmer had managed to save over a lifetime.

For the past six months he had awoken each day and gone to bed each night remembering the discovery of Josephina in the hay barn: nearly beaten to death, her dress torn from her body. Remembering running outside and watching Morrow ride into the distance, the monthly rent as well as his daughter's virtue in his possession. Remembering the nights Josephina had woken up screaming; her inability to eat or sleep; the dark despair she had fallen into that he couldn't bring her out of, no matter how hard he tried. Remembering that morning, walking into the kitchen to find his only living child in the bathtub, her wrists slit with the pair of sewing shears his late wife Lizzie had used to make and mend the family's clothes.

George barely had saved her life, gripping her wounds and screaming entreaties to God. Now Josephina lived in a sanatorium run by the Sisters of the Good Shepherd, spent her days staring out the window while her wrists knit themselves back together.

The old man watched until Damien and his horse were a speck on the horizon before he headed inside.

Damien rode through cattle country, into the wide-open spaces of the Rio Grande Valley. He had checked off the men on his kill list, fulfilling his obligations to his client. Now there was only one thing left to do regarding the violation of Josephina Llewelyn.

That night, he camped on a hillside, eating a can of beans roasted over a fire. A crow landed a few feet from him and steadily hopped closer until it was a foot away. Damien dipped his fork into the can and brought up a single bean, then blew on it until it was cool. He placed it on his palm and held it out to the crow. The bird took the bean in its beak, swallowed, and cocked its head, winking. Damien winked back, and the crow flew away.

He didn't dream that night. In the morning, he rode toward the parish, a half day's journey north, toward Santa Fe. He was pleased to find the trail mostly uninhabited, as he always enjoyed a little solitude after a killing. When the sun sat directly overhead, he finally set his eyes on the parish's white steeple, which poked up from behind a hill studded with sage and cactus.

Damien dismounted and tied the Morgan to a post next to a dry trough. After removing his hat, he pushed through the double wooden doors and headed inside.

Hundreds of votives along the perimeter illuminated the sanctuary. When Damien's eyes adjusted to the dimness, he saw a carving of a crucified Jesus Christ on one of the walls.

He had been fascinated with Christian icons since his youth, when he had lived as an orphan at the Little Sisters of the Poor. He took a seat in a pew in front of the altar and admired the carving. Scanning the sanctuary, he observed the probable inaccuracies in the depiction of this particular form of execution, most notable the fact that the hands were nailed to the cross but the arms weren't bound to it by ties. The weight of the body would cause the nails to rip through the palms, he thought. Regardless, it seemed a particularly gruesome and agonizing way to die, and Damien always found himself awed by this.

Someone in the church cleared his throat, and Damien laid a hand on his revolver.

A Mexican deacon stood in the doorway, a wooden pail of water in one hand, a rag in the other. The man pointed to the floor, and Damien relaxed his gun hand.

"*Convento de monjas*?" Damien asked.

"The nunnery is behind stables," the deacon answered.

Damien walked toward a row of votives at the back of the chapel, produced a few coins from his pocket, and dropped them into the poor box with a clatter.

"*Salud*," said the deacon.

Damien replaced his hat and walked back into the sunshine. As he passed the stables, he spotted a humble adobe building a few hundred feet down a path and headed there. An old nun in a habit swept the front porch.

"Sister. Good day to you."

The nun gave Damien a once-over. As her aged face settled into a mask of disdain, she planted her broom on the wooden porch.

"State your business," she said.

"I'm looking for Miss Josephina Llewelyn. I'm a friend of her father's," he said, hoping to sound as conciliatory as possible.

The nun set the broom against the wall, headed into the convent, and slammed the door behind her.

Damien stepped onto the porch. "My name is Damien Attica," he called out. "I was in the employ of Mr. George Llewelyn, Miss Josephina Llewelyn's father. I was tasked with bringing justice to the cowards who brought her harm. I did so. She no longer needs to fear for her person in that regard."

He listened for any movement or response from within. Hearing none, he stepped off the porch.

The door opened behind him, its rusted hinges squeaking. He turned to find a young woman in the doorway. She was garbed plainly in a simple checked dress, a wooden cross on a string around her neck. Her once-freckled complexion was tanned like leather, a result of the Irish immigrant daughter's lifetime under the desert sun.

"Miss Josephina Llewelyn?"

"Yes."

"You seem well, Miss Llewelyn."

"Josie."

"Ma'am?"

"You can call me Josie."

"Very well, Josie."

"What...what did you do to them?"

Damien was taken aback at the question, and he regretted the condescending tone of his response as soon as he said it.

"Well, Josie, I killed them."

Josie glanced over her shoulder, checking through the screen door for the nun. Damien folded his hands behind his back to project what he hoped was an appropriate, professional demeanor.

"Did...did they suffer, sir?"

Again he was completely unprepared for the question. "Excuse me?"

"When you killed them. Did they feel pain? Fear?"

*Yes, they undoubtedly felt both those things*, Damien thought. The nature of their crimes gave him no pause in the application of torturous methods in their executions.

"Wouldn't want to vex you with the details, Josie, if it's all the same to you," he replied.

Josie arched an eyebrow and took another step forward. "I would hope that they suffered," she said, folding her arms underneath the crucifix dangling around her neck.

Damien wiped the sweat from his brow with his shirt-sleeve. He squinted up at the sky, noting the overwhelming beauty of the thick white clouds that hung above their heads, looking as though God had painted them.

"Let me think on it a moment," he said, and replayed the deaths of Morrow and Balazarus in his mind's eye.

---

Josie's rapist was known to frequent a saloon just outside the Old San Miguel Mission in Tularosa. Damien had tracked him there and waited outside for the better part of an afternoon for him to emerge. When he finally did, Floyd Morrow was stupefied to find his horse no longer hitched to the post outside the saloon. Amused, Damien watched as Morrow spun around on his heels, his whiskered face searching the town for any sign of the steed. Finding none, he walked to the center of the thoroughfare and shouted to all within earshot.

"Who the fuck stole my fucking horse?"

Business continued as usual, the village's men and women picking up the pace of their errands slightly but not enough to demonstrate to Morrow that he was any kind of threat. No, Morrow only preyed on the defenseless, like women milking their cows alone in a barn, Damien thought.

"Goddamn it, someone better fuckin' tell me!" Morrow shouted.

A smiling man leaned against a wall outside the tobacconist's, next to a wooden Indian statue. Morrow squinted his beady eyes at Damien, his pockmarked nose wrinkling into a sneer.

"The fuck you smilin' at, mister?" he asked.

"Is there a reward?" Damien asked.

"For what?"

"For telling you where your horse is."

Morrow blinked, as if he had trouble understanding. "You know who I am, mister?"

"Yes, I do. You're Mr. Morrow."

"And do you know who I work for?"

"Yes, I do. You work for Mr. Greeley."

"That's right," Morrow said. "Your reward for telling me who got off with my horse is I don't stomp your guts out in this here thoroughfare."

Damien hadn't quite made up his mind how he was

going to kill Morrow until just then. He smiled, happy to have a plan in place.

"You ain't gonna be grinnin' much longer, mister, if I don't hear where my horse got up to and what son of a bitch got him there."

"I took your horse, Mr. Morrow."

Morrow raised his hand and pointed to Damien. "*You* did?"

"Yes. His flank is scarred where your spurs tear into his flesh, which makes you not only a cowardly rapist but also a cowardly rapist who mistreats animals." He clucked his tongue and slowly shook his head.

Morrow snorted, spat into the dirt, and went for his gun. Damien reached his first, and, shooting from the hip, put a bullet into Morrow's right knee. Morrow fell backward with a guttural shout, the panicked footsteps of the villagers running for cover filling Damien's ears as he stepped off the walkway.

His countenance crimson, Morrow craned his neck up from the ground. He got up to the sitting position, only to be brought flat on his back again by a swift kick to the face from Damien's boot.

"Who...who the hell are you?" Morrow whimpered.

"You know who I am."

Damien pulled his bowie knife from its sheath, bent over, and cut a deep incision into Morrow's gut from one of his hipbones to the other, just below the navel. Dark blood washed out from the incision like the morning's tide. Damien wiped the blade on his pants then raised his right leg and brought his boot down on Morrow's belly, sending the man's lower intestines squirting into the dirt like rattlesnakes being pitched from a burlap sack.

*That is stomping someone's guts out*, Damien thought,

always privately enjoying making people's clever euphemisms for violence manifest.

He looked into Morrow's wide eyes, pleased to find that while the man was moments from death, he was fully conscious.

"Josephina Llewelyn," Damien said. "The woman you raped on the farm. You are her kill. I am merely the hand."

Morrow gurgled. On more than one occasion, Damien had heard this described as a "death rattle." He hunkered down on his knees and leaned over as the man's body shut down its processes. Before Morrow had a chance to escape further torment, Damien again removed his blade, parting the condemned man's lips and inserting the sharp point into the rotten gums just above his gold front tooth. A quick pound on the hilt with the heel of his hand liberated it from the skull, along with a good bit of Morrow's tongue.

Damien removed his kerchief from his front vest pocket, placed the tooth within, and carefully folded it.

Morrow released his final breath. The last thing he saw before he died was Damien, staring down, eyes as black and impenetrable as a dragonfly's.

———

That had been Morrow. Balazarus was his own deal: britches catching fire, nether regions blasted apart, another violator who had stoked the flames of Damien's sadistic imagination.

Damien kicked at the dirt, Josie's eyes making him feel as though he were being looked *through*, not *at*. He cleared his throat and made a conscious choice not to spit before speaking.

"Morrow went rabbit on me and there was a chase,"

Damien said. "Shot him through the kneecap. Took his front gold tooth while he still breathed as proof for your father. Reckon that caused him some discomfort. Also slit his belly. That's a painful place to be injured, in my experience. It took the man some time to expire."

"I see," Josie said.

"Balazarus—'Colonel' to you and your family, I suppose —I shot him in the buttocks, the material over which caught flame. That happens sometimes. Then I shot him in his private parts before dispatching him with a shell to the face."

Damien took a step back to indicate he was done with his narrative.

"Thank you very much, Mr. Attica," Josie said.

"Damien. You can call me Damien."

"Thank you, Damien."

"You're welcome, Josie."

Josie slipped back inside the convent and shut the door behind her.

# 5

---

*Bennett's Trading Post; New Mexico Territory; October 1855*

Damien guided the Morgan through the ponderosa tree poles that marked the entrance to Bennett's Trading Post, then tied up the horse in a shady spot by a water trough. Once inside, he removed his hat and breathed in the smells of lantern oil, sacks of dry beans, and ground coffee. Bennett was with a customer, a heavily armed Mexican man. Damien browsed an aisle stocked with camping and prospecting gear while he waited for the man to complete his transaction.

Coins clattered on the counter and the customer mumbled his thanks. Bennett's voice came next, cracked and gruff.

"Twist the damn sign."

Damien tipped his hat to the taciturn white-haired man in the green apron, bent and stooped, then did as he asked. The OPEN FOR BUSINESS sign flipped over to CLOSED.

"Lock it."

Damien slid the wrought iron bolt home with a click.

"Any further instructions, Bennett, or does that about cover it?" he asked, hiding his smirk by not turning around.

"Don't you fuckin' sass me, boy," Bennett said.

Taking another deep breath of the warm, comforting smells inside the trading post, Damien headed to the counter. "Didn't mean to delay the day's trade," he said.

Bennett scooped a hunk of chaw with a finger bent by arthritis and jammed it inside his cheek. "If some fame-seeking cowboy with a scatter-gun comes in here following you, I won't be around to trade at all," he said around the tobacco.

Damien shrugged. "No one followed me."

Bennett reached under the counter and brought up a bottle of whiskey.

"You of all people know I don't drink, Bennett."

Bennett returned the shrug, uncorked the bottle, and drank a long pull. "Fine-looking Morgan you're riding. When'd you get him?"

"Recently."

"We'll talk in the back," the old man said. "Away from the windows. Not lookin' to get shot dead just today."

Bennett keyed into a large storeroom, goods piled high against the walls. He lit a lantern then inspected Damien head to toe.

"You look well."

"Well enough, I guess."

Damien perused a shelf filled with small carpenter tools.

"Heard about Morrow," Bennett said.

"Yeah? What'd you hear?"

"Heard his gutted corpse was left in the middle of the road outside that gin house down by Tularosa. You're getting bolder, Damien."

"Had a job to do."

"Morrow was the colonel's man down there," Bennett continued. "No doubt he's heard. Wager there's a price on your hide already."

"The colonel's dead. I killed him." Damien selected a pair of duck-billed pliers from a shelf. "How much are these?"

After lowering himself onto a grain sack, Bennett took another long drink from his whiskey bottle. "I sent that army a book-learned young man, and they returned a killer with sand to spare. Yes indeed."

"Bennett. How much?"

"You tuning a piano? 'Cause that's what those pliers are for."

"And their cost is...what?"

Bennett waved him off.

"Thank you kindly," Damien said.

Bennett set his bottle down. "Morrow was one thing, Damien. He was just a surrogate. But the colonel reported directly to Isaac Greeley. He handled his affairs in those parts. *These* parts, matter of fact. Now you've gone and murdered the man. Greeley *will* come after you. Not to mention every cowpuncher who fancies himself a gun hand who wants to ingratiate himself to the son of a bitch. Greeley knows who you are. You ready for that, boy? 'Cause he's coming. That I promise you."

Damien shrugged. "Everybody knows who I am, Bennett."

A moment later, the pair emerged from the storeroom. "That it?" Bennett asked.

"Sack of coffee. Then I best keep moving."

"Yes. I suppose you best."

Outside the trading post, Bennett shuffled down his steps toward the Morgan, a smile appearing on his face for the first time. He placed a hand on the animal's cheek and produced a sweet plucked from a confection jar on his way out the door. The Morgan licked it up from his palm; Bennett spoke baby talk while the horse chewed the treat.

Damien opened the Morgan's saddlebag, dropped in the piano pliers, and secured the sack of coffee.

"Buy him off you for a hundred dollars," Bennett said, scratching behind the horse's ears as if it were a giant dog.

"Books," Damien said.

"Say again?"

"Books," Damien repeated. "I still read those. Every chance I get. I remember everything you ever taught me. Every word you said. And I got rules. Innocent people don't meet with violence. Not by my hand anyway."

Damien lifted himself onto the saddle as Bennett regarded him with tired, watery eyes. He suspected the old man was nearly blind with cataracts but took pains not to show it. He also suspected this was the last time they would see each other.

"What did I say?" Bennett asked. "You standing there in your army blues. Not sixteen years old. What did I say before you left?"

"You said if I fulfilled just one bit of my potential, the whole world would hear my name."

Damien clicked his heels and rode toward the ponderosa poles, Bennett watching him as he disappeared into the tall pines.

"Much obliged for the goods," he called over his shoulder.

## 6

---

*Buckner Ranch; New Mexico Territory; October 1855*

Damien crept through the trees, saddlebag slung around his back, shotgun at the ready. The forest was quiet, the leaves and branches crunching underfoot unusually loud to his ears. He was firmly in Navajo territory, and a young scout out to prove himself could appear armed with a tomahawk out of nowhere. He arrived at the small clearing with two tree stumps where he usually met his friend, took his hand off the shotgun, and cupped his palm around his mouth.

His birdcall, a bad approximation of a common crow, was answered by a far superior version. Igashu emerged from the trees, a wide grin across his chiseled features. His thick black hair cascaded over muscular shoulders; battle scars burned red by the sun covered his brown skin. The two men embraced.

"Happy to see you, my friend," Damien said.

"It is good you are still alive," Igashu said.

After they both took seats on the stumps, Damien dropped the saddlebag and pulled out a tin can of liver he had procured weeks earlier from a Chinese grocer in the

Utah Territory. He held it out to Igashu, who took it, looking perplexed. Damien then removed his own meal, a can of beans. Igashu spun the can around in his hands, unable to make sense of it.

"Give it here," Damien said, reaching for it.

He sliced the lid off with his bowie and handed it back. Igashu sniffed, grimaced, and offered it back to him.

"Sorry. I don't eat animals, friend," Damien said.

He spooned up some beans and shoved them into his mouth, indicating Igashu should do the same with his food. The Navajo man picked the liver out and held it aloft as though it were the strangest, most unnatural thing he'd ever encountered. Then he tossed it into the forest.

"Could have at least given it a taste first," Damien said, his mouth full. "That can cost four bits."

Damien set his can down, went back into the saddlebag, and brought out the bowler hat he'd worn as a disguise when executing Balazarus a few days earlier. Igashu's eyes lit up at the sight. Damien tossed it to him.

When Igashu set it on his head, a smile breaking across his handsome features, Damien laughed. White men's garments pleased his friend more than any other item he could produce during their transactions—more than weapons or dry goods or even gold, the latter of which he showed no interest in whatsoever.

"Fair trade?" Damien asked.

"Fair trade," Igashu replied.

Igashu reached into a leather pouch slung over his own shoulders, intricately decorated and festooned with hundreds of colorful beads. He brought out a folded envelope secured with a wax seal, "ATTICA" scrawled across the front in ink. Damien took it and held it up to the sun, careful to tear it open so as not to damage its contents.

He unfolded and read:

*Dear Mr. Attica,*

*Your services are requested by Mr. and Mrs. John Buckner of Buckner Ranch in Magdalena. Identify yourself by wearing a red kerchief on your person upon approach, as we are afeared of murderous agents and a dark result. We will look to the east entrance of our property every morning from sun-up until noon until fifteenth November for your appearance. We sincerely hope to make your acquaintance and soon.*

*Sincerely,*
  *John Buckner*

Other words bled through the paper. Damien turned it over:

*Delivered by hand to Indian agent for the recipient. This letter is sealed with the Buckner Ranch mark.*

It was unusual to get new clients so soon after completing a contract, but then Damien's work was unpredictable. He folded the letter and stuffed it into his back pocket. Igashu was admiring his newly acquired hat.

"Igashu. Full moon?"

Igashu nodded. They would meet during the next full moon. If there was another letter, another client, so be it. If not, they would eat; Igashu perhaps would smoke a pipe before parting ways until the next meeting. That was their arrangement over the past several years, the closest human bond Damien had in the world aside from Bennett.

Igashu put on his new hat and rose from his stump. The men again embraced, then headed in opposite directions toward their respective mounts, short distances away.

---

Damien arrived at Buckner Ranch an hour before dawn, using the time to give the Morgan a rest and watch the sun rise. There was something particularly grand about sunrise in New Mexico Territory, as if its border promised a better sky simply by crossing it. As the horizon glowed, he pointed the horse toward the ranch.

An iron archway came into view, and he slowed the animal, reached into his saddlebag, and extracted a red handkerchief and the sheathed bowie. He tied the kerchief around his neck and tucked the knife into the back of his britches. A click of his heels, and the Morgan picked up its pace to a gallop. Soon they were on the ranch.

Damien spotted John Buckner, well dressed and silver haired. The man stepped onto his porch, rifle in hand

"Identify yourself!" Buckner shouted, raising the rifle.

Damien tilted his hat back and pulled down the kerchief from around his neck so it was more plainly visible.

"That's a colorful neckerchief," Buckner called out. "Not too many of those in these parts."

Damien dismounted and slowly approached the porch, arms spread, hands open. "Worn as instructed, Mr. Buckner."

The rancher lowered his rifle. "Do come in, Mr. Attica."

Damien ascended the stairs to the porch and was led inside. The large house was immaculately clean, with fresh-cut wildflowers in jelly jars serving as decor. Buckner went for a bottle of whiskey on the dining room table, then to a cabinet filled with crystal tumblers.

"Whiskey, Mr. Attica?"

"Thank you, no, Mr. Buckner," Damien said, doffing his hat.

Buckner appeared surprised. "It's a bit early, I know," he said. "Won't sway my opinion of you one way or the other."

"Spirits don't agree with me, I find," Damien replied.

Buckner shook his head. "Pity."

The man poured a tall glass of whiskey for himself, swallowed half of it in two large gulps, then gestured to the dining room table. Damien set his hat on it and took a seat across from him.

"You have me at a disadvantage, Mr. Attica," Buckner said. "Whiskey is all I have to offer. That or well water. Unless, of course, you would prefer my wife's rosemary tea." He laughed as if this were an absurd joke.

"Tea would be fine," Damien replied. "Thank you."

There was a silence, Buckner unsure Damien wasn't joking. He wasn't.

"Well then," Buckner said, then called over his shoulder, "Mrs. Buckner. Dearest."

He offered Damien a weak smile, then again reached for his glass. Damien could tell the rancher was nervous, although he couldn't quite figure why.

Mrs. Buckner, a graying woman in a conservative dress buttoned to her chin, stepped into the dining room doorway.

"Ma'am," Damien said.

Mr. Buckner gestured to their guest. "May we trouble you for some tea, darling?" he asked his wife.

"Tea?" Mrs. Buckner asked, obviously not expecting the request.

"Which you enjoy most evenings," Buckner said.

"Yes, of course," Mrs. Buckner said. "I'll see to the kettle."

"Thank you, darling."

Mrs. Buckner headed into the kitchen. A moment later, Damien heard her rooting through a cupboard.

"Didn't mean to be a bother," Damien offered.

"Not at all," said Buckner. "We should be prepared for any eventualities when having guests. I just assumed a man like you...of your profession...would drink whiskey."

"Doesn't agree with me," Damien said with a smile.

"I would like the talk between us to be plain spoken, Mr. Attica."

"That'd be my preference as well, Mr. Buckner."

"First I must know the contents of our conversation won't be repeated outside this meeting. I would like your word on that."

"You have it."

"I also need to know—to understand—how exactly you operate. Or rather, how you intend to..."

Reaching for his glass, Buckner stammered these last words. Damien sat forward in his chair, his hands folded in front of him on the table.

"Sir, if I may..."

Buckner took another drink. Damien continued, making sure to keep his voice low so as not to disturb Mrs. Buckner, who was within earshot only a few feet away in the kitchen.

"You took the pains of finding the Indian called Igashu, managed to get me your message. Tells me you're a pretty canny gentleman. Canny enough to have done his due diligence."

"You're not what I expected," Buckner said.

"I get that a lot," Damien replied. "I'm lettered, Mr. Buckner. And I speak properly when called upon."

"I see that."

"You have a grievance with some individual that needs remedy," Damien continued. "For a price, I will provide the remedy that you seek. It's that simple. Just tell me the particulars, and I'll take it from there. I will obtain proof of death to your satisfaction, and then you'll pay me. After that, we'll never cross paths again. I don't perform my service on women or children, but otherwise I generally tend to find my marks in need of a killing, and I'm amenable to most circumstances. Sound about okay to you, Mr. Buckner?"

Buckner drained his glass. "Yes. Very much so."

"Then tell me about your troubles, at your leisure. I have nowhere else to be."

Mrs. Buckner returned with a tea service on a tray and set it down. She was clearly upset about something. Damien's mind churned trying to identify what it could be.

She poured a pale-yellow liquid that steamed as it hit the delicate porcelain. When she picked it up to hand over to Damien, it rattled on the dish.

Damien took the cup, noting the perspiration ringing her scalp, soaking her hair, and running down her cheek. "Much obliged, ma'am," he said.

Mrs. Buckner all but ran out of the room. The screen door opened and closed. Damien watched through the dining room window as she scurried toward the barn.

He took a sip of tea. "Delicious."

"Cigar, Mr. Attica?"

"No, thank you. Don't smoke."

"No whiskey. No cigar. My goodness, if I didn't know better, I'd think I was conversing with the good Reverend Lawson over at Christ's Calvary." Buckner laughed at his own joke. Then his eyes flicked away, just for a second, to something behind Damien.

Damien yanked the bowie out of its sheath, then spun it around and threw it blade over handle into the rifle-wielding cowboy standing in the corner of the dining room. The blade entered his chest with the force of an ax being buried into a tree stump. The cowboy fell backward, squeezing off a round from his rifle and hitting the whiskey bottle on the table, creating a small explosion of liquid and glass. Damien charged forward, falling onto the cowboy and pushing the knife into the man's body to the hilt. He then withdrew it as the man expired, bringing up a fountain of blood behind it.

Bucker scrambled to his feet, staggering against the wall. Damien fluidly produced a pistol.

"He made me do it! For the love of God! He made me do it!" Buckner shouted.

"Who? Who did?" Damien demanded, pulling back the pistol's hammer. Buckner sank to his knees, his hands outstretched in supplication.

"He said he'd kill me! Kill my wife! Kill my son. For the love of God, please don't shoot!"

Damien pressed the gun against Buckner's forehead. "Who? *Who*?"

"Greeley!"

Damien relaxed his trigger finger and allowed himself a moment's thought. Greeley lived in New York City. He wouldn't deign to mess in the humble affairs of a bunch of prairie folks in New Mexico Territory, even if his own men were being killed. He would just replace them, put a price on Damien's head, and be done with it.

"Greeley's a New York dude. Don't lie to me, Buckner."

"Been in the territory some weeks now. They're outside."

"*They?*"

"His men. Dozens of them. Maybe more. Please...don't sh-shoot."

Damien turned back to the dining room windows to find an armed posse surrounding the perimeter of the ranch house. Bennett's prophetic warning had come to pass: Damien had killed one too many men in his quest to bring justice for the Llewelyns. The contract was for Morrow only, not Balazarus. Now it had come back around on him. He was outgunned.

He lowered his pistol. He hated when Bennett was right about things, and Bennett was pretty much always right about things.

"You out there, Greeley?" he called out.

Jangling spurs parted the crowd of hired guns in two. Isaac Greeley strolled through the gang, squaring the shoulders of his stocky, no-neck frame, rattlesnake skin boots kicking up dust. Damien knew the spurs were just for show, as was the white hat atop his waxen bald dome.

"I am," Greeley called back.

Maddox, Greeley's rotund henchman, stepped ahead of his boss, rifle raised. "Attica, step on out. Slowly," he shouted, whiskered jowls quivering. "Hands high. You know what's waiting outside these walls."

Damien turned to Buckner, who was cowering on the floor. "How much did he pay you?" he asked.

"Nothing. I swear. He said he'd burn the house and hunt us down if I didn't write the letter."

"What did you think I'd do to you if I found out?"

"Please, sir, I beg you," Buckner whined. "I beg you for my life. Please. Please."

Damien plucked the rifle off the dead cowboy's corpse. "Law of averages has one of them peckerwoods putting me down," he said. "But I aim to take most of them with me before I go. You tell Bill Bennett at the trading post what you saw, and we'll call it square. Deal?"

"Yes. Deal. Absolutely, Mr. Attica."

Damien double-checked his ammo while walking back into the kitchen, then crouched behind the cast iron stove. "Greeley!" he shouted. "I'm gonna come out. I got twelve bullets and a blade. The slugs are for the poor souls you paid to back your play. The blade? That's for you."

Damien kicked the screen door open, then dove back for the floor, a hail of bullets punching the kitchen walls above his head. He crawled into the dining room and got to his feet before running in a crouch toward the front door.

"Stay down!" he yelled at Buckner, who already had arranged himself into a fetal position, hands covering his head.

Damien leapt over the dead cowboy and through the door, then ran around the back of the house to be greeted by two pistol-wielding thugs. They barely had time to react before he discharged a shot from both barrels. Thug number one crumpled to the ground, a bullet having passed through the cheek an inch below his left eye socket. Thug two was shot in the jugular, but unlike his partner, he was still very much alive.

The man kicked the dirt, gasping for air, blood jetting from the exit wound. Damien dropped the rifle in exchange for the pistol, grabbed the throat-shot thug by his collar, and brought him to his feet.

He removed his hat and placed it on Throat-Shot's head. Blood burbling from his mouth and down his chin, the man tried to speak. Damien dragged him by the collar along the back of the ranch house.

"Here I come, boys," he hollered, shoving Throat-Shot out into the open.

As the thug staggered forward, gunfire erupted, spinning him like a top. Damien ran around to the other side of the house, pistols raised, and surprised the firing line.

Greeley's men didn't realize they were hitting the wrong target before they were shot themselves. Each bullet found its man perfectly, their bodies falling in a slow wave.

Awestruck, Greeley watched as Damien wiped out his posse, a bemused expression on his face. "I want him alive," he muttered.

"Yes, sir, Mr. Greeley," Maddox said, raising his rifle.

Damien's weapons clicked over empty, and he tossed them. He pulled out the gore-soaked bowie from its sheath and found shelter behind a water barrel next to the porch. A cowboy with a Remington revolver emerged from a hiding place and shot rounds into it.

"He's done, boss!" the cowboy shouted.

Damien had no intention of leaving the world that quietly. He rose from behind the barrel, knife in hand, and stalked toward the cowboy.

"Hell you doing?" the cowboy said, firing but missing.

"Better make the next one count," Damien said, his pace quickening.

Greeley laughed and shook his head in wonder, as if he were watching an illusionist or a circus act. "I'll be damned," he said.

The cowboy backed away as Damien approached him, struggling to aim. He fired his last shot, the bullet grazing Damien's scalp but otherwise doing little to impede his progress.

When Maddox raised his rifle, Greeley gripped the man's wrist, lowering the weapon.

"That dude's good as dead I don't do somethin', Mr. Greeley sir."

"Yeah, well," Greeley said.

Damien embedded the bowie behind the cowboy's Adam's apple, the blade punching out the other side of his neck.

"Jesus, Mary, and Joseph," Greeley said, wincing. "Everything they said he was and more. *Now* you can shoot him. Somewhere he won't bleed out."

Maddox emptied his rifle, hitting Damien in the shoulder, leg, and foot.

Damien lay on his back, looking up at the desert sky and turning what he assumed were his last thoughts to total wonderment at its perfection.

Greeley and Maddox stood over him, eclipsing his view.

"Damien Attica," Greeley said. "We'll have our talk inside, all the same to you."

Maddox smashed his rifle's stock into Damien's forehead, sending him into darkness.

## 7

*Attica Peninsula, Greece; the Month of Thargelion, 435 BC*

For three days, Damien didn't eat or sleep after witnessing the Orphic monk's slaughter on the stone wheel. On the fourth day, Ignatia went in search of him, eventually finding the boy alone by the sea, staring out at the horizon in a daze.

"You must eat something," she said.

Damien shook his head.

Ignatia crouched and took his hands into hers. "Damien, look at me."

When he did so, she wiped away a tear rolling down his cheek.

"I brought you to that room for a purpose," she continued. "We need to talk about why you are here. You can't keep pretending it didn't happen. My hope was that witnessing what you did would shock you out of your silence. Bring it all back perhaps."

For the life of him, Damien couldn't figure out which incident in his past Ignatia kept referring to. He dropped her hands and walked down the beach, so exhausted from lack of sleep and food that he could barely see straight.

Ignatia followed, the pair leaving footprints in the wet sand. "Damien."

He squinted into the light that glittered off the sea. Ignatia put her hand out for him to take.

"Come with me," she said.

---

Damien and Ignatia strolled through a meadow an hour's walk from the shore. She guided him to a shady spot under a tree and sat him down gently in the grass. He awoke hours later with his head on her lap, the sun well on its way to setting.

"How long was I asleep?" he asked.

Ignatia shushed him and pointed a few yards ahead. Damien sat up at what he saw. A family of elk grazed the meadow: a great buck, the mother, and two calves.

"They say Orpheus, may he be blessed, sat under this tree and played his music and sang his songs, and all the animals gathered to listen to him. Right here, in this very place," Ignatia said.

"Is that true?" Damien asked.

Ignatia gave a little shrug and stood up as quietly as she was able. They silently walked through the cool grass toward the elk.

"Tell me how Orpheus, may he be blessed, left this world, Damien," Ignatia whispered.

Damien took a moment to remember his scriptures.

"Orpheus angered the god Apollo," he said softly, "who commanded his May...his *May*..."

"Maenads."

"Who commanded his Maenads to rip him limb from limb."

"Correct. But how in this world or the next could that be so? Orpheus was able to charm any living thing with his words and music."

"They couldn't hear his song," Damien replied, remembering his lessons, "and his music had no effect on them."

"That's right," Ignatia said, squeezing his hand to indicate they were as close as they would get to the elk. The animals kept a watchful eye on the pair but continued to graze.

"Orpheus could have talked to these animals, were he standing here beside us," Ignatia said. "They could have understood him, and he would have understood them. And they would stand here and have a delightful conversation. Did you know that?"

Damien tried to guess what the right answer might be. In his daily classes at the temple, he had a lot of trouble discerning what was true and what was merely fanciful storytelling. The story of Orpheus, upon whose legacy the entire Orphic faith had been built—not to mention the great stone temple in which the faith resided—was one he had trouble getting his head around.

"Yes?" Damien replied.

"Yes, indeed," Ignatia replied. "Orpheus walked these fields and played and sang and talked to the birds and the beasts and even the rocks. The rocks, Damien! They too heard his song and knew his words, and they sang their songs back to him."

Each of the elks took another gentle step forward. Damien's mind filled with questions he was too embarrassed to ask. How did Orpheus and the animals speak to each other and in what language? Did they have voices like humans, or was Orpheus able to speak in theirs? He couldn't imagine what the exchanges would sound like.

"You have a song inside you too," Ignatia said. "It's a very unusual song, I think, and one that others will have a difficult time understanding." She tugged at Damien's sleeve, brought him close, and whispered in his ear. "But it is *your* song and you must learn to sing it."

*Buckner Ranch; New Mexico Territory; October 1855*

Damien sensed his wrists first, burning and bound together...then his feet, cold and floating above the earth. The smell of sweat and blood filled his nostrils as pain radiated from his broken nose. He gasped for breath and opened his one good eye.

"He's awake, Mr. Greeley," Maddox said.

When Damien let his head fall forward, he now understood he was suspended from a rope hanging from the barn's ceiling. He looked up to his hands, purple with lack of circulation, and down at his leg, which was dribbling blood from the bullet hole. The pain there was excruciating, as was the pain from his broken collarbone, which he was fairly certain was threatening to poke out of the skin, if it wasn't already.

Greeley was holding a glass jar up to the light, watching something Damien couldn't make out crawling around inside. Greeley set it down, strolled up to Damien, and stopped a few inches from his face.

Greeley wore the expression of a man who'd just bagged

a prize buffalo. He placed his hand on Damien's chest and pushed him, causing him to swing like a pendulum, the movement making the ropes cut into his wrists even deeper. Damien swallowed the pain as best he could.

"Can you hear me?" Greeley asked.

Damien grunted in affirmation.

"I'm going to ask you a question," Greeley continued, "and if that question is truthfully answered, I promise to dispatch you with merciful haste. However, should you make a heroic attempt at concealing the truth, you will be, shall we say, compelled."

Greeley glanced back toward the jelly jar. Damien saw something crawling up the smooth interior, heard its legs clicking against the glass.

Greeley took a step closer. Another few inches, and Damien would have bitten the man's nose off, but he stayed just out of reach. "Who hired you to assassinate my agents here in the territory?" Greeley asked.

Blood dripped into Damien's eye. He blinked it away but said nothing.

"I'll show uncharacteristic patience and assume it's possible you're not sure which of your murders I'm referring to," Greeley continued. "Balazarus and Morrow. They were in my employ and valuable to my operations. Who paid you to kill them?"

Damien swayed, silent.

Greeley laughed. "Man's got sand, I'll give him that."

"Yes, sir, he sure does," Maddox said, shaking his head.

Damien steeled himself for a knife in the heart as Maddox walked across the barn, blade in hand. But he didn't stick it into Damien's chest. Instead he stepped up on a milking stool and sliced the rope that secured him to the ceiling.

Damien landed on his bad foot first, then on his shoulder. Maddox grabbed him under the armpits and dragged him across the barn floor before hoisting him onto a wooden table.

"You can't even lift a finger to help or nothin', Mr. Greeley, sir," Maddox murmured as he ran the slack rope dangling from Damien's wrist and ankle ties underneath the table. Damien cried out as the ropes went as tight as Maddox could make them. He lay there in excruciating pain, splayed out on the table.

As Maddox ripped Damien's shirt open, the buttons clattered to the ground. "Mr. Attica, I'm going to give you one last opportunity to spare yourself what I understand will be indescribable agony," Greeley said, holding up the jar.

Damien now saw what was inside. At least a dozen bark scorpions skittered around the bottom, none larger than the size of a quarter. He was familiar with the creatures, their venom responsible for more than a few casualties in his unit down in Mexico during the war. Attempts at communicating with them always proved futile. Their stings wouldn't necessarily kill a man but would certainly incapacitate him, making whatever limbs they sunk their tails into paralyzed, bloated, and useless. Damien had no idea what a dozen or more would do to a body. He supposed he was moments away from finding out.

"The naturalist who provided these specimens assured me their venom rivals only that of the king cobra, a snake whose bite kills lions in deepest, darkest Africa. These creatures' toxins dissolve their victim from the inside out. Or so he claims."

Greeley uncapped the jar and held it at a tilt over Damien's bare torso. "Who hired you?"

Damien's eyes rolled over to Maddox, who, with revulsion, watched the scorpions scramble over one another in the jar. He then rolled them over to Greeley, who cupped a hand around his ear and leaned closer to him. Damien hacked up the biggest mouthful of saliva he could muster and spat on Greeley's face, pleased with not only the volume but also its high content of blood and mucous.

Greeley removed a handkerchief, wiped his face, then flipped the jar over and planted its open end onto Damien's bare stomach. The scorpions stung his flesh, sending shock waves of pain radiating from the center of his body toward his limbs. He convulsed on the table, the ropes cutting into his wrists and ankles.

Greeley leaned in as the scorpions scrambled over one another, red welts blooming on Damien's skin. "Tell me the name and I'll have Maddox put one between your eyes. It'll all be over."

Damien bit his tongue until he tasted blood. If he could ride out the pain a few minutes longer, he would die without giving Greeley the satisfaction of his screams.

"Say it," Greeley said, inches from Damien's sweating, reddening face. "It'll take you whole days to die. I'll see to it personally that it does, and that's a promise. Tell me the name, Mr. Attica. Tell me so I can end this for you."

Damien's eyes rolled back in his head as his heart fluttered. He was both freezing and running with sweat, the muscles in his arms and legs spasming.

"What could your employer possibly be to you?" Greeley said. "You're a hired hand, nothing more. There is no honor to be had here. Say it. While you still can."

Damien wheezed, fluid foaming out the sides of his mouth.

"Say it!" Greeley shouted.

Damien froze, paralyzed now. Greeley capped the jar.

"What should I do with him?" Maddox asked.

"Take him out of here. Don't let Mrs. Buckner see the body. Leave him for the animals."

"Yes, sir, Mr. Greeley."

Damien heard the ropes that bound him being sliced, then sensed an impact as his body was dragged off the table and dropped to the ground. Something he assumed were probably his legs slid through the dirt and hay while the darkness behind his eyelids grew brighter. Birdsong and distant thunder filled his ears, along with Maddox's mumbles.

"Yes, sir, Mr. Greeley. Oh, yes, sir. Lucy Maddox's son is here to do your whims and biddies, Mr. Greeley, sir. Don't lift a finger on them golden hands of yours. Wouldn't want to scratch 'em up, Mr. Greeley oh Lord my God."

A much quieter voice—confused and alarmed— emerged in concert with Maddox's. Damien listened, trying not to let Maddox's whining drown it out. He was now on the back of a horse, tied behind the saddle like a bundle of sticks. His deadweight was inflicting considerable stress on the animal's back, not that Maddox cared. Completely paralyzed by the toxins that had flooded his bloodstream, Damien listened to the animal bemoan its labors.

They rode this way for a while. Damien figured Maddox would take him to an empty spot deep in the foothills, his dead body perhaps discovered by a passerby one day.

Bennett wouldn't notice his absence for several weeks, not unless Greeley made it known that the notorious assassin had died by his hand. Then Bennett would face a choice: seek revenge or go about his business and privately mourn the man he called a son. Damien hoped he would choose the latter. Although Bennett was the finest gun hand he'd ever known, Greeley had an entourage of killers, mostly ex-army looking for a paycheck and a chance to keep murdering people under the color of law. Bennett wouldn't get within a mile of the man before being cut down in a hail of bullets. Damien prayed his own bones would be picked clean by hungry buzzards and his disappearance would forever remain a mystery.

After a time, Maddox slid off the horse, the ropes hissing over each other as Damien's ties were removed. Another loud thud resounded, Maddox's breath coming fast from the effort of pulling Damien off the steed and onto the ground.

"Poor son of a bitch."

Maddox clicked his tongue and the horse hooves faded into the distance.

Damien would lie here for some time, deep in the country, with nothing but his own thoughts to keep him company until he expired.

## 9

*Bennett Residence; Jefferson City, Missouri; July 1836*

Damien chose a happy memory on which to meditate as his body slowly died of scorpion venom and exposure. In it he was thirteen, in the field behind the house Bennett had built for himself and his late wife Agnes. Damien had spent the afternoon practicing loading and firing a dueling pistol Bennett claimed to have acquired in France. Although he had pressed Bennett to tell him about the circumstances that had led him overseas to Europe, he had yet to convince him to tell the tale.

Damien reloaded the pistol, carefully pouring the gunpowder so as not to spill so much as a granule, then dropped in a ball. He poked it down with a long stick stripped of its bark, Bennett having lost the ramrod years earlier. He then pulled back the hammer and placed the cap, stood at attention and dramatically brought his arm down, a behavior Bennett had described while recounting a duel he'd witnessed as a boy. Damien aimed for the tin can on a tree stump ten yards away, took a breath, held it, and fired.

The can didn't move. Hearing footsteps behind him, he made a face, knowing what was coming next.

"You're jerking your shoulder when you squeeze the trigger," Bennett said.

Bennett, a man in his thirties with a full head of hair, dirt-covered hands on his hips, shook his head.

"No, I ain't," Damien said.

"No, I'm *not*," Bennett reminded him.

Damien swallowed his anger at having his grammar corrected, something Bennett did half a dozen times a day. If Damien sassed back, Bennett would punish him with a backhand to the mouth.

"No, I'm *not*," Damien said.

"Yes, you are. Enough foolin' around now. Time for your lessons."

"I'll hit it, Bennett," Damien pleaded, pointing to the can.

"Holster that iron, boy."

There would be no further pleading.

"Yes, sir."

Damien walked toward the house, placing the pistol in Bennett's outstretched hand as he passed. Bennett picked up a small rock off the ground at his feet, aimed, and pitched it toward the stump. He hit the tin can dead center, popping it up and over on its side. Damien stood on the porch, watching him.

"Boy, you'd better get your ass inside and..."

He didn't need to finish the sentence. Damien already was through the door like a shot.

Bennett's study was lined with bookshelves, hundreds of tomes Damien couldn't get enough of. He didn't understand half of what he was reading, but it didn't matter. On this day in his memory, his younger self chose *Systema Naturae,* a yellowing book with funny words and detailed drawings of plants and animals. Bennett entered, a cup of coffee in one hand, a glass of milk in the other, and placed them on the rolltop desk.

"When can I have coffee?" Damien asked.

"When I tell you it's time," Bennett replied. "Now where were we?"

Damien found his mark and carefully opened the book, the spine crackling as he laid it flat on the desk. Bennett claimed the book was almost a hundred years old, and by the look of it, he probably was right. Bennett's callused hand smoothed down the page before he rested a finger on the large, intricate drawing in the center of it.

"What are those called?"

"Butterflies, of course."

Bennett gave Damien a little smack upside the back of his head.

"*Anthropoda.* I was just foolin', Bennett."

"Class?"

"*Insecta.*"

"Order?"

Damien shifted in his seat.

"Order?"

"*Lepid...Lepid...Lepidoptera,*" he finally said.

"Kingdom?"

"*Animalia.* That's easy."

"Wasn't easy two weeks ago," Bennett said. "Turn the page."

Another intricate drawing filled the two pages, each half meticulously illustrating the wing of an insect Damien had often seen in nature.

"Ah," Bennett said, coffee on his breath. "The mighty monarch."

"Thought that meant 'king,'" Damien replied.

Bennett brought a pair of wire spectacles from his shirt pocket and leaned over the page. His finger traced under the funny words Damien couldn't pronounce.

"...so named monarch as it is one of the largest of all butterflies, ruling a vast domain. Foul tasting, poisonous specimens. Toxins derive from the milkweed they ingest. Predators learn to avoid them thusly." A sly smile stretched across Bennett's face. "So he's a killer."

"Yeah," Damien said. "Seems to be."

"But is he clever?" Bennett asked.

"How you mean?"

"*Do.*"

Damien bristled but corrected himself. "How *do* you mean?"

"Turn the page."

Damien did, revealing another drawing almost identical to the one that had preceded it, with slight variations to the dark hues on the tips of its wings.

"False monarch," Bennett read, running his finger along Latin verbiage beneath the sketch.

"Meaning 'not true,' right?"

"Very good, Damien."

"So he ain't...*isn't*...poisonous?"

"But to some hungry crow..."

"He could be, so they don't eat him."

Bennett sipped his coffee and tousled the hair on Damien's head. "You understand then."

Damien flipped between the two butterflies for a while before answering. "Oh, yes, sir," he finally said. "I understand."

## 10

---

*Navajo Pueblo, New Mexico Territory; October 1855*

The pain radiating through Damien's broken collarbone jolted him awake; he was still blind and paralyzed but no longer lying in the dirt. He was moving at such a pace that he concluded he was again on the back of a horse. Trying to speak, he could only manage to gurgle the fluid in his throat. The horse's rider clicked his tongue, and the animal slowed to a halt. A hand gently touched Damien's back.

"Damien."

Igashu. Damien again tried to speak, but only produced more gurgling. Igashu patted him to be still. The warm desert sun on his skin, along with the rhythmic pounding of the horse's hooves, lulled him back into unconsciousness.

---

Damien awoke in near darkness, flames in a small clay pot his only light. He made out what appeared to be shadows on the adobe ceiling above, but as his vision adjusted, he realized they were plants and herbs, tied in bunches and suspended to dry. His eyes traveled over the walls decorated with blankets and motifs depicting creatures fashioned from beads. A shaft of light under the wooden door told him it was daytime, but otherwise he had no sense of how long he'd been lying here. He only knew he couldn't move or speak.

He lay like this for hours, the light fading. Then came voices, and the door swung open, Igashu silhouetted against the sunlight. Damien managed a wink, and Igashu stepped to the side, another figure darkening the doorway.

It was an old woman dressed in black, a striped woven blanket around her shoulders. Her silver and turquoise jewelry rattled, her long gray hair tied in thick braids over her chest. Squinting in the low light, she took Igashu by the arm, allowing him to guide her to Damien. When she reached the bed, she stopped, her eyes wide, and put her hand to her mouth to stifle a scream.

The old woman's knees buckled and Igashu caught her, helping her to the floor, leaving Damien curious as to what physical state he must be in to elicit such a reaction. Several young Navajos then entered the room, took the woman by the arms and gently lifted her. She shouted tersely, prompting Igashu and the other men to release her; she then raised her right hand. Igashu and the others left, shutting the door. The medicine woman trembled as she slowly walked to Damien's side, an expression of awe on her face.

To her eyes, Damien was a living corpse, bone thin and dressed in a smock dyed red with what was unmistakably human blood. His head was shaved bald; his neck cut open so deeply that it revealed his larynx. Believing she was in the presence of a chindi—an evil spirit of the dead—she prayed to her ancestors that it wouldn't infect her with its ghostly sickness.

She sang in Navajo, her voice both mournful and beauti-ful, turning for the large woven basket in the corner of the room. Something rattled inside, and she shook it in her hands before placing it on a wooden bench next to the plat-form Damien lay on. The shaman grabbed a heavy black blanket decorating the wall and draped it over him, then laid her hands on his belly. Damien coughed, his body convulsing with the effort, and more thick white foam ran out of his mouth and down his chin. The woman wiped it from his face with her hands as it flowed, then cast the fluid into the clay pot and its fire, which hissed and sparked.

The woman twisted off herbs and leaves from the many bundles hanging from the ceiling and dropped them into a wooden bowl. She set it on the bench and removed the basket top; a four-foot rattlesnake lay within. The shaman rested the reptile's fangs on the bowl's edge and milked its venom over the herbs and leaves, then dropped the rattlesnake onto Damien's chest, laughing heartily as his eyes went wide with fear. She saw this chindi was relatively young and had yet to come to terms with who it was and, perhaps more important, why it was here.

She knew the rattlesnake would no sooner bite the chindi than it would offer itself to an eagle's talons. Her patient didn't seem to know that, however, and she chuckled as she mashed the herbs and venom into a paste with a smooth stone.

Damien's eyes followed the snake as it slithered over his body. He felt no affinity for it, none of the rapport he found with other creatures. Its blind eyes took no mind to the darkness of the room, the tongue instead guiding itself up Damien's chest and toward his face. It stopped just short of his nose, and sat like this for a while.

The shaman swept the snake up and dropped it back

into the basket. She then dipped her hands into the wooden bowl; her fingertips brought up a heap of freshly made poultice and slathered it across Damien's forehead. She sang, soft and melodically, the rhythms soothing. The shaman sighed with relief as the chindi fell into unconsciousness, then said a prayer of thanks to her ancestors for protecting her when called upon. She knew once Damien left, the room must be dismantled, and everything it had contained burned. He would have to take his ghostly sickness with him, leaving no trace.

---

The percussive thrum of Navajo warriors chanting brought Damien from his sleep. The pueblo was enacting some sort of ceremony and he wanted to see it, to feel humans joining together with a purpose other than killing one another. He struggled to his elbows and fell back onto his bed with a sigh of frustration. He wasn't yet fully free of the poison's effects, not to mention his gaping neck and gunshot wounds, still suppurating.

He heaved his right shoulder up and over and rolled onto the floor. He groaned at the impact before twisting himself around so he was facing the door. Damien was glad neither Bennett nor Igashu was present for this spectacle.

He crawled for the door on his elbows, his legs tingling but still paralyzed by the vestiges of the scorpion venom. He gripped each wooden slat of the floor, using them like rungs on a ladder, his teeth grinding with effort. When he finally reached the door, he stopped, rested his forehead on the ground, and caught his breath. When he could, he reached out and pulled the door open.

Painted dancers dressed in feathers and beads circled an

enormous bonfire. Damien felt its heat from thirty yards away and breathed in its warmth. Igashu stood at the dance circle's perimeter; Damien called out his name without hope of being heard over the din. He kept on, finding he could bring up his left knee, letting the rhythm of the drum infect his spirit, channeling its energy into his weakened body.

*Haiya naiya yowo yowa lana ya, na'eye lana heya eye...*

Damien's body absorbed the fire's heat and light, his shivering muscles coming back to life.

Then a woman screamed.

It was the shaman. All music and dancing stopped. The old woman stood near the bonfire, speaking rapidly. As she did, a great commotion erupted among those assembled. One word escaped the lips of everyone present, a word Damien didn't understand.

Chindi.

A dancer with a face painted in white and black stripes dropped his drumming and charged across the circle toward Damien. Igashu protectively leapt in front of him, and they shouted at each other; "chindi" spit from their lips like rotten meat.

The shaman separated the two men, then held up her hand, commanding silence. All was silent save for the crackle of the bonfire.

Igashu came to her side, uttering a single word in Navajo.

"Friends," Damien translated with what little voice he possessed. "That's us, all right."

The shaman glared at Damien for a long time before turning back to her people. She made another proclamation, and they sprang into action, collecting their drums and rattles and evacuating the circle. In a matter of moments, Damien and Igashu were the only ones left by the fire.

Damien repeated the word he kept hearing, doing his best not to mispronounce it. "Igashu, what's a chindi?"

Igashu stood in front of the bonfire, arms to his sides, then crumpled to the ground. He closed his eyes and stuck out his tongue, making Damien laugh, something he hadn't done in so long he couldn't remember the last time he'd done it. Igashu lay in the dirt like this, a growling sound low in his throat.

He stood, twisting his face grotesquely. Damien laughed again, delighted by his very serious friend's pantomime. Igashu lurched toward Damien, his mouth in a snarl, growling.

He relaxed his expression and stood as he normally did. "Chindi," Igashu said. Damien shrugged. "Its meaning will remain a mystery, I suppose. Didn't mean to break up the party, friend, for whatever it's worth."

Igashu picked up a woven blanket and draped it over Damien.

"Could use forty winks, surely," Damien said, then fell back asleep by the roar of the fire.

## 11

*Attica Peninsula, Greece; the Month of Thargelion, 435 BC*

Dried blood coated the stone wheel in the Great Round Room. The group of thirty students whispered to one another, trying to guess its purpose in the day's lesson. Damien's special knowledge of it came with a mixture of smugness and terror. He felt smug that he alone among the students had been privy to a ceremony that usually was forbidden to them, and terrified the class would be called upon to witness the slaughter of another Orphic.

The doors opened, and Master Charos entered. The children jumped to their feet and bowed. "Good morning, Master," they intoned.

"Sit," Master Charos said, and they obeyed.

Master Charos frightened Damien. The teacher was rumored to have been one of the great Spartan warriors and possessed the body of a man who'd been raised to defend Greece with his physical might. He was nearly seven feet tall, with arms and legs so muscular they were larger in circumference than Damien's waist. Even more striking than the man's physical stature was the nature of his war wounds, horrific scars that obliterated the right side of his face. The left side revealed a once handsome man, with its untouched blue eye and neatly trimmed beard. The rest was a mass of burned and mutilated tissue, healed over and difficult to look at. Master Charos also possessed a thundering voice, which pierced Damien to the core every time he spoke.

Master Charos pulled up the sleeves of his tunic, revealing his massive forearms, and gestured toward the wheel. "Who among you has seen this before?" he asked.

The children stole glances at one another, no one saying a word.

"Any idea of its purpose?"

Silence.

"No one can tell me? Can anyone guess?"

A hand shot up.

"Yes, Timon."

"I believe it to be a wheel, Master," the boy offered.

"A wheel."

"Yes, Master."

"Have you ever seen a cart so large that it would require a wheel of this size, Timon?"

"No, Master."

"So it is not really a wheel then, is it? Who else might hazard a guess?" Master Charos searched the room. "Damien."

"Yes, Master?" Damien stood up.

"Do you have anything to offer?"

Damien tried to swallow but was unhappy to find his tongue would not cooperate. "No, Master."

"And why is that?"

"I'm not sure what it is, Master."

"You aren't sure what this is?" the teacher said, taking a

few steps forward. The students craned their necks to take in his full height, as if gazing up the trunk of a forest oak.

"No, Master."

"Were you not recently in this very room witnessing the spilling of Orphic blood upon this object?"

A gasp went through the assembled, and the class looked at Damien, his face hot and red. His eyes watered, and he prayed to the gods he wouldn't cry in front of the other children.

"Yes, Master."

"So you do have some idea then. Please share what you witnessed."

Damien's hands trembled. He balled them into fists, hoping no one would notice. "The Master spoke of the grievous cycle," he said shakily. "She...she..." The sound of the Orphic's slashed windpipe while the man tried to suck in air filled Damien's ears again. He stamped his foot, took a breath, and continued. "...spoke of the wheel of reincarnation. Of the soul returning to its body ten times."

"Very good, Damien," Master Charos said. "Very good. Now tell me, did what you see frighten you?"

Lying to a teacher was forbidden, and Master Charos would know if Damien was telling one. Risking future ridicule from his peers, he spoke the truth.

"Yes, Master."

"Did his blood frighten you?"

"Yes, Master."

"Did his pain frighten you?"

"Yes, Master."

"Did his death frighten you?"

"Yes, Master."

Master Charos sighed. "Then you have much to learn, Damien. All of you do. You may sit."

Damien did so, sweat running down his back.

"Your souls are in bondage!" Master Charos bellowed. "And those souls are divine, your gift from the gods!" He pointed to the mangled half of his face. "*This* is its prison. *This* is the filthy soot of Titan flesh seared from their bones by Almighty Zeus!"

The children bowed their heads. "We are blessed by the gods," they chanted as one.

"You were born of sin, and you live as sinners in the eyes of the gods," Master Charos continued. "And you'll continue to do so in this life and the next. Ten times in total. Bound, as Damien correctly stated, to the circle of reincarnation." Master Charos again pointed to the stone wheel. "*This* is not a wheel, not really. It is instead a *symbol* of a journey each of us will take." He pointed to Damien. "Damien, I pray you will come to understand that what you saw should fill your heart with joy, not fear. For what you witnessed is a soul one step further on its journey toward communion with the gods."

All Damien figured he had seen was a man's throat being cut, but now wasn't the time to say so.

"Yes, Master," he said instead.

---

After dinner, Damien went straight to his room, where he lay in bed and waited for the sun to set. Although he heard the others in the library down the hall playing knuckle-bones and dice, he had no desire to join them. He craved another cup of wine, anything to alleviate the anxiety that stirred in his chest. Praying for dreamless sleep, he closed his eyes.

A quiet knock on the door opened them.

"Come in."

The door cracked open, and Ignatia appeared in the doorway, a krater of wine in her hands. Damien sat up, smiling. It was as if she'd read his mind.

She shut the door and poured the wine into two cups on the wooden desk that faced the window. The setting sun cast a pink light across the ocean waves, the first hints of humidity in the early summer breeze wafting inside. Ignatia sat beside Damien, who took the cup and a grateful swallow. The wine was again undiluted, its calming warmth soothing the knot inside his chest like a balm.

"Damien, I spoke to Master Charos," she began. "He told me about your class today." Damien took another drink. "He only wants what we all want."

"And what is that?" he asked.

Ignatia set down her cup, leaned toward Damien, and peered deeply into his eyes. "For you to remember why you are here."

He swallowed the rest of his wine, slid off his bed, and poured himself another cup from the krater. "I'm here to learn about the gods," he said.

"In a sense, yes, that is true," Ignatia said. "But that isn't what we pray you will remember. To continue on your path, to one day wear your red robe and call yourself Orphic, you first must remember what brought you to the temple in the first place. Do you understand?"

Damien shrugged and drank.

"Put that down. Right now," Ignatia ordered.

Unnerved by her tone, he set the cup on the desk.

"Where were you born?"

Damien opened his mouth to answer, then stopped. His brow crinkled as he scoured his thoughts. He had no choice than to admit the truth. "I don't know."

"And your parents," Ignatia continued. "Who were they? What did they look like?"

Damien again searched his mind. A moment later, his green eyes lit up. "My mother was very beautiful, with golden hair, and she wore a robe as blue as the sea," he said, cheered by the memory.

Ignatia shook her head. "The person you describe was Selene, the woman who took you into the temple and nursed you back to health. But she wasn't your mother."

Panic shot through him as the memory became clearer. In it he lay in a bed, the woman named Selene feeding him broth with a spoon. Ignatia was right.

"And what of your father? Do you remember anything about him?"

Damien stared at the floor, and shrugged.

"Damien, you have come as far in your studies as you can without understanding why you were chosen to reside in the Orphic Temple. We cannot go any further until you do. If too much time passes, you will have grown into a young man and will have to leave, I'm afraid."

Damien's head shot up, his eyes wide. "I don't want to leave!"

"I don't want you to leave either."

"I want to stay here with you!"

"Then you have to remember."

"What about the others? Why are they here? Tell me!"

"Every student is here for his or her own reason, and no two are alike," Ignatia said. "Some are incredibly learned of the sacred scriptures, with an understanding far beyond their years. Others are especially adept at music, with an ear for its creation that would make the gods themselves weep. There are great athletes, with skills that would rival the legends of Olympia. Every child has a special gift, a special *song*. As teachers to Orpheus—may he be blessed—it is our duty to help all of you learn to sing yours."

Damien felt ashamed to find his eyes welling with tears, but before he could stop himself, he was crying. "I don't know what my song is, Ignatia. I don't know why I'm here. I don't know where I came from. I don't know who my mother and father are."

He buried his face in his hands and sobbed. Ignatia let him, offering no comfort beyond her presence. After a while, he caught his breath, wiping his face on a sleeve, his eyes red and swollen.

"I'm sorry."

"Don't be sorry. I think perhaps we're closer than we've ever been."

"I don't feel closer to anything." Damien sniffed. "I feel like I don't even exist. How can someone be alive without a mother and father? Or memories?"

"Your memories are just on the other side of a door," Ignatia explained. "All you have to do is open it. But you will have to do it by yourself. I can't do it for you. No one can."

"I'm afraid."

"Of what?"

"Afraid of everything. The temple. The Orphics. Master Charos. The other children. *Everything*."

Ignatia let a small laugh slip.

"What's funny? Are you mocking me?" Damien asked.

"I don't mock you, no. I laugh because I find myself amazed by what the gods have created. Every day that I'm alive. You say you are afraid of everything, and I struggle to imagine how that could be so. For you see, Damien, when your crimes first brought you to this temple not two years ago, it was *we* who feared *you*."

## 12

---

*Navajo Pueblo, New Mexico Territory; October 1855*

A drumbeat filled Damien's ears. Stirring back into consciousness, he opened his eyes. His vision was blurry before clearing enough for him to see a roaring bonfire—that and a dozen Navajo warriors standing in a circle around him, coyote pelts wrapped around their shoulders, woven black masks covering their faces. Damien sat up with a start, his right shoulder flaring in pain. The warriors stared at him through their featureless masks, the steady drumbeat continuing.

*Bum...bum...bum...bum...*

Black fur and feathers swirled around him. During the war, he had seen more rotting corpses left to bake in the desert than he could count, twisted black faces receding from teeth bleached white by the sun. That was what the masks surrounding him brought to mind. Their brown eyes peered at him through small holes cut into the cloth.

*Bum...bum...bum...bum...*

Damien's searched for Igashu among the circle, but each man was indistinguishable from the next.

Suddenly the drumbeat stopped.

One of the warriors ululated from behind his mask, and the men descended onto Damien. Hands grabbed his arms and legs, dragging him to the bonfire. They released him then backed away, shouting in a language Damien didn't understand. He hadn't been upright like this since the showdown at Buckner's Ranch and relished the opportunity to stand on his feet again. The opportunity was short-lived, though, as all feeling drained from his legs, his knees buckling. Just before he hit the ground, one of the warriors caught him under the arms and brought him back to his feet, then shoved him toward the bonfire. Damien stumbled and tripped, the fire's white-hot coals rushing toward his face, only to be caught again, brought upright, and pushed backward, his arms flailing as he tried to gain his bearings. A sort of game began, the warriors sending Damien across the circle toward each other like children playing catch with a doll.

The shaman watched at the edge of the circle, the woven basket that had contained the rattlesnake cradled in her arms. A young girl stood next to her, clutching the blanket Damien had slept on. Two warriors held him tightly, one on each arm, his shoulder lighting up with pain. The girl walked toward the fire and tossed the blanket into the flames. The fabric exploded as if it had been doused in lantern oil, and the warriors all took a protective step backward. In a flash, the child fled back to the pueblo.

The shaman approached Damien, who was unable to move in the powerful grip of the warriors. One of the men brought Damien to his knees. The shaman stood over him, her eyes red by the light of the fire. She opened the basket and the snake rattled its tail. Fresh terror leapt into Damien as the old woman reached inside and brought out the reptile, its forked tongue shooting from its lipless mouth, tasting the night air. Damien heard the warrior to his right suck in his breath as she tossed the basket aside, the rattlesnake curling around her fingers. The men's grips loosened; Damien was now alone, on his knees before the woman.

The shaman took a step closer, the snake slithering up her arm, burying its head protectively in the crook of her elbow. She grabbed it and brought it back out into the firelight, her fingers squeezing its jaws open, a bead of glistening venom hanging from each fang. The woman's raspy breath steamed from her mouth in the cold air.

"Chindi," she said, and plunged the snake's fangs into the side of Damien's neck.

The poison seeped into his veins, his flesh burning. A moment later, the snake's body went slack, unwinding off the shaman's arm. It dropped to the ground in a heap, dead.

The warriors backed away, shouting in confusion. The shaman's eyebrows arched as she stared at the deceased rattlesnake. A familiar warmth washed over the muscles in Damien's legs, and he was pleased to find he could now stand without assistance.

The shaman reached out toward the wound on his neck and placed her open palm over his heart. Her mouth formed words without sound, her eyes widening, as she listened to a voice only she could hear.

Damien took her wrist, fearing the woman was taking ill, and at his touch she gasped. "What vexes you, healer?" he asked.

The woman shook her head, her breath coming quick. Then, in a language she had never spoken before this moment, whispered to him:

*"Now. You sing. Your song."*

The woman fell forward. The warriors caught her and guided her back toward the pueblo.

The warriors removed their ghost masks, their dark-brown eyes looking Damien over warily as they left the circle. Soon there was nothing but the crackling fire, Igashu, and the dead rattlesnake in a coiled pile at Damien's feet.

Damien picked it up and tossed it into the flames. The snakeskin blackened; when its dark eyes went white with ash, he took his first lurching steps in a week toward the pueblo. He nearly tripped, his extremities half numb and of limited use. Igashu walked to his friend's side and helped him put one foot in front of the other.

They walked this way, like two buddies stumbling out of a saloon after a night of revelry, then arrived at a teepee with a blue bear painted on it. Inside it was warm, with a small fire crackling, thin smoke rising through a vent at the top. After Igashu helped his friend to a bearskin on the floor, Damien collapsed onto it. Although his vision swam and his limbs were shaky, he was in the best shape he'd been in since the assault at Buckner's ranch. Igashu unrolled a blanket to make his own bed on the opposite side of the fire.

"Thank you, old friend," Damien said. "Thank you."

Igashu winked.

Damien used his good arm to bunch the bearskin behind his head into a pillow. The fire's smoke rose out of the teepee, swirling among the stars beyond. He drifted off to sleep, the old woman's words ringing in his ears.

*Now. You sing. Your song.*

---

Rifle fire woke Damien with a start. It was morning, hazy sunlight trickling into the teepee, the smell of the dead campfire in his nostrils. More shots rang out. He groaned as pain radiated through his bad shoulder. He listened to shouting in both English and Navajo, along with the drumbeat of horse hooves. His good hand instinctively went for his gun, then to the small of his back for his knife. But he possessed neither.

Damien half ran, half limped toward the pueblo, a cloud of dust in the air signaling the chaos on the other side. He found a suitable vantage point and peered around the corner, finding Maddox on horseback leading a posse of rifle-wielding men.

The warriors had stopped them just short of entering their structures, standing shoulder to shoulder against the invasion. Their expressions hard, they held weapons they had become justifiably infamous for utilizing. Damien, however, knew these white men were struggling to hide their terror.

Maddox turned to his scout, a sullen Navajo on the horse next to him, dressed in a military jacket draped with beaded necklaces.

"Any of them speak English?" Maddox asked him.

The scout raised a finger and pointed to the line of warriors. Igashu stepped forward, glowering. He carried a rifle affixed with a bayonet, finger on the trigger. Damien counted himself lucky that their first meeting some years ago had resulted in a friendship and not a death match; he wasn't at all sure he would have emerged the victor had it come to one. Maddox tilted his hat back and squinted in the sun.

"Where's Damien Attica?" he asked Igashu.

Igashu said nothing.

"Damien Attica," Maddox said again. "He here?"

Igashu shrugged.

"Thought you said a white man was being doctored to out here," Maddox told his scout.

"No white men here," Igashu said. "White man comes here, white man dies."

Damien had to cover his mouth to keep from shouting with laughter.

"Relations with you people have gone all the way south of cheese, ain't they," Maddox said. "Jesus Christ Almighty."

A fat bearded man among the posse, dressed in a Mexican poncho, raised his six- shooter in the air and called out to the men. "All right, boys! Let's toss the place for Attica! Keep your hands off the women!"

The warriors with rifles raised them in a firing line, while those with axes and long knives made ready for more intimate combat. The white men shouted among them- selves, a few turning and riding out of the posse, unwilling to risk their lives for whatever paltry wage Maddox was paying.

"Whoa, whoa, whoa!" Maddox called out. "Slow it down, ya'll! Let's slow 'er down!" He pointed to the fat man. "Steve! Shut your fuckin' yap!"

Ready to defend the pueblo to the death, the warriors didn't flinch; they merely waited patiently as the white men sorted themselves out.

Damien had seen this patience during the war. Navajos lining up to watch skirmishes from a vantage point, biding their time before killing and plundering whichever side was left for dead on the battlefield. Mexican, American—it didn't matter. They simply stood there, like birds of prey watching a starving animal slowly die.

"I said hold it! *Hold it!*" Maddox shouted. "Boys, lower them smoke poles! I said lower them, goddamn it!"

The posse lowered their guns; the warriors didn't.

Maddox took off his hat and wiped the sweat from his brow, then called out his next words. "Attica! If you can hear me, listen! And listen good! You should've had the good sense to die out there, like you was s'posed to! Now Greeley's huntin' for you. And he's gonna find you! Now I'll tell him you weren't here. But he'll keep at it! Starting with the old man!" Maddox leaned toward Steve, his voice lowered. "What's that old coot's name again?"

"Bennett."

"Bennett!" Maddox hollered.

Adrenaline ripped through Damien's bloodstream at the sound of his friend's name.

"As you well know, Mr. Greeley has a way of asking questions that ain't none too pleasant!" Maddox continued. "If you ain't at Bennett's, he'll keep looking! Might make his way over to the Llewelyn farm! Or the convent, to see George's daughter! Pretty young thing! Remember, you've been told!"

Maddox tugged on his horse's reins and turned back toward the desert. The posse fell in line behind him, the warriors remaining as they were. Only after they were specks on the horizon did they lower their weapons and turn back toward the pueblo.

Women and children gradually materialized from hiding, as did Damien. The pueblo's citizenry stared at him as he headed toward Igashu, undisguised contempt on their faces. Not only was he a threat to them spiritually, but he also had put their physical safety in jeopardy. It was time for him to leave this place, and he knew it.

They walked toward the horse stables. Damien spotted the Morgan, still saddled, drinking from a water trough.

"Igashu, you rascal!"

Damien had never been happier to see a horse in all his

life. He hobbled his way toward the animal as fast as he was able, stumbling through the dirt. Once there, he ran his hand down the Morgan's mane. The animal appeared well fed and healthy. Igashu couldn't hide his smile.

"Thank you," Damien said. "I don't know how to repay you. Don't think there's any way I could."

Damien was extra grateful to find the saddlebag attached, his few cans of beans, his books, even the pliers from the trading post all still inside.

Bennett. He had to get to Bennett.

Damien managed to get his boot situated in the stirrup, almost making it onto the horse when his leg gave out. He fell onto the dirt, flat on his back.

Igashu bent over, hands on his knees, shoulders shaking with laughter.

"Happy to be of amusement to you," Damien muttered.

He rolled onto his stomach and got back to his feet. Igashu was now laughing so hard his eyes were watering.

"Show at the top of every hour," Damien said. "Nickel gets you in the door. Drinks two bits."

He regarded the saddle, trying to come up with a plan. If he was permanently disabled—and there was every reason to believe he was—he would have to devise a method for getting on and off his horse. Walking across the territory for the rest of his life wasn't an option.

Damien had no choice. He would have to mount his horse the way women and children did, a display he highly doubted would strike fear in the hearts of his enemies should they ever observe him doing so.

He gripped the saddle's horn. "Igashu. You ever tell anybody you saw me choke this horn, I'll shoot you dead, friend or not."

He put his boot in the stirrup and pulled himself up,

face crimson with effort. Beads of sweat sprang from his skin as he reached the saddle and then across it like a sack of grain, catching his breath.

"Don't trouble yourself to help, Igashu, I got this. Truly."

He attempted to swing his leg over but failed. He then grabbed his pants leg, pulled the extremity to its destination, planted his hands on the saddle, and pushed himself upright, chest heaving.

"Piece of cake."

Wiping his eyes, Igashu approached his own horse, a golden Palomino with a black handprint on its flank. He got a running start and leapt onto its back.

"Show-off."

They rode until the sun began to fall, steering the horses toward a ravine that would soon be their camp.

---

Damien let his troubles wash out of him as the campfire danced in the darkness. He relished the desert's silence, communion with nature a reliable antidote to his ills. Igashu had packed the bowl of a wooden pipe and now carefully dipped it into the fire's topmost flames. His cheeks puffed as he inhaled the sweet smoke into his lungs. He sat back, his dark eyes glassy.

He passed the pipe across the campfire to Damien, who held up his hand. "Don't smoke. You know that."

Igashu shrugged, reversing the pipe and taking another lungful of smoke, then joined Damien in looking at the stars above.

"Thank you," Damien said after some time. "For what you did. Getting me back on my feet—literally—and all."

"You're welcome," Igashu replied.

"Navajos and the white man," Damien said. "They'll make war on each other soon. White man will win, Igashu. They'll kill every Injun in sight. Just like we did down in Mexico. Won't be but a few of you left. Just enough to dig the graves."

Igashu picked up a branch pulled from a mesquite tree and stoked the campfires flames.

"I hope I'm not around to see it happen," Damien continued, then closed his eyes.

Igashu used his branch to roll a small log into ash. The contents of his pipe had unraveled the mysteries of the universe to him, and he gave himself over to their teachings as Damien slept, for now.

## 13

*Bennett's Trading Post, New Mexico Territory; October 1855*

Damien and Igashu rode through the next day and the day after that, the sky bright and blue and cloudless. When hungry, they shared a can of beans. When thirsty, they sipped from the water bladder dangling off the Palomino's saddle.

The scrub brush soon grew familiar to Damien's eyes, in the peculiar way home always did. After he pointed to the east, the two men steered their way through the crisp fall air toward Bennett's Trading Post.

The stink of brush fire filled their nostrils not long after. A mutual alarm went off between the men, and they instinctively spurred their horses forward. Before long, it became apparent what they were riding toward.

Bennett's Trading Post had been burned to the ground, every inch of it. All that remained was the smell of decay, boiled sap, and a half-acre of charred mountain.

Damien slid off his horse and limped toward the heap of ash. Everything was blackened: the trees, the grass, and all things in the area that had once been alive.

That included Bennett's body, now little more than a ruined skeleton. Something bright and blue had been stuck between the teeth within the rotted skull. Damien stepped heavily toward the corpse. He gently pulled the rain-soaked paper from Bennett's mouth and unfolded it, revealing his own handwriting. They were the words of John McKenzie Anderson, a phantom solicitor concocted to demand justice for the rape of Josephina Llewelyn.

Isaac Greeley had connected the dots and tracked Damien's letter back to its source. Only the territory's trading post stocked blue stationery. The owner's body and all he had worked for had been destroyed in turn.

Damien sank to his knees as he pulled the pages apart.

Bennett was dead. No matter who was killed in retaliation, no matter how great their suffering, nothing on earth could change this singular, immutable fact. Damien reached out a hand and placed it on what had been Bennett's chest, his palm resting on a rib cage made clean by fire and scavenger birds.

Igashu crouched next to him, now understanding that this particular white man meant a great deal to his friend. Bennett's many faces flashed before Damien's eyes: the young buck behind the Missouri storefront counter who had taken him in and given him his first job, the wagon pioneer steering his horses west, the cantankerous proprietor making his stand in a territory unfit for man or beast. Bennett had been all these things and more. And now he was gone.

Damien got to standing unaided, the blue paper wadded in his fist like a ball. His eyes traveled around the patch of forest that was now his old friend's graveyard.

Igashu gripped his rifle, searching the perimeter for danger. Damien stepped through the rubble, most everything from Bennett's stock robbed by Greeley's men. Only a few things remained, ruined either by the fire or the rains that had put them out. One of those things stuck out of the charred earth twenty feet beyond Bennett's corpse, a small mercy that would aid him in the last thing he would do for the man he had called a father.

It was a shovel.

## 14

---

*Nunnery. New Mexico Territory; October 1855*

Damien and Igashu arrived at the convent a day after Bennett's body was remanded to the earth, their horse's heads sagging with fatigue. After they guided them to a puddle formed by the previous evening's rains, their animals greedily lapped the water.

The two men approached the nunnery. They were almost to the front porch when the wooden doors flew open, a nun wielding a double-barreled shotgun charging through them.

"Mother, we come in peace!" Damien shouted.

His childhood, spent in a Catholic orphanage, had given him a healthy fear of the women who had married themselves to Jesus Christ. No man in the territory, no matter how formidable, scared him. Nuns, however, most certainly did.

"I am here to ask your permission to visit with Miss Llewelyn," he continued.

"I should kill you for asking," the nun hissed. "The Lord would judge me fairly for it."

Damien now understood what had happened. Josephina wasn't here anymore. Someone had taken her away.

"How many were there?" he asked.

"Who the hell are you?" the nun barked, peering through the shotgun's sights.

"A friend of the family."

"I doubt that. And the heathen?"

"Igashu is my Injun guide, Mother. He means no harm."

The nun slowly lowered the shotgun. "The girl was taken two nights ago. They kicked in the door. Men reeking of liquor. They will surely suffer the Devil's torments for this."

Damien smiled. "Yes indeed, Mother," he said. "And I'm the man who will see to it that they do."

The nun hitched the hem of her black skirt slightly and came down off the porch. Igashu took a wary step backward.

"How many?" Damien asked.

"It was dark," she replied. "Perhaps a dozen."

"They say anything to you? Anything at all?"

"One of the cowards did. Yes."

"And what did he say?"

The nun took another step toward Damien, a curious smile coming over her face. "He said when Attica comes around, tell him we came to call. May I assume you are he?"

"I am. Damien is the name. Pleased to make your acquaintance," he replied. "Those men won't come back, Mother. You won't ever see them again. I swear it."

"And the girl? Josephina?" she asked.

"I'm betting she's still alive. They figure I'm coming to get her. They figure right."

After Damien tipped his hat, Igashu followed him back to their horses. The nun called out to them. "Gentlemen!" They turned back to the nun. "Go with God then," she said.

Damien squinted in the sun and lowered his hat brim. "Not sure God's the one I'm going with, Mother, but I appreciate the sentiment."

———

They guided their horses back to the trail. Damien whistled, which Igashu found he only did when he was in a particularly good mood.

As Damien eased the Morgan into a trot ahead and his whistling grew louder, the Navajo warrior knew one thing for certain.

Many men would soon die terrible deaths.

## 15

*Llewelyn Farm, New Mexico Territory; October 1855*

Damien and Igashu stopped at the Llewelyn farm on the way to Silver City only to confirm the inevitable. The property was in the state they'd expected to find it: silent but for the meandering of hungry, listless animals.

The cows had managed to knock down a fence on the edge of the property and were grazing on scrub brush in an attempt at keeping their giant stomachs full. The chickens had long since pecked one another to death in the henhouse, the lone survivor picking the bones of the vanquished clean. Several horses whinnied at the sight of them. Igashu rode to their stalls, opened the doors, and set them free.

Damien stepped over the kicked-in kitchen door. There at the table sat George Llewelyn, bound in rope to a wooden chair, castrated. His head was tilted back, genitals stuffed in his mouth, a pool of coagulated blood around his feet where he had bled out. Damien removed his hat and shooed away the flies that buzzed about the corpse.

They had tortured the old farmer to death while interrogating him, no doubt as to Damien's whereabouts in the territory. When the man continued to insist he didn't know, they had committed this atrocity.

Damien carried Llewelyn's putrefied corpse outside. Igashu was in the meadow fifty yards away, leading three horses by their bridles toward the Morgan and the Palomino. Navajos revered horses, and no man of his blood-line would leave one to suffer.

Damien stopped at a headstone not far from the barn. George's name was inscribed on it between a woman named Elizabeth, here memorialized as BELOVED MOTHER AND WIFE, and HENRY, LOVING SON. He set George's body down and retrieved a shovel from the shed, then set about to dig a second grave in as many days.

A couple of hours later, they met back at their horses. Damien gestured toward Igashu's newly acquired herd.

"They doin' okay?" he asked.

Shrugging, Igashu mounted his Palomino. When Damien didn't mount the Morgan, Igashu's face creased into a frown.

"Here's where we go our separate ways, friend," Damien said.

Igashu shouted in Navajo, his arms gesticulating wildly. Damien let him speak his mind before he continued.

"I'm gonna kill a lot of men, Igashu," he said. "A lot of *white* men. You don't want that coming back on you. You or your people."

"We go," Igashu said. "Together."

"No. Igashu. *No.*"

Igashu's jaw clenched and unclenched. Damien didn't budge.

"I'll miss you too, friend," Damien offered. "And I'll see you again. In this world or the next."

Tears sprang in Igashu's eyes. He wiped them away as he spat in the dirt.

"*Yá'át'ééh*," Igashu said.

"What's that mean?" Damien asked. "Goodbye?"

Igashu shook his head. "It means 'I will see you later.'"

---

## 16

*Outside Silver City, New Mexico Territory; October 1855*

As Damien rode through the territory, the loss of Bennett crept around the edges of his mind. He couldn't allow himself to be anchored by grief, a paralyzing state that served no purpose. He needed his wits about him now, needed them to be sharper than ever.

But first he wanted a drink.

He made camp that night, rereading Walt Whitman's *Franklin Evans* cover to cover. The book had a knack for driving out his thirst for liquor, the redemptive ending reminding him that drinking led men such as him only to ruin. But that night the book had little effect. Although Damien hadn't had a drink in over ten years, he still recalled the taste of whiskey, hot and sharp down his gullet. He fell into a restless sleep.

In the morning, a buzz filled his ears, waking him up. Chalking it up to insects that had found his half-eaten can of cold beans, he rolled over. When the buzzing grew louder, he opened his eyes to find three hummingbirds floating above his head, waiting for him to rise from his slumber.

Damien sat up, and the hummingbirds drew closer, cocking their heads from side to side. He raised a finger and one of them perched itself there, winking its tiny left eye. He winked back. "Thank you for the visit, friends. Much appreciated."

The hummingbirds flew away, instantly transforming into black specks against the pale-blue sky. He picked up his can of beans and scooped up the remainder in a few quick bites for his breakfast, his thirst for alcohol unquenchable.

---

The nearest saloon was a day's ride outside of Silver City, so he steered the Morgan there, keeping a safe distance from the wagon trail that connected the town to Santa Fe. Undoubtedly, Greeley's agents were lying in wait along the path, hoping to ambush the most wanted man in the territory.

Ike's Saloon was little more than a shanty house repurposed for paying customers seeking the blunting effects of local moonshine. It stood out against the dull-brown desert, the distillery behind it ejecting thin blue smoke into the chilled air. Damien drew closer to it, the Morgan slowing its pace as if to give him another few moments to think about what he was doing.

He limped through the saloon doors to find it empty, save for three cowpunchers in a darkened corner turning cards. He bellied up to the stretch of wood that served as the bar and folded his hands on it.

Ike the barkeep, a pasty beanstalk wearing a decrepit suit reeking of mothballs, shuffled down to Damien. He reached under the bar and slapped a small glass down, his hand shaking with an inebriate's morning tremors.

"Headed to Greeley?" Ike asked.

Damien's mouth fell open. "What'd you just say?"

"Didn't mean to pry, mister."

"What you just said. Say it. Again."

The bartender nervously cleared his throat. "Only asked if you were headed to Greeley. If you was, I got letters you might deliver in exchange for a libation. Is all. No offense meant."

"None taken," Damien said. "As it happens, I'm only passing through Silver City on my way to points beyond."

Ike coughed wetly, eyes on the bar.

"Silver City is called 'Greeley' now. What I meant, mister."

Damien leaned forward on his stool, now understanding. "Silver City is now known in this territory and points beyond as *Greeley*. That what you're telling me?"

"Yes, sir."

"Such is Isaac Greeley's economic influence."

"Yes, sir."

"That he renamed the town after himself."

"Yes, sir. He renames everything after himself."

"I see," Damien said. "I'll have a drink then."

Ike brought up a bottle of clear liquid, the only drink that he poured. Many men called it by many names, but it got the job done. He carefully topped off Damien's glass then corked the bottle.

"Two bits, stranger," the barkeep said. "Unless you'd trade for delivering my letters."

Damien reached into his pocket and pulled out five dollars in coin. He dropped them on the bar with a clatter and pointed to the bottle.

The barkeep narrowed his watery eyes at the money then at Damien. He picked up the coins, hefted their weight, then tossed them on the shelf behind him, the transaction made good. Damien waved his hand, and the bartender shooed away like a fly.

He held his shot delicately, careful not to spill a drop. He brought it to his nostrils, his throat stinging at the smell. He would drink this one, then another, then another. His burning bloodlust would be cooled, at least for a little while. That would have to do, for now.

Just as Damien opened his mouth to toss back the drink, an early spring day from his boyhood came to mind. He sat like this as it returned to him, his glass an inch from his lips.

---

Damien, fifteen years old, was chopping wood in Bennett's front yard, a hateful chore but one he always did without complaint. The back door opened and slapped shut behind him.

He buried the hatchet in the wood and wiped his brow. "Almost finished, sir."

Bennett walked down the staircase, his footsteps slow and deliberate in a way that belied his displeasure at something. Damien rolled his eyes before turning his head. When he did, panic bolted from his toes up through his chest at the sight of what Bennett was carrying.

It was a whiskey bottle, half empty.

"Somethin' wrong, Bennett?" Damien asked.

Bennett held up the bottle, his finger pointed two inches above the line where the liquor met the glass.

"'Fore I went to bed last night this was here," he said, his brow pinched. "Now it's here." He tapped his finger where the whiskey now sat. "You got an explanation?"

"No. No, sir."

Bennett grimaced. A beating, possibly a severe one, was in the offing. Damien took a step backward, contemplating running from the house and living the rest of his days on the streets of Jefferson City rather than face the man's wrath.

"You didn't drink from this bottle, boy? That what you're telling me?"

"Yes, sir. That's what I'm saying."

Bennett's nostrils flared. Damien cut his losses while he still could.

"I...I lied. I did. Drink some. Just a taste."

Bennett stalked toward Damien with a deliberation that made the hairs rise on his neck. He pulled the cork out of the bottle and shoved it into Damien's hand, wrapping his fingers around the glass.

"Finish it."

"I don't want any more, sir."

"*Finish the goddamn bottle!*" Bennett roared.

Damien took a long slug, his esophagus burning.

"More."

Damien obeyed.

"More."

He dropped the bottle from his lips with a retch. "I...I can't..."

Bennett grabbed the bottle with one hand and the scruff of Damien's neck with the other, pouring the whiskey down the boy's throat. Damien choked and sputtered and gasped as the brown liquid was emptied into his guts.

Bennett's face had turned purple with rage. "Drink it! Drink it up! Drink it all!" he shouted. Damien fell to his knees and vomited in the dirt. "There you go!" Bennett roared, pulling a pistol from his shirtwaist and handing it to Damien. "Take this."

Damien moaned, drooling vomit.

"*Take it.*"

Damien yanked the weapon from the man's hands. Bennett pointed to a tree in the center of the front yard.

"Hit that crabapple."

Damien swiveled to the tree to find a solitary apple, green and worm ridden, dangling from its branch.

"*Hit. It.*"

His vision swimming, Damien raised the pistol.

"What's the matter?" Bennett snapped. "You could hit apples off that there tree yesterday. And the day before that. And the day before that. You can't hit it now?"

Damien brought the pistol up and fired, missing his target by several yards.

"Try again!"

Damien weaved on his feet, closing one eye, desperate to find his aim.

"*Shoot, goddamn it!*"

After one last futile attempt, Bennett stripped the gun from his hands. "You want to lay waste to your fucking brains, you'll not do it here. That understood, boy?"

Bennett shoved him to the ground, and Damien heaved his guts into the dirt.

---

Damien set his shot on the bar, untouched, and cried.

The bartender politely moved down the bar, wiping it down with a filthy rag.

Damien continued to weep. A voice full of whiskey shouted from the back in response.

"Will you shut the *fuck* up?"

Damien turned to the voice, his face streaked with tears. A drunken cowboy sat at the shadowed table in the corner with his friends, a poker game laid out, mocking smiles on their faces.

"Yeah, you! We're tryin' to have ourselves a card game over here, and now we gotta listen to you carrying on? Fuck that. Shut up."

No longer crying, Damien slid off his stool.

The cowboy clapped his hands. "Well! You one bad hoot owl, ain'tcha? I dunno, boys. This dude looks mail-ordered to me."

The men laughed and sipped their drinks. The cowboy stood, revealing the holstered pistols hanging heavily off his leather belt.

"What you say, Molly? Wanna step outside for a minute? I'll give you something to cry about."

Damien allowed him to close the distance between them.

"I asked you something, Molly," the cowboy spat.

Damien imagined grabbing the bottle of moonshine by its neck, shattering it on the bar, and slicing its jagged edges against the cowboy's forehead. How it would unclasp the man's skin like a lady's purse, blood running down his face like rain off a windowpane.

"What the hell?" the cowboy said, backing up toward the table.

Damien envisioned one of the companions opening fire. He would use the cowboy as a human shield, the man's head snapping forward as bullets pierced his spine. He would take the dead man's pistols and shoot the smaller of the two in the chest. The bigger one would run for the door, abandoning his friends. Large men with small agendas always did that, Damien found.

"Holy *shit*," the cowboy said, and now his friends saw it too.

Damien would catch the big cowboy by the shirt collar before he could make his escape; he'd shove him face first through the plate-glass window that spanned the bar's entrance. The man would crawl through the dirt, and Damien would flip him onto his back with his boot tip.

Ike came around, getting an angle on what had the men so upset. When he gazed upon Damien's face, he raced out of his own saloon.

Damien guessed the cowboy would beg for his life. "You chose the wrong friends," Damien would say—that or something very much like it. He would raise a pistol by its barrel and smash the butt into the cowboy's face.

The two men at the poker table ran out after the bartender.

Damien would keep smashing it, over and over and over and over, until the cowboy's head split like a pumpkin. He then would get to his feet and stomp the man's forehead with the heel of a boot until his brains spurted out of his ears like jelly.

He imagined these violent events but did not act upon them.

The cowboy sank to his knees.

Damien's eyes were black as ravens and shining. He held out his hand. "Guns," he said, his voice reverberating inside the cowboy's skull. "Give them to me."

The cowboy laid his pistols on the floor in front of Damien's boots like a penitent offering a sacrifice at an altar.

"Go," Damien said. "Tell others what you have seen."

The cowboy fled.

Damien picked up the weapons and holstered them. He walked outside, and the black stallion ran past him in a blur.

*Faster,* it said.

Damien remembered Colonel James Balazarus's wall of animal trophies and gave chase.

*Faster.*

He remembered the rapist Morrow, on his back, intestines in the dirt.

*Faster.*

Bennett, burned to a crisp.

*Faster.*

George Llewelyn, unmanned.

*Faster.*

And he remembered Josephina Llewelyn, first raped facedown in the hay, and now again ripped from her bed, Greeley's prisoner.

*Faster.*

Damien sprinted beside the Morgan, nearly passing it, then leapt onto the saddle. The Morgan spirited him across the desert plain, wild shrieks filling the air, Damien not realizing it was the sound of his own voice.

He charged forward on the Morgan toward Greeley, New Mexico Territory, his mouth open in a howling scream.

# PART II

## THE COMANCHE MOON

## 17

*Attica Peninsula, Greece; the Month of Skirophorion, 435 BC*

The children sat in a bowl-shaped meadow that overlooked the sea, each with a caged bird set in the grass before them. Master Praxis, a slight man with thin shoulders barely holding up his white tunic, paced the rows of students, the twittering of the birds melding with the crashing waves below.

"Within these gilded cages are, quite clearly, birds," he announced, his nasal voice struggling to be heard over the crashing waves. "In the not-so-distant past, they were free to fly about the sky and lay their eggs and generally do whatever a bird sees fit to do. Now they are your prisoners. Do you understand, children?"

"Yes Master," the children answered as one.

"These creatures are now your charges. You are responsible for them. If and when they eat, if and when they drink, if and when they die. It is entirely up to you. May I suggest that the gods—may they be blessed—would frown upon the latter?"

"Yes Master," the children answered.

"Are there any questions?"

Hands shot up across the meadow.

"Yes, Korrina," Master Praxis said, pointing to a girl with her hair tied up in a satin bow.

"Master Praxis, may I name mine Lysandra?"

"I want to name mine Myron!" shouted a boy.

The children spoke out of turn as they tried to come up with a superior name for their respective bird. Master Praxis listened patiently, his arms crossed. After a while, he raised an eyebrow, and the chatter died down.

"Korrina, you asked Master if you may name the bird you've been instructed to care for 'Lysandra.' Is that correct?"

"Yes, Master," Korrina replied.

"And when you sought Master's permission to do so, you used the word 'mine.' Yes?"

"Yes, Master."

"Why?"

The question took Korrina aback. When no words came forth, Master Praxis raised his hand. "Allow me to help you with this, child," he said, and walked to the center of the group, the children's heads turning to follow him as he did.

"Korrina used the word 'mine' because she believes that the bird is *hers*. That the bird is *her* property, the way one possesses a drinking cup or a charm worn around one's neck. In fact, the bird is no such thing. It is a creation of the gods—may they be blessed. It was born of their brows and thus can never be the property of man, woman, or child. Do you understand, children?"

"Yes, Master," the class replied.

"The birds before you can never and may never be named. If you must call them something, call them 'birds,' for that is what they are. My advice is to call them nothing, which you will find they will reciprocate. To them you are a giant creature, a Titan peering through the bars of a prisoner's cell. They only wonder when they will be freed and allowed to take back to the skies, which they were born to do. Am I clear?"

"Yes, Master," the children replied.

"Very good. For the rest of the afternoon, you will spend time with your respective bird and that bird only. You are not to speak or play or generally carry on with a fellow classmate. If you do speak, speak to the bird, though I highly doubt it will understand a word you have to say. My further advice, should you wish to take it, is to *listen*, rather than impose upon it your loud, frightening human prattling. Am I understood?"

"Yes, Master."

"Class dismissed."

The children leapt to their feet, gingerly grasping the handle of their birdcages and holding them up to their faces, cooing at the birds within. Most ignored Master Praxis's advice and spoke to them at once, introducing themselves by name and assuring them they were pretty birds, good birds, that they would be well taken care of. Sparrows, crows, doves, pigeons and all manner of Grecian fowl chirped and tweeted, filling the seaside valley with song. Master Praxis walked up the hill back toward the temple, his arms behind his back, whistling tunelessly.

Damien, who always had positioned himself toward the back of the class, sat still, a tiny cage in his lap. In it was a little finch, all its feathers yellow except on the head, which were black. It hopped from its perch to the floor of the cage then back up again, ceaseless peeping emitting from its beak. Damien made his way down toward the beach, cage dangling from his hand.

He liked that the sound of the ocean surf drowned out the other children's voices as well as the anxious thoughts that played nonstop in his head. The cool beach sand gave under his footsteps as he walked the coastline. The finch hopped around its cage. After some time, he found the rock he liked and sat upon it, gently set the finch on another rock next to him, and stared at the sea.

His days at the temple were numbered. Try as he might, he couldn't fulfill the task Ignatia and the masters had set upon him: to remember where he had come from. Who he'd been born to and why he was here. Everything before his first night in the temple dormitory, when he was spoon-fed hot soup and had a cool cloth pressed against his forehead, was a blank.

Damien closed his eyes and let the crashing waves and sea air wash over him. He steadied his breathing as best he could, trying to stave off a full-blown attack on his jangled nerves. He hugged his knees tighter and buried his face in his arms. He sat like this for a long while, and then a small voice spoke.

*The ocean is forever, and you are a child of the gods.*

His head shot up. He looked left, then right, trying to identify who had spoken, but the beach was empty.

*The ocean is forever, and you are a child of the gods.*

Damien leapt to his feet and spun around, expecting to find one of the boys taunting him. There was nothing but rocks and sand.

"Who said that?" he asked. "Who's speaking to me?"

No response came.

The tide was rising enough that his sitting rock would soon be consumed by it, so he headed back to the temple. He brushed sand off the back of his smock and picked up the birdcage by its handle. What he found inside it stopped him in his tracks.

The finch was not chirping, was not hopping, was in fact not moving or doing anything. It sat on its perch, head cocked to the side, unmistakably looking directly up at Damien.

He lowered the cage and stared back at the bird. He took a step to the right, and the bird turned its head, following him. He took a step the left and the bird did the same thing.

"Clever bird, aren't you?" Damien said, embarrassed to have asked it aloud. Cold seawater splashed against the back of his knees. He lifted the cage and started his way back down the beach.

He walked for a while, careful not to swing the cage and disturb the finch. Shortly into his walk, his thoughts again went dark. He would be terribly lonely outside of the temple; he was sure of that. There would be no one to talk to, no Ignatia to soothe him, no wine to wash away the incessant thrum of anxiety that beat inside his chest. If he could, he would have made up a story about his past to satisfy their requirements, but that would never work—Ignatia and the masters were only waiting for him to tell them what they already knew. He was desperate for any shred of memory, any clue. He cried, hoping no one would hear him.

*The ocean is forever, and you are a child of the gods.*

"Who keeps saying that?" Damien shouted.

He turned around to the empty beach but saw nothing behind him but his own footprints.

At dinner that night, the children ate hot barley bread slathered with sheep butter, the birdcages lining the long wooden tables in the dining hall. The birds' voices echoed off the stone walls while the students fed their charges bits of their bread. Damien sat at the end of a long row, watching as his finch hopped about the bottom of his cage, gobbling up the crumbs he tossed its way. One of the boys sitting across from him, a redhead named Gallus, stopped feeding his bird, a large black crow, and tossed a bit of bread at Damien, bouncing it off his chest.

"Is it true? What they say about you?" Gallus asked.

Damien didn't respond; he only glared at the boy.

"Well? Is it?"

"I don't know what you're talking about," Damien finally said, his voice low.

"Yes, you do. You must."

Damien shook his head. Gallus sighed, and called out to a boy farther down the table.

"Borus."

"What?" said the heavyset boy, who was attempting to convince his canary to jump to his finger.

"C'mere."

Borus pushed himself back from the table and walked over to Gallus, who pointed at Damien.

"What does everybody say about him?"

Borus didn't hesitate. "That he's a wolf boy."

Gallus nodded. "See?"

Damien fidgeted in his seat. "What...what does that mean?" he asked Gallus.

"It means your mummy was a wolf. And your daddy was a wolf too. But the gods made sure you were born a boy."

"But you're not a boy," Borus told Damien, picking his nose and wiping it on his smock.

"No, you're not," Gallus continued. "Because you eat wild animals the same way wolves do. Deer and rabbits and such."

"No, I don't," Damien replied.

"Sure you do," said Gallus, evenly. "Everybody knows it."

Nothing about the boys' attitudes belied any sort of mockery or derision. They appeared to be merely stating facts.

"No, I don't," Damien insisted.

Gallus and Borus shot each other a look. Borus shrugged.

"Then why were you all covered in blood and leaves and such?" Gallus asked.

"When?" Damien replied.

"What do you mean, when?" Borus said. "How could you not remember something like that?"

"When you came here. When the nurses brought you inside," Gallus continued. "We all saw it."

Damien stared at the two boys, his vision swimming.

"Oh, come off it," Gallus said, and called down the table to another student. "Aja. Aja!"

Aja, a dark-haired girl running a gentle finger down a mourning dove's feathers, rolled her eyes over to Gallus.

"Remember what you said? That night they brought the wolf boy in?"

"Don't call him that," Aja said.

"Why not?"

"It's mean."

"How is it mean?" Gallus protested. "I rather like wolves."

"Damien doesn't have teeth like a wolf," Borus offered.

"Never mind. Aja. Tell him what you said."

She shook her head. "I don't want to."

"Come on."

"Leave me alone."

"She asked why you were naked," Gallus told Damien. "Where your clothes had gone. The nurse carrying you said, 'Animals don't wear clothes.'"

"Doesn't make him a wolf, though, does it?" Borus asked.

"What else could he be?" Gallus replied.

Damien couldn't breathe. His mouth was so dry he couldn't swallow.

"You all right?" Borus asked.

Sweat sprang out across his palms. He felt cold, weightless.

"You okay?" said Gallus.

Damien shot up and ran for the dining hall doors. He shoved them open and raced down the hall, his feet slapping against the stone floor. He ran until he reached his room, where he slammed the door shut and slid to the floor, panic washing out of him and pooling around his shaking body.

For one brief moment, Damien had seen himself the way the other children had those two short years ago—and the nurses and masters too. It was the night he had been brought into the temple for the first time, shivering and naked and soaking wet—not with rain but human blood.

He recalled being wrapped up in the arms of an older woman in a long blue dress, her embrace the first warm touch in as long as he could remember. His hands, pale and trembling, were caked in blood, so thick and dark the nurses initially had mistaken it for mud. Yet there had been no rain, hadn't been for some time.

He had blinked against the torchlight illuminating the dark hallways near the temple's entryway. Children, dozens of them, had trickled out of their rooms to watch the spectacle of the naked, bloody boy being carried inside by a small parade of nursemaids, who then had rushed him into an empty room and closed the wooden door behind them.

And that's all Damien remembered.

———

He spent the night curled in a ball on his bedroom floor, then woke the next morning to three loud knocks on his door. He opened it to reveal Master Praxis on the other side. In his right hand dangled a birdcage, the black-and-yellow finch chirping within.

Damien took a step back and opened his mouth to offer an explanation. Master Praxis held up a hand, silencing him, and pointed to the stool in front of the wooden table Damien was expected to use for study. He sat obediently, folding his hands in his lap, his eyes on the floor.

"Look at me, child."

Damien did.

"Is this not the bird that was entrusted to your care?"

"Yes, Master."

"The bird Master instructed you to provide food, water, and shelter?"

"Yes, Master."

"Then why am I holding it in my hand? Why did a servant bring it to me from the dining hall? And why did said servant discover it abandoned next to a plate of half-eaten bread?"

"Master…"

"I am disappointed in you, Damien of Attica. Very disappointed indeed."

Damien hung his head.

"No, no. No one feels sorry for you, boy. You reside as a

student in the great Orphic Temple. You are fed and clothed and sleep in a warm bed. You are instructed in the ways of Orpheus—may he be blessed. Don't you dare feel sorry for what you have brought upon yourself."

"Yes, Master."

"You will be punished."

"Yes, Master."

"Wash your face."

---

Damien was made to pick the blackberries that he and the other children often enjoyed with their breakfast. Only after clearing an entire patch was he relieved of his punishment. A taciturn nurse oversaw his afternoon of labor and later wrapped bandages over his swollen, bloody fingers, which had been ravaged by the tiny thorns underneath every delicate piece of fruit. Afterward, filled with self-pity, he retired to his room.

The finch bounced around in its cage, cheerful as always. Damien lay down and put a pillow over his head to muffle the noise. Exhausted from the day's work, he was nearly asleep when the tiny voice again spoke its familiar words.

*The ocean is forever, and you are a child of the gods.*

Damien sat up. The room was empty, save for the finch, which was perfectly still, like a little statue. Its head was cocked to the side, the better to look Damien directly in the eyes. He swung his legs over his bed, leaned into the cage, and peered through the bars, inches from the bird.

It didn't move so much as a feather.

It did, however, wink.

Damien took a deep breath and raised his hand to knock on the great oak door before him. He hesitated, the bird fluttering in the cage giving away his presence.

"Enter," said a voice behind the door.

Master Praxis sat behind a desk piled high with scrolls and parchment. He peered at a document through a thick looking glass, his right eye magnified to the size of an apple as he read. Damien quietly closed the door.

"Young Damien. Back from the blackberry patches, I see."

"Yes, Master."

"Difficult pickings, eh?"

"Yes, Master."

"Well, go on then. Sit."

Damien walked to the wooden chair in front of the old man's desk, carefully set the birdcage on the floor next to him, and sat.

A giant painting depicting the hero Herakles and the beast Cerberus covered the wall behind the Master, and Damien found himself getting lost in the intricacies of the work. The teacher swiveled around to look at it.

"Came with the room, I'm afraid. Do you like it?"

"Very much, Master."

"Truth be told, I find it a bit pedestrian. They just sort of stand there. Lacks imagination. Only my opinion, of course. What draws you to it? And don't say the color."

Damien studied the painting for a few moments more before replying. "I like the serpents coming from Cerberus's mane," he said.

"Oh? Why that in particular?"

Damien considered his answer. "Because," he finally said, "they are his friends."

Master Praxis smiled. "Indeed." The finch chirped, and he pointed to the cage. "And how are you two getting along?"

Damien shifted in his seat. "That's what I came to speak with you about, Master...if I may."

"Proceed."

Damien peered at his hands as though he would find the words he was looking for written across their palms. All he found was a thin sheen of sweat. "My bird...*the* bird... is...*unusual*, Master."

"How so?"

"It..." Damien began, then stopped himself.

"Yes?"

"It...it..."

Damien let out a long breath. "I think it speaks to me, Master."

Master Praxis's bushy eyebrows shot up. He laid the parchment in his hand aside and pushed the glass away on its swivel. "It speaks to you."

"Yes, Master."

The old man sat forward, his chair creaking, and folded his hands in front of him on the great oak desk. "You're very...*unusual* yourself. Aren't you, Damien? To borrow the word you used to describe the creature I placed in your care."

Damien shrugged. "I suppose so. Most people think I am."

"It's not an insult, boy. Far from it. Just an observation."

Master Praxis lifted a krater from a clay dish, poured wine into two small cups, and passed one to his student.

As Damien gratefully swallowed the red liquid, the tension melted out of his shoulders.

"I understand something of an ultimatum has been put to you," Master Praxis said. "A demand upon your memory. A full understanding of the journey that brought you to this temple. Is this the case?"

"Yes, Master."

"Sounds dreadful."

Damien laughed then covered his mouth, embarrassed.

"I do believe that's the first time I've ever heard you laugh, young man," Master Praxis said, and swallowed his cup of wine in one gulp. "You say the bird seated on the floor beside you 'speaks' to you. Is that what you're telling me?"

"Yes, Master. As clearly as you are speaking to me now," Damien replied, his tongue loosened by the wine.

Master Praxis chuckled. "Well, then, Damien. That leaves only one question before us." The teacher leaned forward, eyes twinkling. "Whatever in the world does it have to say?"

# 18

---

*Greeley, New Mexico Territory; November 1855*

The beggar lurched through the thoroughfare, reeking of excrement. Passersby reversed direction, pinching their noses or exclaiming their disgust. The wretched creature hadn't been seen in the streets of Greeley before today, and not one citizen had bade him welcome or made an offer to help. Not until Mrs. Truitt of The Greeley Temperance League made her way down a wooden sidewalk, fresh from her morning shopping at the general store.

The beggar hid his features under a pitiful mask made from a burlap sack, one eye peering out into the world through a single hole. He was draped in a horse blanket, his tattered clothes sodden. Mrs. Truitt observed him for a while as he dragged his lame left leg, his weight thrown onto his walking stick. Allowing him another moment without aid would be unforgivable in the eyes of the Lord, so Mrs. Truitt reorganized the bundle of parcels in her arms and stepped out into the muck.

The smell wafting off the man nearly sent her back to

the sidewalk, but instead she pulled out a handkerchief and placed it over her nose.

"Sir? Good sir, here," she said, holding up her hand in greeting.

The beggar stopped and slowly twisted his head to her, his green eye wide.

"Do you require my assistance, dear man?" she asked.

The beggar grunted.

"What is your name?"

The beggar's eye rolled up in his head, mucus churning in his throat. He trembled slightly, a low unintelligible sound emitting from behind the mask.

"No. Please. Is your tongue dumb, sir?"

The beggar grunted again.

"Of course. God forgive me. Trouble yourself to speak no further."

Mrs. Truitt was pleased to find a few pedestrians slowing to take in the scene. She had worked mightily to bring a Christian influence to this whiskey-soaked strip of dirt in the middle of the desert and always relished an opportunity to lead by example.

"Let's try this," Mrs. Truitt said, turning back to the beggar. "I will ask you a question, and you nod for yes and shake your head for no. How about that?"

The beggar nodded.

"Are you hungry?"

The beggar nodded.

"Of course you are. Are you injured? You seem to be dragging your leg. Do you need to see a doctor?"

The beggar shook his head.

"Very good. There's a church just on the other side of the thoroughfare. Christ's Calvary. We will go there at once."

Mrs. Truitt spun around to the citizens who had paused

to take in the unusual scene. She held out her parcels in her arms and raised her voice to the small crowd. "Who will take these goods to my husband at his place of business while I attend to this poor soul?"

Her husband, Mr. Truitt, was less than thirty yards to the east, butchering hogs in a tent bearing his name. The assembled stared blankly at one another until a slight man raised his hand. "Happy to, Mrs. Truitt," he said.

"God bless you, Liam. How very *good* of you."

Liam collected the groceries from her arms into his and backed away, the pungent scent of fecal matter wafting off the hooded man overpowering him.

"Come, sir, please," Mrs. Truitt said with a dramatic sweep of her arm. "Let us go to Christ's Calvary, where you will be ministered to in the eyes of the Lord."

The beggar followed Mrs. Truitt down the road, leg dragging.

---

Christ's Calvary was a structure designed to be the first thing one saw when approaching the town of Greeley. The steeple contained an iron bell that had been delivered by stagecoach from Kansas City, Isaac Greeley himself having paid for its passage. He had suggested to Mrs. Truitt and the other women of the Temperance League that perhaps the church should be named after him in return. Mrs. Truitt then had the awkward task of informing Mr. Greeley that churches were named for either saints or the Lord Jesus Christ himself, not after mortal men, no matter how generous. The man acquiesced, settling on a placard prominently displayed near the poor box just inside the entrance proclaiming the bell a "generous gift from our esteemed benefactor, Mr. Isaac Greeley."

Mrs. Truitt led the beggar to an empty stall in the horse stables, where she pushed the wooden gate open to reveal a bed of straw.

"It's not much, I'm afraid, but it will get you out of the mud. Please rest while I fetch you something to eat."

The beggar swiveled his head, his eye canvassing his new shelter. The rumbling in his chest returned.

"Are you all right?' she asked. "What's the matter?"

Mrs. Truitt took a step back. The foul-smelling man dressed in rags reached out a shaky hand. A whisper emerged from behind his mask. "God...bless...you...ma'am."

Tears sprang into the woman's eyes. "My dear man, God bless *you*. Please rest yourself. I will fetch you some meat from my husband's butchery."

She turned on a heel, holding the hem of her skirt with one hand, the other dabbing her wet cheeks with a handkerchief.

Damien waited a while to make sure she was definitely gone before pulling off his mask.

He drank in the fresh air gratefully, stretching his arms over his head and bringing them down to his toes, spine cracking. He had walked for nearly five miles in this disguise, his body contorted, leg dragging.

Damien pulled off the horse blanket and then his shirt. His skin was itching so badly that he couldn't scratch it hard or fast enough, his fingernails leaving red streaks over his shit-smeared flesh. Having had no idea animal excrement could cause such a reaction, he cast his eyes desperately about the stalls for a source of water. A moment later, he found a milk pail half full of murky rainwater and nearly shouted with joy as he poured it over his chest and back.

Damien had spent the previous morning walking behind the Morgan as it grazed on the thin white patches of desert grass. When the animal finally moved its bowels, he stared at the pile, black flies collecting on its greasy surface, trying to come up with a solid plan B. There was no alternative. A beggar, especially one appearing to hide a deformity, would be subject to immediate harassment in a small town like Greeley. Idiots and mongoloids were given no quarter in the frontier towns of the new West, and if Damien were to have to defend himself, his identity would be revealed. The only thing that might prevent this could be found in the stinking heap at his feet.

He wiped himself down and got back into his costume, wincing at the smell.

Mrs. Truitt found her beggar curled in the hay, asleep. She set down a crumpled yellow ball of newspaper next to him, crossed herself, and backed out of the stall. When her footsteps faded, Damien sat up and pulled off his mask with a gasp. Today was Saturday. He wasn't sure how he would get through the next twenty hours waiting for Sunday Mass to begin.

He unfolded the paper to reveal a pile of steaming tripe. Although Damien had no taste for the meat, he appreciated the gesture. Mrs. Truitt, for all her obvious self-right-eousness and probable friendly dealings with Isaac Greeley, was a good person. Damien never had split hairs when it came to people's character. Most were good, and well meaning, even if flawed in other ways. Besides, he didn't have time to sort out the sort of bad from the just plain evil. There were so many of the latter to kill.

An image in the corner of the crumpled newspaper caught his eye. He slid it out from under the tripe and held it up to the sunlight. There, in newsprint, was a drawing of his face, or at least a crude approximation of it. Squiggly black lines had been drawn across his forehead to indicate an expression of meanness. Underneath, in bold type, the following proclamation appeared:

WANTED FOR MURDER: THE COWARDLY ASSASSIN DAMIEN ATTICA. DEAD OR ALIVE. REWARD: $100.

"A hundred dollars?" Damien asked aloud. "That's all?"

He dropped the paper. Up in the northern half of the territory the price on his head had gone up to nearly a thousand dollars in golden nuggets before he was through with the Bannon Gang, a corrupt outfit of lawmen who used the power of their badges to inflict all manner of injustices on the populace. Maybe Balazarus and Morrow didn't quite rate the same. Damien comforted himself with the knowledge that the bounty would no doubt rise dramatically and soon.

## 19

*Christ's Calvary Church; Greeley, New Mexico Territory; November 1855*

The church bell clanged at the stroke of nine. Mrs. Truitt, dressed in her Sunday finery, led her husband across the thoroughfare to Christ's Calvary, the townsfolk quietly filing in around her. Mr. Truitt was suffering his way through a rather serious hangover, mopping his brow as his wife led him through the stables. When the couple arrived, they found the beggar propped up in a corner of the stall.

"Sir? Good sir?" Mrs. Truitt said, her hands on her knees as if calling to a puppy.

The beggar awoke with a start, coughing wetly.

"You must come into the church with us, as our guest," Mrs. Truitt said. "Come."

She extended her hand, and Damien stood unsteadily. Mrs. Truitt elbowed her husband, and the portly man stepped forward to help, only to be repelled by the scent of manure emanating from Damien. Mr. Truitt ran for the stall opposite, where he vomited into a pile of straw.

"I feel better, dear," he said, wiping his mouth.

The Truitts walked ahead of Damien, who lurched behind them. They found the church packed to capacity, the air thick and warm, a stark contrast to the near freezing fall-morning air outside. The murmuring congregation fell silent at the sight of the stooped man squinting out of his burlap mask.

Mrs. Truitt addressed them in her high, clipped voice. "Dear citizens, do not be alarmed, for within this man's strange ensemble is a lamb of God. 'It is a sin to despise one's neighbor, but blessed is the one kind to the needy.' Proverbs, fourteen-twenty one."

Mrs. Truitt pulled Damien along by the shoulder, her arm sweeping as if conducting an orchestra as she spoke.

"This pitiable man has sought out this community in the hopes of mercy and redemption. I beseech you to welcome him as I have."

With that, Mrs. Truitt led Damien down the aisle, the townsfolk gripping their noses as he passed. Damien fell into a pew near the back, now seated inside a building for the first time since convalescing at the pueblo. He was hoping for a long service, the stiff wooden bench already doing wonders on his aching back.

Mrs. Truitt and her husband sat down a few rows ahead. Reverend Lawson, a ginger-haired man of considerable girth, walked to the pulpit, a Bible tucked under his arm. He cleared his throat and had taken a wheezing breath to utter the service's first words when the church's double doors opened with a whoosh.

Isaac Greeley entered, immaculately dressed in a gray frock coat and a top hat. Maddox and another man followed him closely, both armed. The trio's boots thudded along the floorboards, heads turning as they made their way to the front pew.

Greeley doffed his hat and handed it to Maddox, who along with the other cowboy remained standing, each on either side of the pew, hands folded in front of them.

"Mr. Greeley."

"Reverend."

"How good of you to join us at Sunday worship."

"Happy to be here. Let's get to it."

Nervous chuckles rose from the crowd. Damien shifted in his seat, his heart beating so hard he was sure it could be heard in the next row over. It took every ounce of discipline he had not to rip off his hood, strip Maddox of his gun, and execute Greeley in the middle of the church for all to see. In fact, he wasn't sure he could last the whole service without doing just that.

Reverend Lawson read several passages from Leviticus, then Job. He gave a fiery sermon about the disintegration of the Christian family in the face of Western expansion, as well as the duty of all the men in attendance to stay mindful of their husbandly duties to the women and children they had left Back East. His fists clenched in his lap, Damien didn't hear a word of it.

As the sermon neared its conclusion, the congregation rose to sing "God's Grace on Thee." Greeley sang the loudest, his baritone soaring to the rafters. Neither Maddox nor the other bodyguard participated in the singing and hadn't moved a muscle during the service. They just stood there, hands folded.

The song concluded and the congregation resumed their seats. Greeley did not, however; instead he stepped out of the pew and walked to the pulpit. The reverend vacated it with a slight bow and supplicating grin.

Greeley rebuttoned his coat and took in the crowd with a steely glare. "'Mornin'," he said.

"Good morning, sir," the crowd replied.

"How about that bell? You like the bell, do you?"

Appreciative murmurs filled the room. Greeley held up a hand, commanding silence.

"Fine, fine. I had that bell sent here at great expense from Kansas City. Very expensive bell."

Greeley pointed to another man in the front row, who stood and bowed, much like the reverend had.

"'Mornin' sir."

"What's your name again?

"Phineas. Uh, Finn, sir."

"Finn. You used a word to describe that bell at the ribbon cutting, didn't you?"

"Sir?"

"Yes, I'm sure it was you."

A woman Damien assumed to be Finn's wife stared up at her husband, wide eyes communicating silent, urgent thoughts.

Finn stammered his next words. "I-I-I think the bell's... I...I-I-I think the bell's tremendous, sir!" He sat back down so hard the pew wobbled.

"Tremendous!" Greeley said. "Yes. That was the word. *Tremendous*. I think so too. Now I didn't get up here to talk about the bell, tremendous though it is. No. There is, as many of you know, a much more pressing matter that directly affects all of us in this wonderful, God-fearing community."

Greeley exhaled, gripped the pulpit, and shook his head.

"I needn't remind you that we have lost two of our finest citizens in recent months. Lost to a cowardly, sinister operator who has cost you nice people many a good night's rest. I speak, of course, of that gutless, spineless yellow-belly, Damien Attica."

Greeley canvassed the crowd, brow furrowed.

"I took out an advertisement in yesterday's newspaper at my own expense. I have placed similar notices across this and the surrounding territories, all at considerable cost. Excluding the bounty I will pay personally, of course, to the man courageous enough to bring down this dastardly son of a bitch by hook or by crook!"

A woman gasped, and Greeley placed a hand on his chest.

"Forgive my obscenity, ma'am. You see before you a good man brought low by sorrow. Sorrow at the needless loss of the war hero Colonel James Balazarus and the esteemed Mr. Morrow, both of whom gave so much to this citizenry and whom you all held in such high regard."

Greeley balled his right hand into a fist and slammed it on the pulpit, causing not a few of those present to jump in their seats.

"Those great men shall be avenged!" he bellowed, his bald head flushing. "Their deaths will not have been in vain!"

"God bless you, Mr. Greeley, sir!" a man shouted, and the room broke into applause. Greeley smiled as people rose to their feet. He basked in the standing ovation for a while then held up in his hands.

"Good people, please," he said over the noise. "Please resume your seats."

The room quieted down and the congregation sat as instructed.

"Thank you. That did my heart good," Greeley continued. "It is an honor to be among such fine people. It goes without saying that I do none of this for my own glory but for yours. For your safety. For your peace of mind. I am but your humble servant. And I will leave you with this."

Greeley raised his right hand, fingers spread.

"I hereby raise the bounty on Damien Attica's head to five hundred dollars."

More applause.

"Five. Hundred. Dollars. Spread the word. And in Jesus's name, let us bring his reign of terror to an end!"

The standing ovation resumed. Maddox appeared at Greeley's side as if on cue, handing over the top hat. Greeley placed it on his head and waved to either pew as he marched down the aisle, shaking outstretched hands. He worked the crowd, Maddox and his cohort warily searching the sea of faces, gun hands at the ready. Damien stayed in his seat, watching the spectacle.

Greeley saw him, stopped in his tracks, and raised a hand.

"Silence!" he shouted.

Greeley tilted the brim of his top hat back and bent forward, eyes narrowing.

Damien held his breath as Greeley stared into the burlap mask's eyehole. Damien blinked.

Greeley held out a hand, and Maddox reached into his vest and pulled out a leather pouch. He shook out a coin, which Greeley took and offered to Damien.

"Here, my good man. Take it."

Damien lifted his palm, receiving the token. He couldn't know what it was that had given Greeley pause.

The eye peering out of the beggar's mask had been black as pitch. Then he had blinked, and it was green again.

"Vigilance is all!" Greeley announced, then parted the church doors, striding out into the sunshine.

Damien waited until the last parishioner had passed

before he followed the Truitts outside. Greeley waved to the crowd, his bodyguards flanking him as he backed up toward the hotel down the muddy thoroughfare. The establishment was adorned with new brass lettering proclaiming it the Greeley Hotel. As its owner went inside, Damien pondered how he, the most wanted man in the territory, could manage to check in for the night.

## 20

*Parlor House; Greeley, New Mexico Territory; November 1855*

Madame Alice sat by her upstairs window, the beggar limping to her doorstep one floor below. She rose from her chair then paused to brush away a bit of cigarillo ash from the plush red upholstery. She then turned the brass doorknob of her bedchamber and descended the staircase, sweeping past one of her employees in the midst of vigorous copulation with a Mexican cowboy. Business was damn good, particularly for a Sunday.

She arrived outside to find her bouncer, an Irishman named Capper Dan, doing what he did best: chasing off the riffraff.

"Ima give yer stinkun fuckin' ass 'un mere chunce tuh tern round 'fore uh run muh fist in yer oogly bazoo," the big Irishman growled at the beggar in his indecipherable brogue.

Madame Alice placed a well-manicured hand on Dan's hairy neck. "Good work, Danny. Go inside and have yourself a drink."

He sighed. "Yes'm."

Capper Dan went inside, and Madame Alice faced the beggar unaided. "We service all manner of man in this here establishment," she said, a painted eyebrow arched. "This ain't no frilly Kansas City whorehouse. Greaser, nigger, heathen, dwarf—you name it, we fuck it. Providing you're holding. Cash, is what I mean, in case I failed to make myself clear." She took a step to the side, gesturing to the open door. "*Entre, monsieur,*" she said, and the beggar shuffled into the parlor, Madame Alice holding her breath against the odor as he passed, smiling all the while.

Once inside the foyer, the beggar straightened his shoulders and pulled off his mask. Alice's eyes went wide, and she caught herself, regaining her composure.

"Mr. Attica, I presume," she said.

"How do you know who I am?"

"Everyone knows who you are, honey. Posters don't quite do you justice, though. Any hope of escaping this most welcome of introductions without getting my throat slit?"

"I got rules, ma'am," Damien replied. "Innocent people don't meet with violence. Not by my hand anyway."

"How magnanimous," Madame Alice said, running a finger down his chest. "You look like you'd be grateful for a hot bath from one of my girls. If the stories about you hold an ounce of truth, you're certainly good for it."

Damien gently clasped Madame Alice's wrist and lowered her hand. "I'd be grateful for a bath," he said. "The girl won't be necessary. And yes, I can pay. I can pay for the bath and the shelter and your cooperation. Whatever the cost."

Madame Alice took Damien by the arm and pulled him toward the staircase. "Then let's get you fixed up nice and proper, cowboy," she said, leading him up the stairs.

Damien scrubbed his skin raw, the powdered chlorine of lime for which he had paid a dollar misting his vision and burning his nose. It was glorious. A young woman dressed in a red lace corset watched from the doorway, studying him curiously.

"You're sure you don't want any help with your bath, mister?" she cooed. The man in the soapy water had a kind face and hadn't harassed her one bit. Hadn't yet acknowledged her presence at all, in fact.

"I'm just fine, ma'am," Damien said, stepping out of the water, hands covering his privates. "A thousand pardons."

"Oh, you're pardoned, Mr. Attica," said the woman.

"Damien. Call me Damien."

"You're pardoned, Damien."

"And what's your name, if I may ask?"

"You can call me whatever you like, Damien."

The young woman held a towel at the ready. Damien took it and ran the clean cotton over his face and neck.

"I'd like to call you by your name."

The woman crossed her arms. "No foolin'?"

"No foolin'," Damien said, tousling his hair dry.

"Well, then. My name's Betsy."

"Please to meet you, Betsy. Now I got one thing to ask of you. Just one little thing."

"Anything, Damien."

"Any chance you ladies have a nice can of beans you could spare? I'll pay top dollar."

Damien sat in his room, eating piping-hot beans with a clean fork off a clean plate, dressed in a silk bathrobe. Between the meal and the bath, he felt like a new man. He scraped the dish bare then tilted it into his mouth, slurping up the juice. He dabbed his lips with the cloth napkin and lay back on the bed, resting his head on a feather pillow for the first time since leaving Bennett's for the war more than a decade earlier.

He almost had faded into sleep when the door creaked open. His hand instinctively gripped the pistol at his side but relaxed as Madame Alice slipped inside.

She sauntered across the room toward Damien, a glass of whiskey in each hand. Damien sat up and she handed him one, clinking it.

"Cheers," she said.

"Cheers," Damien replied, and set it on the nightstand. Alice downed her drink then pointed to Damien's untouched glass.

"Don't drink with whores? Is that it?"

He shrugged. "Don't drink at all."

"You don't drink."

"No, ma'am."

"Damien, you call me 'ma'am,' and I think my dearly departed Meemaw is standing behind me like the Ghost of Christmas Past. Call me Alice."

"As you like, Alice."

"Better."

Alice reached over, drank Damien's whiskey for him, and sat in the chair opposite his bed, fanning her skirt over her knee-high leather boots.

"How were those beans?"

"Excellent. Thank you. Nice and hot."

"We got steak, you know. Capper Dan roasts a mean T-bone."

"Don't eat meat."

"You don't eat meat."

"No."

"You don't drink whiskey and you don't eat meat."

"That's correct."

Madame Alice shouted with laughter, pulling a silver cigarette case out of her décolletage and plucking out her smoke of choice. She handed it across to Damien, who opened his mouth to speak.

"No, no," Alice said, withdrawing the cigarettes. "Let me guess."

"Don't smoke," Damien and Alice said in unison.

Now Alice was really laughing. Damien retrieved a candle from the mirrored bureau and gallantly held it out for her.

Alice exhaled smoke and shook her head, tendrils of dyed red hair brushing over her freckled shoulders. "You're not at all what I expected," she said.

"I get that a lot," Damien replied.

Alice puffed on her cigarette. "Well, sir, I aim to please, and if you'll permit me, entertain. So tell me. What *do* you like to do?"

No one had ever asked Damien that. He glanced out the window, noting the curious way the world outside appeared when viewed through the thin, warped glass. After a long while, he spoke.

"I like...reading."

"Reading."

"Yes. And I like sitting by the fire."

"Like a fireplace? I like that too," Alice said, drawing on her cigarette.

"Never had a fireplace. Well, Bennett did. I meant more like a campfire. Under the stars."

"Who's Bennett?" Alice asked, her voice low and soft. She had a way of making Damien want to talk to her, made him feel he was interesting and the things he thought about were interesting. It was part of the service he was paying for, but at this particular moment he didn't care.

"Bennett was my father. Well, not really my father."

"But like a father," Alice said.

"Yes."

"He pass away?"

"Yes."

"I'm sorry to hear that, Damien."

"Thank you."

Alice stubbed her cigarette out and brushed her dyed red hair away from her shoulders. When she started to unclasp the buttons of her waistcoat, Damien turned back toward the window.

He was fully aware of the sexual act but had absolutely no interest in it, having spent long nights in the army listening to other men describe in lurid detail their conquests with women, their prowess with them, and the physical attributes of those left behind back home. Damien always gamely went along, but it was always an act. He'd never had attraction for or need of sexual congress with women, or men for that matter—he understood that too was a thing in the world. More than anything, he dreaded moments like the one he was in now.

Sensing this, Alice dropped her hands. "I can fetch you a younger girl, if that's what you like."

Damien shook his head. "It isn't that, Alice. It isn't that at all."

Alice regarded him curiously for a moment, then

plunked herself on the bed next to him, her perfume light and sweet in the air. "Damien. Let me ask you something. You ever read *A Christmas Carol*?"

Damien grinned. "When you referenced the Ghost of Christmas Past earlier, I very much wanted to inquire the same of you," he said.

"Then why didn't you?"

"I..." He stopped himself. "I don't know."

"Well, I *have* read it, a bunch of times in fact, and not just at Christmas either," Alice replied.

"I enjoyed it very much. *Very* much," Damien offered.

The pair spent the better part of the next several hours talking about the book and a great many others. Damien confessed his admiration for the writings of Walt Whitman, Alice of Catharine Sedgwick. Both had memorized favorite soliloquies from the works of Shakespeare and recited them to the other's mutual delight. They didn't notice the setting sun, or the candles burning out, tendrils of smoke wafting through the dark still air. At one point Alice lay on her side. Damien joined her, and he spoke of Bennett's library and his hundreds of tomes and his daily lessons as a boy until his eyes grew heavy and finally closed. Alice waited until she was sure he was deep in sleep and only then rose from the bed, taking pains not to jostle him awake.

She picked up his pistol and placed it next to his open palm. If he needed it, it would be there. She let herself out of the room and quietly pulled the door closed behind her. Damien didn't stir. He lay like this until dawn, the rattling and clattering of a stagecoach being loaded across the thoroughfare bringing him out of his slumber.

He opened his eyes and spent the next half a minute trying to discern where in the world he was. The previous evening's conversation with Alice drifted back into his memory, and his head whipped around, looking for his pistols. One was holstered on the belt hanging off the back of the upholstered chair, just as he had left it, the other next to the imprint of his sleeping body. The thin wooden door to his room had been all there was between him and any of the men in Greeley who had a mind to capture or kill him. Fortunately for Damien, Madame Alice and those in her employ were trustworthy, or at the very least their trust was for sale.

Teamsters labored in front of the Greeley Hotel. The stagecoach was enormous, its bright-red cushioned seats visible even from the second story's vantage point. The rippled glass made specifics impossible to observe, so Damien yanked the window up, the wooden frame splintering. He shook his head at the poor craftsmanship and peered at the scene below.

Upon further inspection, he realized the expensive coach would soon contain a person of means, and he could hazard a guess as to who that person was. Up to this point, the territory had no wealth beyond the white Eastern entrepreneurs trickling in from New York, Boston, and other cities overrun by vermin and disease, hoping to escape their stifling conditions and make a new stand out west. Greeley was the only man in a thousand miles who could afford to summon transportation as well appointed as this.

As if on cue, the man emerged, Maddox at his side.

Damien had held himself in check in the church and did so now, resisting the impulse to run down the stairs in his silk bathrobe into the thoroughfare, guns blazing. He would have killed Greeley and possibly even Maddox, only to be cut down by any number of the men in the vicinity with iron hanging off their cow-skin belts, either out of misplaced duty to Greeley or the five-hundred-dollar bounty Damien's body would fetch. His corpse would lie in the dirt, dressed in silk, the newspapers proclaiming the famous assassin's comical death in a bathrobe, fresh from the local whorehouse. That would just not do. That would not do at all.

Josephina Llewelyn was nowhere in sight. Had she been in either man's clutches, Damien would have sacrificed dignity in the name of his sworn mission, but thankfully it needn't come to that. For now he just observed, undetected.

Greeley took a seat in the coach and Maddox doffed his hat, the teamster taking the gesture as a sign to get going. A flick of the driver's wrist, and the horses trotted forward. Maddox stood and waved until the stagecoach rounded the bend at the end of the thoroughfare and was gone.

What Greeley's thug did next brought Damien to his feet. It had only been a small gesture, but what that gesture implied told him all he needed to know.

Maddox hadn't put his hat back on. Instead he had licked his palm and run it across his thinning hair, smoothing it down, then gone back inside the hotel, hat tucked under his arm.

Josephina Llewelyn was a captive inside the Greeley Hotel; of this Damien had no doubt.

## 21

*Parlor House; Greeley, New Mexico Territory; November 1855*

It stood to reason that at least one of the men posted guard at the Greeley Hotel eventually would be relieved of duty and that this man would use his time off to walk the twenty paces across the thoroughfare and into the swinging doors of the town's only cathouse. Damien sat in his room all day, waiting for this to take place. As he scooped up the last bits of a second plate of beans, this one seasoned with a sprig of rosemary, two cowboys emerged onto the hotel's front porch, discussing who would go in first. Damien set his plate down and listened from the partially open window, their voices carrying through the crisp air.

Ned, a heavyset man with a blond beard who was missing most of his upper teeth, spat a long line of tobacco off the porch and rested his thumbs in his gun belt.

"Wouldn't mind a piece of pussy tonight, tell you what."

Charlie, a man of Damien's approximate height and complexion with a patch over his left eye, spat a glob not far from Ned's and grunted his affirmation.

"Ain't that the fucking truth?"

"Greeley really expect Attica's just gonna ride up here in front, pretty as you please?" Charlie asked.

"Guess so," Ned said with a shrug.

"That ain't likely. Attica's long gone. He a triggerman. Got no stake in this. Nobody's payin' him."

"S'pose you're right."

Charlie and Ned stared at the Parlor House's brightly lit windows, the occupants within shielded from the harsh realities of life in the territory by thin red curtains. Charlie's head nodded in time with 'Camptown Ladies', the piano's melody irresistible.

"We could take turns," Charlie offered.

"How's that, Charlie?" Ned replied.

"One fella goes, then the other is my meaning."

"No, dumb ass. I'm sayin' how do we do that? Maddox wants two men out here on post."

"Aw, hell. That ol' boy is on his second bottle already. He ain't long for this night."

Ned spat again. "You think he depredated her?"

"What's that mean?" Charlie asked.

"Forced himself on her."

"Greeley would kill him if he tried. You never know, though."

"Yeah, but Greeley ain't here," Ned said.

Ned shook his head and ran his finger around his gums, adjusting his chaw. His next words were garbled by this finger, but clear enough for Charlie to let out a whoop and start running toward the Parlor House.

"You go first," Ned had said.

While Charlie was downstairs enjoying his first whiskey and shyly canvassing the parlor's girls, Damien was upstairs, fully dressed and armed, sipping a cup of chamomile tea in a chair across from Alice. The madam had set out candles, an indulgence even for a business as successful as hers, and the pair enjoyed the flicker of the lights while they sipped their tea.

"They're French," Alice said.

"Sounds expensive," Damien said.

"Oh, they are. But I love the way they smell."

Damien leaned forward and sniffed the air then sat back. "My olfactory senses might be impacted from too many blows to the head, Alice, but I must confess I can't smell a thing."

Alice laughed. "Precisely. Precisely, Damien. These candles have been crafted in such a way that they elicit no odor. Isn't that grand?"

Damien sipped his tea. "Remembering what candles smelled like back in the service, yeah, Alice, I see your point. Pretty grand."

When he set down his empty teacup, Alice rose for the private bar near her four-poster bed, and poured herself a tall glass of whiskey.

"You're something of a hero to me and the girls, you know," she said, leaning against the bar.

"How's that?"

"Killing Morrow like you did. And that Colonel whoever."

"Balazarus."

Alice nodded. "Yeah, him. He was a sick twist, let me tell you. Got his jollies beating up the girls. Had a thing for choking them until they passed out during, you know, the act. Nothing we could do about it, not with him working for Greeley and all."

Damien gritted his teeth at this new information.

"Is it true what they say?" Alice asked, walking from the bar and returning to her seat. "How you went about killing him?"

"That depends," he said. "What do they say?"

Alice leaned forward. "That you shot him in the balls?"

"Yes," Damien replied. "As a matter of fact, I did."

"Ha!" Alice shouted. "Before he was dead or after?"

"Before."

"You are my kind of man, Damien."

He reached for the teapot, poured himself another cup, then set it back on its doily, his expression grim. "Alice. I am many things to many people. But I am no kind of man."

The smile faded from Alice's face.

She could see now how tired he was, his cheekbones jutting through the skin; his scarred, swollen knuckles and their skeletal fingers. Alice wanted to say something to him and made a start to do so, when a door opening and closing in the adjoining parlor room turned both of their heads.

"That's them," Alice whispered.

Damien rose from the chair, hand on a pistol, and headed for the door.

---

Betsy danced an inebriated Charlie around the room next door, the cleavage pushed up to her chin mesmerizing him as they twirled in a slow circle.

"I'll be your prairie nymph tonight if you let me, Charlie," she drawled.

"Mercy me," said Charlie.

"Charlie's a handsome name. Handsome name for a handsome man."

"You're just blowing sunshine now."

Betsy pulled him in close. "Strong-looking man too. You a saddle stiff, Charlie?"

"Used to be. Work for Mr. Greeley now."

"Well, sound the goose!" Betsy shouted. "Mr. Greeley! That mean I have to fuck you for free?"

Charlie stumbled backward onto the bed, slurring his answer. "Well, them's drinks downstairs was free. Don't rightly know about the rest."

Betsy hiked her skirt and straddled Charlie, pushing him flat on his back. "I'm gonna go into that other room and sweeten my honey pot, Charlie. When I get back, I want that big pecker of yours right an' ready. Can you do that for me, Charlie?"

"Do my best," Charlie replied, his words muffled by Betsy's breasts, which now rested on his face.

She jumped up and sailed through the door adjoining the two rooms then closed it behind her. Once on the other side, she faced Damien and Alice with a sly smile.

"He's all yours."

"You sure that's one of Greeley's?" Damien asked.

"Third thing to come out of his mouth."

"Patch over one eye?"

"That's the one."

"Good," he said, then reached into his back pocket and produced a small handmade leather pouch.

"That Injun?" Betsy asked.

Nodding, Damien plucked a gold coin from within and lay it next to the porcelain teapot.

"Your money's no good here, mister," Alice said.

"I insist."

"Insist all you like," she retorted. "Way I see it, you puttin' Morrow and that fat bastard colonel six feet under saved us ten times that coin of yours in visits from Doc Hansen all by itself. In this house, you're on credit."

Damien retrieved the coin. "In that case, Alice, I'll make sure to stop by again once I'm through with my business with Greeley. And perhaps we can split another pot of tea and discuss stories and poems and all manner of things."

Alice grinned. "I would like that very much, Damien."

Damien gave a courtly bow to Alice and Betsy and placed his hat on his head. He walked into the adjoining room and quietly closed the door behind him.

---

Charlie was sitting on the edge of the bed, vigorously working a hand over his nether regions. Upon seeing Damien, he threw his hands straight into the air.

"Oh, Jesus me!" he shouted. "I beg you not to shoot me, Mr. Attica! Or cut me or bring any manner of harm to my person! I have no quarrel with you! I'm just a hired hand, sir!"

"Look at me," Damien said.

Charlie obeyed, wincing as his good eye met Damien's.

"Where is she?" Damien asked.

"At the hotel, sir. Right across the way there."

"Which floor?"

"Second, sir. First door on the left as you walk up the stairs."

"How many men?"

"Three 'sides me. No, four. Maddox up there too. No one really thought you'd show, Mr. Attica."

"Anyone violate her? You, for example?"

"Not me, sir, no! No, uh-uh! One ol' boy tried, but Maddox put a stop to that."

"What's his name? The one who tried?"

"Willy. Don't know the surname."

"And he's over there right now?" Damien asked.

"Yes, sir."

"And Greeley?"

"Far as what, sir?"

"Where did he go this morning?"

"No idea, sir."

Damien whipped out a pistol, stalked across the room, and placed the barrel against Charlie's temple.

"Swear to God! He comes and goes! Where, not nobody tell me!"

Damien lowered his pistol, the truth evident in young Charlie's voice.

"You ain't gonna shoot me then?"

"No."

"May...may I pull my trousers up, sir?"

"No."

Damien began to undress. "Take off your shirt," he told Charlie. "And that patch on your eye."

## 22

*Greeley Hotel; Greeley, New Mexico Territory; November 1855*

Damien, dressed in Charlie's clothes, hat, and eye patch, staggered out from the saloon and into the moonlight. When he gripped Capper Dan's arm for balance, the formidable Irishman shoved him off his person and face-down into the dirt.

Capper Dan recognized the eye patch, having stared at the man wearing it across the thoroughfare for the last two weeks. He cupped his hands around his mouth and called out to the men guarding the hotel.

"Dis yer boo-ey?"

Ned, in the middle of telling a filthy joke, turned his head from Spivey, a hulking farm boy Greeley was grooming for Maddox's position should his right hand man ever be put out of commission in the line of duty.

"Hell's that you say, Irish?" Ned called back.

"*I sed*," Capper Dan roared, "*is dis yer boo-ey?*"

Ned and Spivey looked to the man in the dirt.

"Aw, hell. That you, Charlie?" Ned yelled, and started toward him.

Spivey followed, calling over his shoulder for more help. "Willy! Get your ass out here and come help get Charlie up inside! Come on now!"

Willy, rifle slung across his back on a tattered rope, made no move to descend from the hotel's balcony and offer a hand. He just took it all in through bored, half-lidded eyes.

"Goddamn, boy, you've done got yourself roostered something awful!" Ned said, picking Damien up by his ankles.

As Spivey took his arms, Damien made sure to keep his chin tucked and face hidden as they carried him across the way to the hotel. Spivey cast a hateful glance up at Willy as they walked him through the front door.

"Don't you be puttin' no salty looks my direction," Willy spat.

Once inside, they carried Damien around a front desk decorated with elk antlers; mounted above it was the head of a tusked wild boar. Spivey walked backward, toward the staircase, and then Ned stopped, out of breath.

"Fuck you think you're going?" Spivey asked.

"Up the stairs."

"I ain't carrying this sack of shit up no goddamn stairs."

"Well, where you want to put 'im?" Ned said. "Here on the floor? Over there on Mr. Greeley's fine furniture? Nuh-uh."

Spivey continued upward. When they reached the midpoint of the staircase Ned dropped Damien's legs. Damien winced as his shins connected with the hardwood.

"Gimme an arm," Ned said. "I can pull him."

When they reached the second floor, they hefted Damien onto a bed so pungent with body odor that his eyes watered. The mattress sank as he landed on it facedown.

Willy sauntered in from the balcony and leaned in the doorway.

"You are one lazy bastard, Willy," Ned said.

"Ya'll looked like you had the sitch'ation in hand," Willy drawled.

"You'd better keep that ugly ass of yours awake out there, Willy. I catch you sleepin' on watch again, you and me gonna have some strong words."

"Tell you what, Ned," Willy continued. "Them two marbles of yours make out Attica riding up the thoroughfare, blastin' his smoke wagons, you lemme know. I'll be on my feet faster than a buttered bullet."

"Like to see that," Ned sniffed. He and Spivey stalked out of the room, down the stairs, and back to their posts.

Damien remained motionless until he was sure all three men had resumed their former positions, then quietly got to his feet. He took off the eye patch, reached down into his boot, and pulled out a blade.

Willy had just put a fresh pinch of tobacco in his cheek when Damien palmed his face from behind, gliding the blade across his throat from one ear to the other. He severed the man's larynx on the first pass and pulled Willy's head back, widening the wound. In a few seconds, Willy's knees buckled, and Damien eased the body to the slatted wood. Blood pooled out fast and black around the dead man's head, creeping toward the balcony's edge. Then it spilled over.

A few feet below, something dripped onto Spivey's shoulder. He put a hand out, checking for rain.

"Hell you doing?" Ned asked.

"Somethin's pissin' down on me."

"Probably Willy squirtin' the dirt."

"He'd better not. Willy!" Spivey yelled. "You takin' a leak off there?"

Silence. Then more drops. Ned reached out his hand, catching a few on his skin, and held his palm up to the torchlight.

"Ned," Spivey said. "*Ned.*"

Ned went slack-jawed as blood ran down his palm.

"*Ned.*" Spivey pointed across the thoroughfare.

Charlie was running out of the Parlor House, naked. He scrambled up onto a horse, kicked his bare feet against its sides, and rode as fast as he could out of town, flesh jiggling all the way.

Ned and Spivey looked at Charlie, then each other, then straight up to Damien on the balcony, his head haloed by the full moon.

"Gentlemen," Damien said.

"Oh, my dear Lord in heaven," Ned replied.

"Just call me Damien. Tell me, where is Isaac Greeley?"

"Sir, I have no earthly idea, and that is the God's truth," Ned said, mouth hanging open.

"I believe you. And what about you? Do you know where Isaac Greeley is?"

Trembling, Spivey shook his head.

"I believe you too. Now. Tell me this: where is Maddox? Is he in one of these rooms?"

"Last door on the right, hall right behind you, sir," Ned said.

"Thank you. Now, you may go. And should you see Mr. Greeley in your travels, please tell him I'll be coming to see him directly."

"Yes, sir, Mr. Attica," Ned said. He and Spivey raced down the thoroughfare faster than Damien had ever seen anyone run.

Damien left a trail of bloody boot prints as he walked down the hall to the last door on the right. He twisted the knob and poked his head inside; the sour smell of whiskey breath filled the room as Maddox lay flat on his back, gut rising and falling with his snores.

Damien gingerly removed the rifle clutched in the man's sleeping hands and brought it off his chest. He set it on the wall by the door, gripped Maddox's leg, and shook it.

"Maddox."

Shifting his weight, Maddox mumbled something unintelligible.

"It's me, Maddox. I want to ask you something."

Maddox's eyes popped open, and he sucked in his breath.

Damien stood above him, half of his narrow face glowing in the moonlight, cheek sunken, eye socket shadowed, his thin lips creased into a smile.

"Where is Isaac Greeley?" he asked.

Maddox began to hyperventilate.

"Tell me," Damien said, his voice low.

Maddox lifted his head, ever so slowly pressed his hand against the bed frame, and scooted himself up to a half sitting position.

"I-I...I don't know where he is," he said.

"I see. When's the last time you saw him?" Damien asked.

"About a week ago, honestly."

Damien sighed. "No, Maddox, it has not been a week, and you are not being honest."

Damien took a seat at the end of the bed, the wooden bed frame creaking. He pointed out the warped glass window, the light so bright he almost had to squint.

"Do you know what kind of moon that is, Maddox?"

"N-no."

"Sure you do. Look at it."

Maddox's eyes flicked up and to the left. "F-full moon?" he managed to answer.

"Well, you're half right," Damien continued. "That there is what's called a Comanche moon. At least down in Texas. Do you know why they call it a Comanche moon?"

Maddox shook his head.

"Because the Comanche Indians do their raiding by its light." Damien plucked his hat off his head and hung it on a bedpost. "I'd been in the army for about a year when I got captured," he went on. "Bivouacked in some village—I don't remember which. One night they came, under a moon just like that one out there. The Comanches. Didn't make a sound. We fought 'em, sure, even killed a few. They were *relentless*—that's the word I'd use. They started with the men, about fifty of us at the time. When they were finished, it was just me and two others. Then they killed the civilian men left in the village. Mexicans, you know. Then the children and babies. Then they raped the women, every single one. Grandmothers even. Then they killed them. About a hundred, hundred fifty raped and dead in the span of an hour."

Damien adjusted his sleeves and crossed a boot over his knee, Willy's blood shiny on the sole.

"They led us, me and the last two in my squadron, east. Ropes tied around our necks, walking behind their horses. For two days. They never said a word. Figured they'd kill us any minute of each of those days, but they didn't lay a hand on us. Fed us, watered us, let us sleep as much as we were able to under guard. On the third day we arrived at their camp, really a small village. They put us in one of their huts, what some call a teepee, walled off with buffalo hide. A Comanche about our age comes in, face painted all white. He sits across from us, makes a fire, smokes a pipe. Turns out he speaks English."

The sweat that had formed on Maddox's forehead rolled down his face.

"He asks us where the other soldiers were," Damien continued. "Where they were stationed, what their next moves in the area were going to be. Excellent English, truly. Well, the truth was we didn't know. They had managed to take into captivity three greenhorns who barely knew how to salute and march properly, much less be entrusted with vital army intelligence. The Comanche patiently listened to us as we explained all this, a lot like I'm listening to you now. Very calm. He asked us a few more questions, then let us turn in for the evening. The two boys I was with lay there all night crying and calling out to Jesus and Mama and anyone else they could think of. Me? I was guessing something...*extraordinary* was going to happen in the morning. Was fairly excited, if I'm being honest. And when the sun rose, it turned out I had guessed right."

Damien gripped the edges of his boot and began to work it off his foot.

"They marched the three of us out to the middle of this field. All the grass, maybe three acres, was hacked down to the nub. In the center of the field, a hole had been dug. Not a grave. It was just deep enough for a man to stand in and still see over the top."

Damien set the boot on the floor, revealing a threadbare cotton sock.

"They took one of the men from our outfit, fella named Peter, and dropped him in that hole. Two of the Comanches held him down in there, and another filled in the dirt, right up to his neck. Pushed it down tight too. Boy couldn't move. Then one of those Comanches brought out a blade and cut his eyelids off."

Maddox let out a small whine like a dog begging for scraps at the table. Damien crossed his socked foot back over his knee.

"Now you might be asking yourself what me and the other fella were up to. Well, they had taken one of our boots off, like this. Then nailed us to the earth, into the soil. Like this."

Damien removed his sock and held up his foot in the moonlight. A thick, knotted scar jutted from between his toes.

"Six- or eight-inch peg made from animal bone. Right in that little web of flesh there. Hurt like I don't know what. Simple but effective. You moved so much as an inch to your right or left, it was like stickin' your foot into a wasp's nest. So we sat there, pegged down, with a view of what was to happen next."

Damien started to put his sock back on.

"You ever have what's called a staring contest with someone? That's what Bennett called it. Bennett, the man you helped kill and burn up out yonder? When I was a kid, he'd play it with me. You look at each other and try not to blink. Well, if you haven't, let me tell you, it's hard. Your eyes get dry and they start to sting a little. Then a little more. Then a whole lot more. Then you blink and you lose."

Damien pulled his sock up to his knee. Maddox trembled so hard the bed jostled.

"Let's try a round. You stare at me, and I'll stare at you. The first man who blinks loses."

Damien sat forward, green eyes wide. Lips quivering,

Maddox stared back. A few beads of sweat dropped into his eyes, and he blinked.

"See! It's hard!" Damien said. "Very difficult indeed. Now imagine that except without any eyelids. No relief whatsoever. That was Peter's fate, you see? By the time that noonday sun rose high and hot and bright over that meadow, he got to screaming. Boy, did he ever scream. We sat there, held fast, listening to those screams for the better part of that first day. After a while they grew so weary of all that hollerin' that same Comanche took that same blade and went over and cut that boy's tongue out of his head."

Damien picked up his boot and shook out a pebble.

"I say 'first day' because his ordeal was far from over. He lasted like that, buried there, for a good long while. No food or water. Just bleedin' out. Now they fed *us*, and when they did we ate. And they gave us water too, and when they did we drank. But not Peter. No. They just left him there, maimed. I learned that word from Bennett. *Maimed*. It's the right word for what he was."

Damien set the boot on the floor and slid his foot back inside. Then he crossed his other boot over his knee and yanked that one off.

"So Peter finally dies. Comanche comes and pulls the pegs out, marches us back to the tepee. We weren't quite able to march at this point, just sort of hopped on our one good foot. Comanche lights a fire, smokes a pipe. Asks us again. Where's the rest of the army? What are their plans? And so on and so forth. The other soldier—his name was Timothy—starts bawling and pleading and begging, swearing up and down: 'I don't know nuthin' and blah, blah, blah. All of it the truth. Comanche finishes his pipe and we're dragged back out to the field."

Damien let the boot fall to the floor and massaged his foot.

"'Scuse me. Dogs are barking."

He massaged it a while longer then pulled the second sock off.

"Where was I? Oh, yes. The field. They already had pulled Peter's corpse out, and in its place they had dropped a pole, a pine tree pole stripped of its bark. And in this big, wide circle, they had laid a ring of branches, maybe knee-high. About, oh, twenty or thirty feet out. So they drag Timothy toward this pole, him kicking and screaming all the way and peg me back to the ground..."

Damien crossed his left foot over his right knee, a scar identical to that found between the toes of his right on display for Maddox's eyes.

"...like so. So there I am, again, and out there in the center of the meadow is Timothy, being lashed to the pole. They tie him good and tight, and I'm sitting there thinking, *What in the world are these people going to do now?* If they were going to burn him, the fire wouldn't be anywhere close enough to touch him. Let me tell you something, Maddox. I learned a great deal from the Comanches that day. Learned a great deal about how with just a little bit of thinking and a little bit of know-how you can exceed people's expectations beyond their wildest imaginations."

Chuckling, Damien slipped his sock back on.

"The women come out next. Comanche women, mothers and daughters. And they get on their hands and knees and go about setting this big ring of branches on fire. Takes a while for the sticks to really get going. And I'm sitting there half out of my mind with physical discomfort, unable to comprehend what they were getting up to. Once the fire started raging, you know what those Comanche women did, Maddox?"

Maddox remained silent.

"Maddox, I asked you a question."

"N-no. I d-don't."

"They put the flames out."

Damien picked up his boot and slid his foot inside, wincing.

"Well, not *completely* out. They brought out these blankets and waved at the smoke, sending it out of the circle, *away* from Timothy. They waved them and waved them until the sticks were ash. And under this ring of ash they were making, you could see this kind of dark red glow. Then the women and girls stepped out of the circle and walked back toward the tepees. And all of us, me and a hundred Comanches, watched, silent as church, waiting for what was going to happen next. Do you know what happened next?"

Maddox shook his head.

"Timothy started to scream. Just all of a sudden. And I'm thinking, *This is some red-man magic, 'cause I don't see a thing touching him.* Not a flame, not a blade...hell, not a mosquito! While he's writhing around on this pole screaming and hollering, I finally see it. I see it and...well, sir, you could have knocked me over with a feather. Know what I saw?"

Maddox again shook his head.

"Timothy was *shimmering.* You know what that word means? Shimmering? It means he was sort of wavy like, the way the horizon dances and twists on a hot summer day. You ever look through the other side of a campfire you know what I'm talking about. The way you can *see* the heat? That's what I was seeing. The *heat.* And it hits me. They weren't *burning* young Timothy to death. Oh, no, sir." Damien leaned in to Maddox and whispered. "They were *roasting* him. *Alive.*"

A dark stain blossomed across the sheets as Maddox lost control of his bladder. The whining returned, high in his throat.

"Next thing I knew, these young warriors appear at the edges of the circle. Nine, ten years old. They jump into the ring, feel the heat, jump out. Some kind of test of manhood...I'm not sure at first. Then one of the boys jumps in and stays in. Runs up to Timothy, who's screamed himself hoarse. Takes one of Timothy's fingers..."

Damien raised his index finger to Maddox and placed it inches from his face.

"...and breaks it. Runs out of the circle hollering, such is the heat. Next boy does the same. Different finger, of course. Then another. Then another. Then the biggest boy goes into the ring with bone and thread. And he sews Timothy's mouth shut."

Damien walked to the window, taking in the view of the thoroughfare.

"No screaming after that. Just Timothy cooked low and slow, the way Bennett used to roast his hogs. Anyhow, the fire went out, eventually, and they cut him down, eventually. Pulled the peg out of my foot and dragged me back to the tepee."

Damien studied the moon's features in the clear night sky.

"Comanche comes back in, makes a fire. Smokes a pipe. Asks me where the army is, where it's headed next. I don't beg or cry or anything like that. I'm just sitting there trying to imagine how much worse my death could possibly be than Timothy's. His own passing had been...hell, ten times worse than Peter's, and now here I was. What were they gonna do to me? Didn't get a wink of sleep that night trying to guess."

Damien retrieved his hat from the bedpost.

"Next morning, right before dawn, I hear this great commotion. The two Comanches guarding me run out through the hut flap, and then there's that sound. That thundering sound. Sound of fifty rifles going off all at once. It was the army. Army I was fighting for. They had found the Injuns' camp."

Damien set his hat on his head and walked toward Maddox's weapon leaning against the wall.

"Comanche fought to the last man, but we had cannons. The women who could, fled. The rest..." He trailed off, picking up the rifle. "After my feet healed up sufficient, I got put back into the rotation. Back in the fight. But I never forgot what I saw during those days I spent with the Comanches. Never stopped wondering, if the army hadn't arrived, what they would have done to me. How much torment I would've endured."

Damien lifted the rifle and pressed the barrel into the center of Maddox's chest. His eyes clouded dark gray, then went pitch-black, a sight so unbelievable Maddox convinced himself that it hadn't happened, that it had merely been a trick of the light.

"Maddox, I am going to give you ten seconds to tell me where Isaac Greeley is. Just ten seconds. If you lie, I'll know. Don't tell me, or lie, and your passing will put those two boy's tortures to shame. I swear on Bennett's grave I will do everything to ensure that no man in this world will have died as badly as you."

A stench filled the air as Maddox released his bowels under the bedsheets.

"One," Damien counted. "Two."

"He's in the mountains," Maddox managed, his voice thin and weak. "Southeast. There's a wagon trail starts half a day's ride from the edge of town. Anybody can show you. You follow it to the end, and you're at the mountain. Loggers cleared a path straight up; just follow that. Everyone knows where Greeley is and what he's got up to."

"Let me hear it from you first," Damien said.

"Building a fort. Fort for ex-soldiers and the like who still want to be fightin' the heathens. Guns for hire. Play for pay. Mercenaries."

"*Mercenaries*. That's a good word. How many?"

Maddox shrugged. "I dunno. A lot."

"He's building a fort to protect his interests in the area is what you're saying."

"Yes. That's it exactly."

"That rings of truth. Thank you, Maddox."

"You're welcome."

"I'm gonna execute you now, but in the customary manner, and not in the way of the Comanche or my variations thereof."

"Thank you," Maddox said, and squeezed his eyes shut.

Damien raised the rifle and leveled it at the bridge of Maddox's nose.

"This is for Bennett," he said, and pulled the trigger.

---

The gunshot across the hall woke Josie from her sleep with a start. She made a move to sit up then remembered where she was, tied down to a bed on the second floor of the Greeley Hotel. There were footsteps, then her room's doorknob rattling, and then the door opened to reveal the outline of a thin man in a hat, his face impossible to make out in the darkness.

"Come at me and I'll scratch your eyes out, I swear to God," Josie shouted, hoping the other guards would hear.

The man took a step forward, showing his features in the moonlight. She recognized him from their conversation at the convent.

"Hello, Josie," the man said.

"Hello, Damien," she replied.

# PART III

## DAMIEN'S SONG

## 23

*Attica Peninsula, Greece; the Month of Skirophorion, 435 BC*

Once again the children were assembled in the meadow, the caged birds' songs muffled by the crashing waves below. Master Praxis strolled through the class, peering down at his students and inspecting the condition of their charges. When he raised a hand, the children's chattering ceased.

"Each of you has spent the last five days looking after these birds," he said. "Five days of ensuring they had food, water, and shelter. And they all still draw air. That's something, I suppose."

Gallus shot his hand up. "Master. Mine ate so very much. It's quite difficult to find worms about the temple, and that's all he wants to eat."

As the others laughed, Gallus scowled at them. Master Praxis clucked his tongue and the laughter stopped.

"Gallus, much like Korrina five days past, you referred to your bird as *mine*. Do you not remember my admonition that doing so is an insult to the gods?"

"Yes, Master. Sorry, Master."

"Do not apologize to me. Apologize to the gods during nightly prayers."

"Yes, Master."

"The crow in your care, Gallus, is quite large indeed. I can imagine its dietary requirements exceeded that of many of the other birds, such as the canary. Or the mourning dove."

"She sings beautifully, Master," Aja said.

"Or perhaps, even, the wee finch," Master Praxis continued, looking halfway across the meadow.

The children's heads swiveled toward Damien.

He sat alone, arms hugging his knees, the caged finch at his side.

"Now then," Master Praxis said, "you also may recall my instructions to *listen* rather than *speak* to the birds. Does anyone remember this?"

Aja's hand shot up, and the other students followed.

"I see. Well, then, I should think all of you are bursting at the seams to share your remarkable anecdotes. Aja, your hand went up first, as always. Do tell us what this mourning dove had to say to you."

Aja slowly lowered her hand, her face red with embarrassment.

"Aja?" Master Praxis took a step toward her. "Don't leave us in suspense."

"Master, I..." Aja trailed off, looking at her dove, then back at the teacher. "I'm sorry, Master, I don't understand the question."

"I think the question is perfectly clear," Master Praxis replied. "I gave this class specific instructions to listen to these birds. You recalled this instruction and now seem eager to share what it said to you. Or did *I* misunderstand?"

"I apologize, Master. I do remember your instructions,

but I...I'm afraid I don't...What does Master mean by 'What did the bird say?'"

"Am I not speaking the native tongue?" Master Praxis said with irritation. "How much clearer can I possibly be?"

Gallus raised his hand. "Master, it's just that birds don't talk, do they?"

"Young man, did you just tell us that birds don't talk?"

"Yes, Master."

"Gallus, this great temple has been named for the prophet Orpheus—may he be blessed. A prophet whose music so enthralled the creatures of this earth that the very stones under his feet sang their songs to him. A man who spoke with the animals the way I am speaking to you now. And you sit here in his temple and tell me 'Birds don't talk'? Is that what you're doing, Gallus? Understand I know that you speak for the class when you do."

"Orpheus—may he be blessed—was a great prophet, Master, as you say," Gallus said. "But we're just ordinary children."

"*Ordinary* children? *Ordinary* children do not study at the Orphic Temple. Each and every one of you possesses an *extraordinary* gift, one you are here to nurture and develop in honor of the gods who bestowed them upon you."

"Yes, Master."

Master Praxis cinched the belt on his robe tighter and nodded curtly, putting the matter to an end, then pointed to Damien.

"Damien of Attica, come to the front of the class."

A gasp came from the group, and Damien went white. He started toward the front as Master Praxis snapped his fingers.

"The bird, Damien, bring the bird."

Damien spun on his heel and grabbed the cage. As he

did, the finch bounced from the floor to its perch and back again. Damien arrived at the front, his eyes glued to his feet.

"Damien, a few days ago you came to my office and told me something very interesting. I want you to share what you said with the rest of the class."

Damien's face was so hot he was sure it would burst into flames.

"Damien."

He tried to swallow, but his tongue was dry as sand. Two dozen of his fellow classmates stared at him, mouths slightly open in anticipation of what exactly he would say.

"Damien."

Damien released the breath he'd been holding. "I said...I thought maybe my...*the* bird. Had maybe. Said something."

Gasps filled the meadow.

"*Silence*," Master Praxis demanded, and silence was immediately had. "Continue, Damien. What did the bird say? Please share it with us."

"It said. It said..." Damien trailed off. The finch sat silently on its perch, staring up at him as expectantly as the children. "He said that the ocean is forever and that I am a child of the gods."

The class broke into laughter.

Damien endured this, his watering eyes riveted to the finch. Master Praxis folded his hands behind his back and waited as the children whooped and hollered.

"Shut up! Don't be mean! Stop it!" Aja yelled, and a few other girls joined her. After several minutes of shouting and carrying on, an uneasy quiet finally settled over the meadow.

"Thank you, Damien," Master Praxis said, wandering among the children and peering at the clouds. "Your laughter is curious to me, children, in that you seem so uncurious yourselves. A fellow student has revealed that a bird in his care, a wee finch, spoke to him. The bird told him, and I quote, that the ocean is forever, and that he, Damien, is a child of the gods. I happen to think both these things are true. I for one would have quite enjoyed hearing Damien tell us exactly where and how this extraordinary occurrence took place. What the bird's voice sounded like. You all have disappointed Master very, very much."

Borus rose to his feet and pointed to Damien. "We think he's a liar, Master. He only wants attention."

Gallus stood behind him. "I agree, Master. The wolf...*Damien* is only causing trouble for the rest of us. Making it seem he's very special and we aren't. He can't prove that the bird spoke to him. At least we're being honest. We want to learn Master's ways, and Damien just wants to show off."

The other children clapped in agreement. Right now Damien wanted to crawl into a hole and die. He stared at the ground beneath his feet, the needles of grass swaying in the sea breeze. The clapping died down and the class awaited Master Praxis's response.

"Accusing a fellow student of lying and cheating is a very serious offense, children," he said. "Very serious, indeed. It is not taken lightly."

"We don't want Damien to get in trouble," Aja offered.

"Yes, we do!" Gallus shouted.

"No, we don't!" Aja snapped at him. "Master, perhaps Damien could prove it to us."

"Prove it, Aja? How?" Master Praxis asked.

"Perhaps he could ask the bird to speak to him in front of the class."

More chatter erupted among the children, some of them

shouting their agreement. The moment Master Praxis raised a hand, the shouting stopped.

"Damien, are you willing to indulge your fellow student's request? To demonstrate your communication with the bird?"

Damien was sure he would pass out from fear. All eyes were on him. It was like a nightmare he couldn't wake up from.

"Damien?" Master Praxis asked.

Damien's heartbeat filled his ears. He crouched and locked eyes with the finch.

"I can't hear anything," a boy said from the back.

"He...he hasn't said anything," Damien stammered.

Aja shushed the class. "Quiet! Let him concentrate!"

All Damien could think to do was beg. Beg the bird to say something, anything, the way it had on the beach. Just a word would do. Anything to save him from total humiliation in front of a group of children who already considered him a freak, an outcast, the "wolf boy."

He stared deeply into the bird's tiny eyes and implored it with his mind to *Please, please, please say something. Save me from this. Please.*

The finch cocked its head.

*Open the cages*, it said.

Damien's eyebrows rose and his mouth opened in a smile. "See! I told you!" he shouted to the class.

"I didn't hear anything!" Gallus shouted back.

"Me neither!" Borus said. The children talked all at once, asking one another if they had heard the bird speak.

"He just spoke! I heard him! You all must have too!" Damien said, his face flushing.

The children continued to holler their protestations that in fact no, they hadn't heard a thing. Although Master Praxis was a patient man, that patience finally had reached its limits.

"*Enough!*"

The students plopped back onto the grass, silent as mice.

Master Praxis regarded Damien, his expression solemn. "Now Damien, I too must confess I didn't hear the bird speak."

"He did speak, Master. I swear to the gods he did," Damien pleaded.

"You misunderstand me. I didn't say I don't believe that it spoke. I said I didn't hear it. For you see, Damien, I *could* not hear it, even if I wanted to. Now, what did it say?"

"It said...it said to open the cages," Damien mumbled.

"Open the cages," Master Praxis repeated.

"Yes, Master."

A low murmur went through the class. Gallus raised his hand.

"Gallus."

"Master, if we open the cages, the birds will fly away. What if Damien is having a laugh? What if this is a prank?"

Master Praxis cocked his head to the side, birdlike. "A prank?"

"Yes, Master. To make us lose our clever birds, whom we've grown so very fond of."

"Damien? Is this a joke?" Master Praxis asked.

"No, Master."

"There you are, Gallus. He says it's not. Every student in this temple is on the honor system, thus Damien's word is his bond. I presume this assuages your concerns?"

Gallus bowed his head. "Yes, Master."

"Very good. Now then, this finch has asked us to open

the birdcages. I propose we do what it says and see what happens."

Not one student moved.

"Children. Open the cages. Now."

The children's hands went to work. Hinges squeaked as every door on every cage was opened wide.

At first nothing happened. The birds stayed on their perches, as before. Then Aja's dove hopped out onto the grass. Then Gallus's crow strode out, squawking. Then Borus's canary flapped its wings and fluttered outside, free. Soon all the birds were in the grass, pecking the ground and singing.

"Why aren't they flying?" asked Aja. The children twisted their heads around, taking in the sight of all the birds bouncing through the grass.

"Damien, what about this bird?" Master Praxis asked, gesturing to the finch in its cage.

"Oh, yes," Damien said, and slid the lock open. He opened the door and the finch flew out, up, and landed on his head.

Gallus pointed and laughed, the finch chirping in Damien's hair. Several others joined Gallus in his mocking laughter, when all at once the birds took to the skies, their beating wings drowning out the noise.

Everyone fell silent as the birds circled above. Then, as if of one mind, they dove straight for Damien. All the birds, twenty-five in all, found a landing space on his body. Even the large crow took his place on a foot, and the finch made way for the dove by jumping onto the ridge of Damien's right ear.

The birds twittered and sang and covered Damien from head to toe. A sparrow leapt from his shoulder to his right pinkie, which Damien extended as stiffly as he could, hoping the perch was sufficient.

Damien moved only his eyes to Master Praxis, who was grinning widely. He turned to the children, all of whom were wide-eyed and openmouthed.

"Class," Master Praxis said, "is dismissed."

## 24

---

*Greeley Hotel; Greeley, New Mexico Territory; November 1855*

Damien loosened Josie's ties and she sat up in bed.

"Thank you."

"You're welcome." He turned up the oil lamp on the bureau, brightening the room. "I'll step outside and give you time to get yourself together."

"There's men here," Josie said. "All over the place."

"Those men are gone now," Damien said. "That rifle blast you heard was the last of 'em. Those who ran won't come back...I guarantee it."

"Who did you shoot?" she asked as she rubbed her wrists, which were raw with rope burn.

"That just there was Maddox," Damien replied.

"He's the only one Greeley ever spoke with."

"Yes, ma'am. Maddox was his second."

Damien backed out of the room, tipping his hat. He walked the halls of the hotel then stopped at a large oil painting hung above the staircase. It depicted a US Army Calvary in a battle with a tribe of Apaches, smoke billowing from half a dozen cannons placed haphazardly across the landscape. Everything from what the Apaches were wearing to a comical rendering of a man felled by cannon fire was wrong. Damien had witnessed plenty of men hit by cannonballs, and they didn't look anything like the soldier in the picture, who appeared to have been merely knocked off his feet and suffering from a twisted back. All the white men still had their scalps attached to their skulls, another unlikely scenario given the numbers they were battling.

"Artistic license," Damien muttered. "That's what you called this sort of thing, Bennett. The gap that sometimes exists between fiction and reality. That's this, all right."

He ambled down the hallway and peeked into the room Maddox had slept in. The man was still very much dead, splayed across the mattress in a puddle of his own filth. His eyes were open, pointed lifelessly at the rotund belly protruding from underneath his bed shirt. Damien shut the door, feeling sorry for whichever Mexican would be tasked with cleaning up the mess.

Josie stepped out of her room, smoothing down her dress. "Who were you talking to?" she asked.

"Myself, Josie. I do that sometimes."

"I confess I do as well," she said.

"I think we all do. Now. How's your person? You injured in any way?" Damien asked.

"No, I'm fine. Well, my neck's a little stiff. But I'm all right."

"That's good to hear. May I ask you a question that's a touch more delicate?"

"Sure."

"Did any of those men violate you, Josie?"

"No," she said. "Greeley wouldn't let any of them near me."

"That's also good to hear."

Damien gestured for the stairs. They descended them and walked into the crisp night air.

Once they were outside, Josie took a deep breath. Damien pointed to the Parlor House across the quiet thoroughfare.

"Good chow over yonder, if you're hungry."

"My daddy's dead, isn't he?" Josie asked.

Damien met her penetrating stare.

"Isn't he?"

Damien nodded.

"How?"

"Josie, I don't think you want to know the—"

"How?"

Damien took off his hat and rubbed his tired eyes. He would spare her the details of her father's castration and tell a simple tale that ended on the immutable truth: he was cold, dead, and in the ground.

"They shot him, Josie. I found your mother's headstone and buried him next to her. I did it right and proper, six feet deep. He'll be ready come the resurrection."

Josie took this in for a moment. "Thank you," she finally replied.

They were silent for a time, Damien unsure what to say. Willy's blood still dripped off the balcony, hitting the dirt. The first light of day was a thin pink band on the horizon, signaling the sunrise to come. Damien didn't want the two of them in town when it rose, what with Greeley's hotel containing two dead bodies at his hand.

"Got a horse idling not too far from town. Figure we set you up with one from Maddox's departed posse and ride out to it," he suggested.

"And then what?" Josie asked.

"And then...then I'll see to it that you get back to your homestead. Back to your land."

Josie wiped the tears from her cheeks. "No."

Damien wasn't sure what she meant or what to say in response. "Did you say—"

"No. I said no. That's not where we're going."

"I see," Damien replied. "Where *would* you like to go then?"

"I want to go where Isaac Greeley is," she said. "And kill him."

Damien took a step back from Josie. She wore the expression of someone who had made up her mind on something, and that decision was unswayable.

"Josie, my plan was to get you home, then find Greeley and execute him," he said. "You don't have to worry yourself on that account. Isaac Greeley will die and die soon."

"Yes. And you'll take me to him. And I will do the killing. I can't pretend I could do it alone. I will need your help. And I'll pay. I ask for no charity," she said.

"Josie..."

"Daddy used to take Eastern types out hunting. Men in fancy suits who'd never held a rifle in their life. He'd take them out to where the deer were, hand them the rifle, and they'd shoot them. That's what it'll be like. You'll be my hunting guide. And I'll compensate you for your time."

Here was a situation Damien hadn't anticipated. He scratched the back of his head, his face scrunched up in thought.

"So it's settled then," she said.

"Josie, it's going to be pretty rough going from here on out. Greeley's paying a bunch of men to back his stake out here. Ex-military types. Like me."

"There's no one like you," Josie said.

"That's kind of you to say, but Greeley nearly killed me once. I don't figure I'll be coming back down that mountain, tell the truth. I think this is a one-way ride. I couldn't have your death on my conscience."

"You underestimate yourself," she said.

"Bennett used to say that. Funny to hear it again. And you might be right, Josie. But there's going to be a lot of bloodshed. You'll need a pretty strong stomach for it."

"I grew up on a pig farm," Josie countered. "I've seen my share of throats cut."

"I don't need the help, Josie."

"Couldn't hurt."

"Oh, yes it could," Damien said. "Yes, it could. The road to hell is paved with good intentions, as the saying goes. People don't realize what killing a man does to the spirit. They think they know, but they don't. Saw a lot of boys come sort of what'd I'd call 'unhinged' after their first kill in the war. It's no way to live."

"I'm going," Josie said. "With or without you."

"Josie, I'll say just one more thing. And after I've said it, I will abide by your decision. All I ask is that you listen. Really and truly. Deal?"

Josie nodded.

"When I was a kid working in Bennett's store up in Missouri, this French fur trapper comes in and offers us five hundred dollars to set him up with a store of his own in town. Teach him the trade, like. The gentleman wanted to sell cheese. Cheese like they do in France, he says. Bennett explained that the life of a store keep wasn't all it was cut out to be. That you just sort of stand there hoping and praying people will walk through the door and buy something. Just staring outside trying to *will* people to come in and part with their money. Said that it wasn't any kind of life to recommend. That perhaps he could simply *buy* some cheese and *eat* the cheese and leave the storekeeping to the store keeps. And that's what I'm saying to you, Josie. I'm saying maybe leave the killing of Isaac Greeley to a killer."

Josie shrugged. "That all?"

"Your mind is set then," Damien said.

"Yes, sir."

Damien started for the edge of town. Josie hitched up her hem and followed.

———

Josie took Maddox's horse, a Missouri Trotter that reminded Damien of his childhood. They crested the hill overlooking Greeley, New Mexico, and down the other side.

"Maybe you should see your father's grave once before we depart. Pay respects and all," Damien said.

She shook her head. "You're just trying to get me home. Figure maybe if you do I'll lose my nerve and want to stay."

"No, ma'am," Damien replied. "Just making sure you do what needs doing before we depart. Hear me when I say this. You and me? We're marching to our deaths. That is something you must understand."

Josie spoke her next words to the sunrise. "This world of men...they do whatever they want. Whenever they want. To whomever they want. They lie. They cheat. They steal. They rape. They kill. And nobody does a thing about it."

Her brown eyes narrowed as the sun rose higher, the piercing light washing over their faces.

"Well, I'm doing something about it," she continued. "If killing this man is the last thing I ever do, so be it. But I won't go home. I won't sit by and let the Isaac Greeleys of the world do what they do and get away with it. Not anymore." She shielded her eyes from the sun. "Unless this is all just about you getting paid up front."

"It isn't anything of the sort," Damien said.

"Then what is it?"

"This is about you understanding a fundamental truth that's escaped every self-professed killer I've ever met."

"And that is?"

"And that is killing someone out of vengeance will not fill the hole in your soul. That I personally guarantee. You think marching up there and putting a bullet in Greeley's head, if such a thing is even possible, will settle the restless vexations in your spirit. It won't. If anything, it'll only cause you more grief. More pain. More suffering."

"So what do I do then?" Josie asked. "Go home and read my Bible and do my knitting and wait for a gentleman to ride along past my dead daddy's farm and sweep me off my feet? Like nothing ever happened? Is that what I'm supposed to do?"

"Maybe it is, Josie. Damned if I know. But lust for blood is not a virtue. It's a sin, and those of us who count ourselves Death's practitioner will surely see the gates of hell. Make no mistake about that. I am a killer, Josie. It's in my nature. I've lived far longer than anyone might have expected, especially me. You want to ride by my side? Want to play judge, jury, and executioner? Then it is for your own reasons and no other. I have no absolution to offer you. None whatsoever."

Damien patted the Morgan's flank and rode toward the wagon trail that led from Greeley into the desert wilderness.

Josie followed without hesitation.

## 25

*Wagon Trail, New Mexico Territory; November 1855*

Around noon, the trail split east, as Maddox said it would, the ground scattered with hoof prints and wagon-wheel tracks.

"We need to get off the main trail," Damien said. "We'll ride parallel. It'll give us half a chance if we encounter any operators lying in wait. Make sense?"

"Yes, sir," Josie said.

Damien steered the Morgan away from the wagon trail proper. The late-fall weather made the day mercifully temperate. He always enjoyed a long ride in cool weather. He allowed his thoughts to drift with the breeze: pleasant memories of winter evenings by Bennett's fire with a good book and summer days spent working by his side. At one point he forgot where he was riding altogether, the hypnotic drone of desert locusts lulling him into a trance.

"We never discussed your fee," Josie said, riding alongside him. "Don't you think that's a matter to bring to its conclusion 'fore we ride much farther?"

"Fee?"

"For helping me kill Greeley. What other fee is there?"

"Aha," Damien said. "That fee."

"Well, then? Name a number."

Damien gently tugged the Morgan's reins, bringing it to a stop. Josie did the same, her horse turning around in a full circle before bending its neck to the gnarled scrub brush sticking out among the drifts of desert sand.

"Truth is I don't have a figure 'cause I'm not doing this for pay," Damien said. "I told you I was gonna ride out and kill Greeley, and that's what I'm gonna do. You said you were going with come hell or high water, so here you are. And that's about the size of it."

"That doesn't make sense," Josie retorted. "What business you got with Greeley?"

"Greeley's who killed the man I called a father," Damien said. "Name was Bennett. Greeley murdered Bennett and your pa in revenge for the killings of Balazarus and Morrow. Balazarus and Morrow were killed in revenge for the violation you suffered, that having been set in motion by your pa contacting me. And so here we are. 'Come full circle' is the phrase I'd use."

"It never ends. The violence. Does it?" Josie asked.

"Doesn't seem to, no."

"What'd my father pay you?" Josie said. "I'll pay the same. Sell the farm if I have to."

"Normally I don't disclose the particulars of my business dealings with clients," Damien said. "However, as he was a blood relation and has shuffled his mortal coil, I will make an exception. The man paid me fifty dollars."

"Fifty dollars."

"Yes, ma'am."

"You killed two men for fifty dollars."

"Well, that's a tale in itself. Short version is no, I killed

Morrow for fifty dollars. Then I got to thinking that your pa deserved financial compensation for the loss he was suffering while you were convalescing at the nunnery. In attempting to extract that money from Balazarus, a dispute ensued, and I executed him also. As well, it should be mentioned, the young capper in his employ wielding a shotgun. Felt a bit bad about that but have since chalked it up in my mind to extenuating circumstances."

Josie shook her head and wiped away the hair the cool breeze had blown into her face. "What is it to you?" she asked.

"What is what to me?"

"All this killing."

"It's like I told you. I am a killer. I kill people."

"But not for the money. I'm right, aren't I?"

"You aren't wrong."

"So then. Why?"

Damien pondered the question for a while. "You know when you got an itch?" he finally said. "Real bad one, say, on your back? Where it's hard to reach?" Josie nodded. "You go up to a tree and rub around on the bark and scratch that itch? You know how good that feels?"

"I suppose. Yes," Josie replied.

"That's kinda what it's like," he continued. "It's an itch I have that's hard to scratch. But when I get to it and take care of it, I feel better."

"Killing people makes you feel good," Josie said. "That what you're sayin'?"

A thunderstorm rumbled fifty miles south of their position, flashes of lightning glowing within the titanic white thunderhead.

"Not all people," Damien replied. "Not you, for instance.

Not your pa. But certain people? Yeah. People that need killing. Makes me feel good. Yes."

Josie clicked her heels against the Trotter. "We'd better keep on," she said.

"Yes, ma'am. We'd better," Damien replied, and coaxed the Morgan ahead.

They rode in silence for the rest of the afternoon, the wind picking up. Damien thought they were in for a night of rain, but the storm in the distance eventually broke, painting the sky with a brilliant sunset. Neither rider asked to stop, although both wanted to. Instead they craned their necks to watch the firestorm of color and light as their horses trudged forward. When it was nearly dark, Damien pointed to a low-lying patch of scrub. They rode to it and got to work on the first night's camp.

Josie pretended to sleep for some time before finally giving in to insomnia. She sat up on her horse blanket to find Damien also awake, stoking the campfire coals with the branch of an ancient cottonwood. He glanced up, his thin face flickering in the flames' light.

She wrapped the blanket around herself and looked skyward. The stars were so thick and bright she felt as though she were falling into them. When she could no longer bear the sensation, she lay on her side, watching the sparks from the fire scatter from their logs and fade into nothing in the cold dirt. A few moments later, she sat back up.

"Can't sleep," she said holding her palms toward the flames.

"Always hard to sleep the first night in a new bed, I find,"

Damien said. "Especially when that bed is the ground in the middle of nowhere."

For a time, they sat without speaking then caught each other's glance. Josie stared back into the fire.

"Speak your mind," Damien said. "I can tell there's something on it."

He handed the stick to her. She rolled a log to catch its opposite side and tightened the blanket around her shoulders.

"How many men have you killed?" Josie asked. Damien shot her a look, and she shook her head. "I gave offense," she said. "Forget I asked. Apologies."

"I'm not offended. Just never been asked that question before. It's a fair one."

"It's none of my business."

"Business or not, it's what I'd be wondering if I were sitting on the opposite side of that fire."

"You don't have to answer."

"Do you really want to know?"

"Yes, I really do," she said.

"Maddox back there brought the total number to ninety-eight," Damien said.

Josie dropped her stick and sat forward. "Ninety-eight," she repeated.

Damien nodded. "Every last one worthy of their sentence. I do my diligence."

"You've killed *ninety-eight* people?"

"Ninety-eight *men*. No women or children. I got rules."

"That's incredible!"

"Is it?"

"I'd say so!"

"That doesn't count my time in the army, which was a different kind of killing," Damien said. "Had a drill instructor, big Irish fella, used to say we weren't being trained to kill people—we were being trained how to shoot a rifle properly. Then, when we marched into Mexico and the Mexicans tried to kill *us,* we could make an informed choice about what to do next, and if we decided to defend ourselves, at least we'd know how to shoot."

"Can't imagine what that war was like," Josie said.

"And you don't want to."

Josie gazed into the fire. "Does it give you bad dreams sometimes?"

"Bad dreams?"

"Yeah."

Damien reached for the branch, and she handed it to him. He held it in the white-hot ash until it caught flame. "Can't say that it does. I do dream sometimes, though. It's always the same. Least the parts I can remember."

He brought the flaming stick up into the air, twirling it, making red contrails as it cooled.

"Tell me," she said.

"Not much to tell," he replied. "It's me in the dream—that much I know. I'm maybe ten or eleven years old, thereabouts. I'm not in Missouri. I'm somewhere else, by the sea."

"The sea?"

"Yeah. And you know something? Never seen it myself. Seen lakes, seen rivers, but never the sea. But in this dream it's right there. And I'm in this meadow, like. Grass is nice and cool beneath my feet. Watch the waves like this a while...seems like forever. Then I hear this voice. Woman's voice. I turn around, and there on top of the hill is this great big white... I don't know what to call it. Bigger than a church, that's for sure. White, like I said, and made of stone. Gigantic. And this woman's waving at me, and calling me in for supper."

"Who is she?" Josie asked.

Damien shrugged. "Don't know. Can't make out her face. I just wave back and turn around and look back out to the water. Like I can't stop looking at it. Rather go hungry than move two feet from where I'm standing. After a while she stops calling me. And then I wake up."

"That sounds like a good dream. Peaceful."

"It is that, Josie. Yes."

A coyote howled in the darkness beyond, close by.

"What about you?" Damien asked.

"I have bad dreams," Josie said.

When she didn't elaborate further, Damien set the branch next to the fire and picked up the bedroll at his side.

"Best get some shut-eye if we can," he said. "We got another full day's ride 'fore we reach the logger trail. Only gets harder from there."

"'Night then, Damien."

"Night, Josie. Hear anything, do give a holler."

---

Damien had been asleep only a few minutes when a hand gripped his shoulder. Without opening his eyes, he reached out and grabbed the wrist and flipped the person onto their back while drawing his blade. By the time his eyes opened —less than a second—he found himself atop a terrified Josie.

"Josie! God Almighty, you gave me a start," he said, helping her to her feet. "A thousand apologies."

He sheathed his blade, and Josie pointed to their camp's perimeter. "Damien," she whispered. "*Look!*"

He already knew what had Josie in such a state. She clung to his arm as he guided her closer to the fire.

"It's all right," Damien said. "They won't hurt you."

A pack of coyotes a dozen strong had encircled the camp, glowing eyes fixed on the duo. A few tails wagged but otherwise they stood their ground, heads turning and watching every move the two humans made.

"That ain't natural, them being so close like that," Josie said. "These animals have the sickness. I've seen it in dogs on the farm. Had to put 'em down."

"They're not sick." Damien walked toward the alpha coyote, who stood only a few feet from the fire.

"Damien! Be careful!"

"They aren't here to cause trouble."

"You can't know that!"

Josie spun around as a coyote positioned itself behind her. She hiked up her skirt and kicked dirt in its face.

"Git! Git on now!" she shouted.

Damien looked into the alpha coyote's eyes. He asked it to order the pack to back away, said they were frightening his friend. The coyote bowed its head and apologized for the intrusion. Damien held out his open palm, and the animal sniffed his fingers.

"He bites, you're done for!" Josie yelled. "You get the canine madness, you won't want to take so much as a sip of water! I've seen it. Back off him now!"

Damien crouched and rubbed the fur between the coyote's ears. The coyote closed its eyes, then hunkered down on its belly, as did every single other coyote surrounding the fire, in turn. Josie could only watch, dumbfounded.

"They're just looking for a warm fire to rest themselves, Josie, is all. They aren't sick and they mean us no harm. Trust me on this. Will you trust me?"

Speechless, she turned in a circle. The coyotes yawned and lay their heads on the dirt.

"Let's get back to some shut-eye," Damien said, spreading out on top of his bedroll. "Anyone comes riding by, this bunch'll wake us up with their yapping, believe me. 'Skittish' is my word for 'em."

He plopped his hat over his face and folded his arms across his chest. A few seconds passed before he began snoring loudly.

Josie got back down on her horse blanket, keeping a wary eye on the sleeping coyotes, waiting for one to spring awake and attack. None did, at least not for the hour she spent awake watching them. Eventually she too drifted off to sleep, more out of extreme fatigue than a willingness to let her guard down. The two slept like this, along with the coyotes, until just past the break of dawn.

## 26

*Attica Peninsula, Greece; the Month of Skirophorion, 435 BC*

As he slept on the desert floor that night, Damien dreamed before awaking in the cool grass overlooking the sea. When he did, Ignatia called to him, but he ignored her request that he join the evening meal, just as he would recount over two thousand years later to Josie, across the fire.

Ignatia walked down the temple's steps and stood by Damien, taking in the view. After a while she turned to the finch on his left shoulder.

"Does he always sit there like that?" she asked, a bemused smile on her face.

"Yes," he answered.

"Does he ever leave your side?"

"Sometimes. To go hunt for worms, I guess."

"May I pet him?" Ignatia asked.

"If you like."

She gingerly patted the bird on the head with her finger. The finch chirped. "Clever little one, isn't he? Does he have a name?"

"Master Praxis says we aren't to give any bird a name," Damien said.

"Has he told you his name? That's what I meant."

"No. He hasn't."

"Well, if your mood isn't too sour, the evening meal is being served. Roasted squash, which I know you enjoy very much."

"Thank you, but I'm not hungry."

"You should eat, Damien."

"I said I'm not hungry."

"You should eat."

Damien wasn't going to win this particular battle of wills. He walked back toward the temple, the finch on his shoulder. Ignatia looked out at the sea for a while longer then followed him inside.

---

That evening, Damien sat at the end of an empty table, several seats away from the next student. Since that afternoon in Master Praxis's class, the mocking had stopped, but not one of the children spoke to him. Many regarded him with undisguised contempt, others jealousy, a few something akin to fear. Damien now ate alone and would read alone and play alone. Except for the finch, of course, who was his constant companion.

He picked at his squash, finally leaving it for his krater of wine. Its effects were increased on an emptier stomach. He drained his cup and immediately thirsted for more, resentful that the children were allowed only one serving per meal, whereas the masters enjoyed what seemed to be an unlimited amount. He longed to sit at their table, filling his glass over and over and discussing philosophy, art, and music, not having to endure the mindless prattling of his childish classmates. He resigned himself to solitude, save for the occasional interactions he enjoyed with his finch.

They were speaking to each other more and more these days. They weren't conversations, just Damien listening as the bird spoke its thoughts, which were becoming clearer to him over time. He pushed his plate of squash away and retreated to his room, wishing to write down the bird's daily musings before he forgot them.

Once safely inside his room, he slid his chair in front of the door, then crawled under the bed. Finding his diary wedged between two stones in the wall, he unfolded the parchment. He traced his finger down each phrase—all written in the order the finch had spoken them:

*The ocean is forever.*
*In the south the wind goes warm.*
*At night I fly by the stars.*
*Today I saw farther than I ever had.*
*The leaves are green in spring.*
*There is perfect quiet in the sky's solitude.*
*The clouds are mountains I must climb.*

Damien plucked the sharpened reed he used to write with from another crevice in the wall, then held it out in the last remaining sunlight of the day. There was just enough squid ink in the tip for the few words he needed to write. He scratched them out carefully, so as not to tear the parchment:

*The moon is a reflection in the sea of sky.*

The finch always followed each phrase with "and you are a child of the gods," but Damien didn't have enough ink to write it down every time. The ink he possessed had been stolen from Master Praxis's office, not enough for him to notice but another raid surely would cause suspicion. He blew on the parchment until he was satisfied it was dry, then refolded it and put it back in its hiding place. Filled with melancholy as the dark orange hues of the sunset traveled across the ceiling, he crawled on top of his bed.

Damien would be asked to leave soon. He saw it in the eyes of the masters, heard it in the tone of Ignatia's voice. They were pulling back from him, preparing for the day when they would send him into the wilderness, into exile.

Once again, he had considered crafting a story, making up the series of events that had brought him to the temple covered in blood, half starved. Every child who resided there had been brought in for a specific skill, a specific talent. The temple was not for the abandoned or the motherless—no, there were other places for them throughout Greece. The Orphic sects were very particular about who they allowed to pass through their doors. To stay, Damien would have to develop and nurture his talents, whatever those might be. All he currently had to show the masters was a proclivity for attracting birds, a skill also shared by the great stone statues in Athens. But it wasn't enough.

He racked his brain for the last events before his first night in the temple. He recalled the air was so hot and thick with humidity that it was difficult to breathe. Tree frogs—what must have been thousands—were chirping in the surrounding forest. He was light-headed, barefoot, and staggering over roots and fallen branches from a recent storm. His chest was slick with what felt like sweat, but the substance was dark, almost black in the moonlight. Then came a man's voice, somewhere far away but close enough that his words were carried by the wind.

"Greetings, child," he had said. "I mean you no harm."

That was all Damien could remember.

He wasn't born in the temple. He also wasn't raised by wolves in the forest, as the children took delight in telling him. So where did he come from? Who were his parents? Did he have brothers or sisters? Although he had asked these questions in the days following his rescue, the masters gently had insisted that it was he who must tell them. They said it in such a way that Damien knew *they* knew the answers, which infuriated him. What could be gained by their withholding this information?

After months of study with the Orphics, Damien finally understood.

The gods bestowed each child's gift upon them. Each recipient was then tasked with developing that talent, nurturing it, and giving themselves over to the mastery of it every day of their lives. The Orphic masters were there to guide them, but only the child could put in the necessary work. To do otherwise was an insult to the divinities who had blessed them. The quest for communion with the gods began with this basic concept.

If Damien didn't understand what gift he had to develop, there was nothing for the masters to do. His bed and food would go to another child, one more deserving.

———

He had been asleep for hours when a faint knocking came at his door. He rolled off his bed and dragged the chair away, steeling himself for a prank from one of the other boys. To his surprise it was Ignatia, her face illuminated by the candle in her hand.

"Dress yourself and come with me, Damien," she whispered. "Hurry."

After he threw his smock over his bedclothes, she led him down the hallway through the dormitories. Then they were outside, cutting through the cold grass toward the part of the temple where the masters kept quarters.

Once they were inside, Ignatia took Damien by the hand, squeezing it tightly in an unspoken demand for silence. Damien walked as lightly as he could as they rushed down the hall to Master Praxis's chambers. He saw the glow of candlelight emanating from underneath the wooden door. When they reached it, Ignatia pushed it open without knocking, as if Master Praxis were expecting her. He glanced up from his work, his eyes bright and alert for such a late hour.

"Shut the door, Ignatia, please," he whispered.

Ignatia did so, Damien's chest tight with anticipation of what was coming next. He figured this was the way it would be done after all, his caretakers quietly removing him from the temple in the dead of night. In the morning the other children would wonder where he was, but not for long. He would be forgotten in no time.

"Come here, child," Master Praxis said, extending a wrinkled hand.

Damien obeyed, doing his best not to burst into tears. He would leave the temple bravely. He didn't want Master Praxis's and Ignatia's last impressions of him to be that of a sniveling coward. They would tell the other students of the courage he displayed, and that's how he would be remembered. The wolf boy no one knew what to do with who left the temple to go live among his own kind. It was something, anyway.

Master Praxis took Damien's hand and encased it between his own. "Damien. Oh, Damien. I have prayed on this moment so."

A lump formed in Damien's throat. Ready for the inevitable, he took a deep breath and stared the master straight in the eyes.

"Many, many times the masters have asked you to go deep within your memory," Master Praxis said, gripping Damien's hand. "To remember the events that brought you here. Your mind's eye protects your heart, child. It will not let you see. But you must see. You *must* see, Damien."

Master Praxis released his hand and opened a wooden chest behind his desk. He removed something heavily swaddled in linens and rested it on the desk between them.

"This is yours, Damien. I return it to you now. It is up to you if you remove this cloth and look upon it. For when you do, you will again see. You will never be the same boy once you do."

Master Praxis sat back in his chair, brow furrowed. Ignatia folded her hands together as if to say, *I can't help you now*.

Damien reached over and rested his hand on the cloth. "If I don't remember, I will have to leave the temple, won't I?"

Master Praxis nodded solemnly. "Yes."

"And this will help me remember. But when I do, it will change me. Into someone else."

"Not someone else," Master Praxis said. "It will reveal your true self. Who you really are." He leaned forward in his chair. "*What* you really are."

Winter was coming, and Damien imagined how cold

and hungry he would be in the wilderness, fending for himself. He thought about how much he had come to enjoy his room, his fire, and the daily kraters of warm wine.

He again reached out and pressed his hand to the cloth, then picked it up, surprised to find how light it was. He then took the edge of the cotton between two fingers and unraveled it. The cotton swaddling dropped to the floor in thin strips as the object inside emerged.

It was something red.

When Damien pulled away the last of the covering, he dropped it as if it were on fire. It fell to the floor with a clatter, and he stepped back, stumbling into the bookcase behind him. Ignatia made a move to go to him, but Master Praxis stopped her with a hand on her arm.

"Let him be."

Damien stared down at the object for some time. Then he picked it up again and turned it over in the light of the fire, the skin on his fingers taking away some of the blood covering it.

It was the jawbone of a small deer. Damien knew it was a deer, because he remembered the skull from which it was taken. He also remembered the men who had hunted it and skinned it. And he remembered what he had done with the bone and how it had come to be soaked in blood.

He remembered everything.

## 27

*Wagon Trail, New Mexico Territory; November 1855*

When Josie awoke, the coyotes were gone, only their paw prints left behind. She studied them for a while in the early light, unsure how any of what she had witnessed was possible. Coyotes were frightened of humans, but these animals had been as calm and friendly as farmhouse dogs.

She looked at Damien. His eyes were moving rapidly beneath their lids. A moment later, they opened and he sucked in his breath, coming back to himself.

"You were having a bad dream," Josie said. "Weren't you?"

"Reckon I was."

She nodded. "It happens."

Damien patted his knife and gripped the pistols hanging from their holsters on his waist, their presence reassuring. The two went about breaking down the camp, Josie rolling up their beds, Damien stoking the last embers of the fire. The horses were almost ready to ride when he approached her, hands behind his back.

"Figure we'd have a little breakfast 'fore we ride on," he said.

"Sounds good to me."

"Pick one."

"One what?"

"Hand."

Josie pointed to Damien's left shoulder. He brought his hand around and held out a can of beans.

"Beans!" she exclaimed. "For breakfast?"

"You picked left."

"What was in the other hand?"

Damien revealed the right one, also holding a can of beans.

"You got something against bacon?" she asked.

———

After breakfast they rode on. The wagon trail rose in elevation, and their ability to ride alongside it came to an end. Damien pointed to the landscape, which started to curve toward the pine-forest-covered mountains ahead.

"I see it," Josie called out.

Damien slowed his horse to a stop and she did the same. "We'll have to ride on the main trail from here on out," he said. "That's a precarious situation to put ourselves in."

"Was gonna happen eventually."

Damien wiped his forehead and pointed to Maddox's rifle, which was tied to the Trotter's saddle. "How handy do you think you are with that? Truthfully," he asked.

"I can shoot a rifle good as any man," she said.

"Pigs and such? On the farm?"

"What's on your mind, Damien? Say it plain."

"Sayin' things will get more and more treacherous closer

we get to Isaac Greeley. Time's coming when you're going to be using that to kill a man, maybe several. Thought maybe you and I would have a talk before it all goes down."

Josie pulled the rifle from its ties and checked its ammo. Then she leveled it at Damien. "All ears."

"Don't concern yourself with that right-between-the-eyes hokum you read about in the newspapers," he said. "All you have to do is put your man down. Understand what I'm getting at?"

"I do," Josie said.

"When they shoot back, that's when it gets a bit unnerving," Damien continued. "You just keep firing, one man down, then move onto the next. These saps Greeley's paying are only doing it for the money. I served with most of them. Inebriates, all. But make no mistake—these are US Army–trained infantryman. When called upon, they'll put a bullet in you."

"That where you learned all this?" Josie asked.

Damien laughed.

"Now there's a sound I never expected to hear come from you," Josie said, smiling. "You should do that more —laugh."

Damien's eyes fixed on the trail and followed it until it disappeared into the pines. "Only thing I learned in that army is what the white man will do to claim a godforsaken patch of cactus as his sovereign territory," he said.

"It was a terrible war. Lost my brother Henry in it," Josie said.

"And here we are all these years later. Not a Mexican in sight. Now we're fixing to go and murder our own tribe. Bennett always said life was a funny thing. Guess this is the kind of situation he was talking about."

---

## 28

*Logging Trail, New Mexico Territory; November 1855*

The pine tree shadows turned like the hands of the clock as the sun fell over from afternoon to evening. Damien and Josie were now deep into the mountain forest, Steller's jays in the branches above their heads, jeering and fat with the piñon nuts they'd feasted on during the late summer. They tilted their heads as the duo passed, the high black feathers on their heads bobbing from side to side.

Damien stopped his horse and listened to them, then raised his hat, thanking them. "Something's up there," he whispered.

Josie peered down the trail. "I don't see anything," she whispered back.

He put a finger to his lips and held up his hand. Josie slowed the Trotter as Damien rode ahead, his hand on one of the pistols holstered to his belt. Soon he reached the point where the trail became a small hill and disappeared down the other side.

When a jay squawked just overhead, Josie jumped in her saddle. "You hush up," she told the bird.

She pulled the rifle up and gripped the cool barrel in her hands. She then canvassed the surrounding forest, and the trail behind her. All was still.

Fifteen of the slowest minutes Josie had ever counted passed. She comforted herself that there had been no gunfire, no hollering. Surely if Damien had encountered anyone, they would have presented themselves. She was about to ride ahead to alleviate her anxiety when a man giggled.

Damien emerged from the trees, his hand on the shoulder of a fellow half his size. His newfound companion was balding and badly sunburned, and his face was covered in sawdust, which clung to his sweat. When he smiled, he revealed half the teeth he would be expected to have at his age, and he cradled a clay jug protectively against his sunken chest. Damien and the man weren't twenty feet away when the smell of moonshine filled Josie's nostrils.

The man kept giggling as if he were remembering something funny. Damien pointed to Josie high in her saddle. "Ambrose, this is Miss Llewelyn," he said. "Miss Llewelyn, this is Ambrose, whose acquaintance I made just a moment ago."

Ambrose bowed at the waist, the liquid in his jug sloshing.

"Howdy do, ma'am?" he said in a nasal, high-pitched Kentucky twang. "Please ta meet'cha."

"Likewise, Ambrose," Josie said, raising an eyebrow at Damien, who winked at her.

"This man was just telling me a joke, like," Damien said. "Tell it to her."

Ambrose raised the jug to his lips and drank deeply. He lowered it and swallowed, then gasped. The smell wafted up to Josie, making her eyes water.

"While passin' a house on a road, two Virginia salesmen spots a mighty peculiar chimney, unfinished, and it attracts they's attentions," Ambrose slurred. "They ask this flaxen-haired urchin standin' near that there house if it done 'drawed well.' Whereupon the aforementioned urchin giveth them the stingin' retort: 'Yes, it draws all the attention of the damned fools that pass this here road!'"

Ambrose again dissolved into giggles, slapping one of the well-worn knees on his sodden trousers.

"Yes, it draws all the attention of the damned fools that pass this here road!" he repeated, tears running out of his puffy eyes.

"That's a good one, Ambrose," Josie offered. "Where'd you hear that?"

"Read it in one o' them newspapers once," Ambrose replied, bringing the jug up again. "Cain't never forget since."

"Ambrose has a timber claim in these mountains," Damien said. "He's been bringing logs out of here for...what was it? Five years?"

"Five a'so them years ago, yessir," Ambrose said, smacking his lips, a bit of moonshine dribbling from the corners.

"But over the last few months you've been working for somebody. What was his name again?" Damien asked.

"Greeley's the man's name," Ambrose replied. "Yankee from Back East. Banker or the like, I reckon. He own e'ry lil thing 'round these parts." He waggled his finger toward the surrounding trees. "All a'dat. Bastard's got us clear cuttin' the top of the mountain too. Like this." The man pointed to the bald circle of skin on top of his head. "Bad fer the soil, what it is."

"What's that?" Josie asked. "Clear cuttin', I mean?"

"They're chopping all the trees down," Damien said. "Old hands like Ambrose here know you have to trim forests in a certain way to maintain their integrity. His boss has them cutting everything at once."

"What he said," Ambrose chimed in.

"Any idea what Greeley's doing that for?" Josie asked. "Why he's choppin' down all those trees?"

"Buildin' a fort. Only word fer it," Ambrose replied. "Got some o' dem boys shaving them timber poles sharp up top, real sharp. Buildin' a wall, what he's doin'. 'Tween him and e'rybody else, like."

"And where is this fort exactly?" Damien prodded.

"Some miles yonder," Ambrose replied. "Though I wouldn't get too close to it, I was you. Got some soldier boys up there off their chumps, you git'ma meaning. Ain't right in the head, some o' dem."

"Well, Ambrose, whatever that boss of yours is paying you, it's not enough," Damien said, walking to the Morgan and unbuttoning a pouch on the saddlebag. He removed a silver coin and handed it to the man.

Ambrose grinned his gap-toothed smile and shuffled to it, plucking it from Damien's fingers and turning it over in the light.

"What's this fer?" he asked. "You want you's a dram? Make it me'self."

"Don't drink," Damien said.

"Well, I feel sorry for ya," Ambrose replied, letting out a fresh salvo of laughter. This round was infectious, with Damien and Josie joining in. "What's it fer then?"

"For the information. And the joke."

Damien put his foot in the stirrup and pulled himself onto the Morgan. "You take good care, Ambrose."

"You do the same, mister. Never did get your name."

"Name's Damien Attica," he replied, and rode ahead, leaving Josie to witness Ambrose drop the jug of moonshine at his feet. Ambrose didn't acknowledge her as she rode past him, just stared at Damien as he guided the Morgan back over the hill, as if he had just seen a ghost.

---

Josie and Damien made camp in a thicket of pine trees well off the road, the horses happy to graze on the nuts they found scattered on the ground. The cold mountain air clung to Josie's skin, even though she was wrapped in the thickest blanket they carried between them. Damien hadn't said a word for more than an hour, only scraped his knife against a smooth stone. The sound had gone from annoying to terrifying in short order, not only for what a freshly sharpened blade portended but also the fact that Josie couldn't see her hand in front of her face in the moonless night.

"Damien."

"Hmm?"

"Could you...not do that right now, please?"

The scraping stopped.

"You all right?"

"I'm fine," she lied. "Just...cold."

She heard Damien adjust his position against the tree trunk he sat against.

"Come over here then," he said. "We'll sit together under both blankets. One body will keep the other warm. And before your mind even entertains the notion that this is some sort of ungentlemanly proposition, know that such things couldn't be further from my mind."

Josie somehow already had known this. Damien had never once looked at her in the way most men did, had never hinted at even the slightest attraction for her. She got to her feet and carefully walked through the darkness, hand extended ahead of her, feeling for trees. She took Damien's hand and lowered herself next to him. She then threw her horse blanket over them, and they pressed against each other, each slipping an arm around the other's waist. She was amazed at how thin he was, how his ribs jutted from his skin so much she could have counted them with her fingers. They leaned their heads against the tree and in no time were fast asleep.

## 29

*Attica Peninsula, Greece; the Month of Skirophorion, 435 BC*

Damien held the bloodied deer bone in his hand as his memory flooded back. Master Praxis and Ignatia listened to him intently as he told his story. He recalled the events of a hot summer day that eventually brought him to the Orphic Temple.

---

*Outside the City of Athens, Greece; the Month of Hekatombaion, 437 BC*

Damien's father would soon be back from his day in Athens, and he rushed his chores in anticipation of it. He couldn't keep the smile off his face as he milked the last of the family's sheep then ran back up to the house with the bucket dangling from his hand. His mother Euthalia already was in the doorway, hands on her hips, black hair sweeping across her preternaturally youthful features in the summer breeze.

"Damien, you spill one drop of that milk, I'll tell Papa."

"I won't, Mama," he said, slowing his pace. She met him halfway and took the bucket from him. Unable to hide her smile, she set the milk down and embraced her son.

"Do you think he was chosen, Damien?" she asked.

"He was. I'm sure of it, Mama," he said.

"Shall we be standing in the doorway, waiting to greet him?"

"Yes!" Damien exclaimed.

"I think so too."

Soon they were doing exactly that, squeezing each other's hands, waiting.

"What's taking him so long?" Damien asked.

"Look at the sun," his mother said. "He'll not be back until it's nearly set. Time has slowed only for us."

They waited and waited. When the afternoon light began to change, the familiar figure of his papa appeared at the bottom of the hill.

"Mama, look!" Damien shouted.

"*Shhh*. Let him tell us. One way or the other."

Damien's father Leon, a towering figure of a man six and a half feet tall, ambled up the road, his tunic wafting around his legs in the early-evening breeze. Damien scrutinized his face, hoping for a clue as to what might have transpired in the city. The big man waved at his wife and child, offering no hint one way or the other.

"I can't tell, Mama. Can you?"

"No. I can't."

She gripped Damien's hand. When his father was nearly up the hill, he called out to them. "I will have my wash before I come inside," he said.

"Yes," Euthalia replied. "Of course."

Leon went to the well, where he cranked the handle and brought up a fresh bucket of water. He splashed water over his face and neck, then rubbed it across his enormous arms.

"Ah," he said. "That's grand."

"Leon," Euthalia said, "are you going to tell us?"

"Tell you what?" Leon replied.

"What happened today, of course!"

"Well, let's see," Leon said. "I rode into town in a wagon filled with fresh straw, which was very pleasant indeed. So pleasant I took a short nap, in fact. Once there, I visited a house with the most wonderful bread you've ever smelled, and I ate some with olives for my breakfast. It was delicious."

"Leon!" his mother shouted. "You know what I mean!"

"*And* there," his father continued, "I was asked to represent Athens in the Olympic Games."

"Thank the gods!" his mother cried, and she and Damien ran to him.

Leon laughed in his deep baritone and pulled them close. "'Thank the gods' is right. I am a blessed man. A blessed man. No more so than for having the two of you to share my life with."

Damien tugged at Leon's belt. "Who will you wrestle, Papa?"

"That is not up to me, son. But whoever it is, they should ready themselves for quite a contest."

"Show me the moves you'll use!" Damien shouted, hopping around in the dirt. "Do them on me!"

"Damien, he just washed up for supper. You can play later," Euthalia scolded him.

Leon got down on one knee. "Come here, boy."

Damien rushed to his father. The big man's black beard glinted in the sunlight, as did his green eyes, which studied his son's face.

"Ready, son?"

"I'm ready Papa."

Leon pointed to the back of his neck. "Put a hand here. And here," he instructed, slapping his left shoulder.

Damien did as told, his father's body as thick and solid as the stone wall that ringed the perimeter of their farm.

"Now I will say, 'Ready, wrestle,' and wrestle we shall. But not before I say it. So I ask you again: are you ready? Really ready?"

"Yes, Papa!"

"Where are your feet?"

Damien adjusted his footing in the manner his father had instructed him many times before.

"Good. Now. Ready? *Wrestle*."

In one swooping motion Leon scooped Damien up in his arms, then dropped him, catching the boy by the ankles. Damien squealed with glee as he dangled from his father's grip.

"Tonight we sacrifice a lamb to the gods and drink wine," Leon said. "There is much to celebrate."

"Indeed there is," Euthalia replied, and they started back inside the house.

———

That night they ate lamb on the bone and drank the finest wine from the cellar. Leon told his wife and son how he was chosen, how it was announced before some of the most distinguished men on the city council.

"There is a possibility—not a promise, mind you, but a possibility—that I also will receive the honor of lighting the Olympic torch in the opening ceremonies."

Euthalia nearly dropped her cup into her lap. "Leon, that's wonderful."

"Things will change for us, you know," he continued. "People will recognize us, want to speak to us in the market and in the city streets. The name 'Attica' will be known 'round the world, for good or for ill. We must be ready for that."

"It's almost too much to contemplate," Euthalia replied. "We are so very blessed."

Leon gripped their hands. "The gods smile down on us," he said. "We already had all we could ever ask for. Good soil, in a land where that is pitifully rare. Healthy animals, which provide us with milk and wool, and the flesh we dine on. Grapes, sun kissed by Helios, that make our wine. We never have suffered illness or plague. And now this. We are *too* blessed, is what we are." Leon leaned over and kissed his wife's cheek. "And now, to sleep. Our work waits for us in the morning, same as ever."

Damien and his mother cleared the table, and soon Damien had washed his face for bed. He pulled the covers to his chin and received his good-night kiss from Euthalia, knowing he would be unable to fall asleep.

He lay awake thinking of the stadium, how it would sound to hear thousands of Athenians cheering his father's name. Leon would emerge from the games victorious, of course— the world's champion, bowing gallantly to receive his olive branch. Damien wanted the games to take place tomorrow, not in two weeks. He didn't think he could bear the wait.

A rapping at the front door jolted him from his fantasy. He quietly slid from his bed and ran into the family room. Leon already was there, dressed in his bedclothes.

"Who is it?" his father said, a hand on the door. A

quieter mumble came from the other side, and Leon opened it. "Nicomedes," he said, surprise in his tone. "Is anything the matter?"

"No, good Leon, no. Quite the opposite," a raspy voice said in reply.

Damien cleared his throat and Leon turned to him, revealing an old man in the doorway, wrapped heavily in a fine purple tunic.

"Son, you should be in bed," Leon said.

"Sorry, Papa. I heard the knocking."

"Nicomedes, this is my son, Damien."

"Hello, my boy," Nicomedes said with a smile.

"Hello, sir. Welcome to our home."

"And now back to bed," Leon said, and Damien obeyed.

When he rounded the corner, he crouched low to the floor and peered around the wall, spying.

"Please sit," Leon continued. "Can I offer you anything? Wine?"

"No, no, no. I will be brief," Nicomedes replied.

The two men sat at the wooden dining table, facing each other. Damien crouched even lower.

"I felt it best we had this conversation outside the city walls," Nicomedes said. "It is not for anyone to know about outside of this house. Do you understand?"

"Yes," Leon said. "Of course."

"I apologize for the late hour, but such things can't be avoided in situations such as this. Therefore I will come straight to the point. The games. You will wrestle Milo of Croton."

Leon sat back in his chair, an expression on his face Damien had never seen before.

"Milo of Croton is beneath my class, Nicomedes. It

wouldn't be fair," Leon said. "I will surely best him in the ring. I could do so with one arm tied behind my back."

"Leon, you will do no such thing. You will wrestle Milo of Croton before the gods and man, and you will lose."

Leon sat there, stunned into silence. "I'm sorry," he finally said. "What did you say?"

Nicomedes reached out and picked up a pair of dice that Damien and his father played games with from time to time. He rolled them around in his right hand, looking at them and not at Leon when he again spoke.

"I am a man of considerable wealth, Leon, though I was not born that way. I made it all on my own, using my wits. Wasn't easy. I'm not proud of how I acquired much of it and what I continue to do to maintain it. But maintain it I must. Without men like me, there would be no games. No libraries. No communal altars or baths. 'He who pays the piper calls the tune.' Doesn't have to make sense. It just is." Nicomedes rolled the dice across the table. "There is more money than you can conceive of riding on the outcome of every event in these games. Who wins and who loses is not determined by skill or the gods, but by men. And I say you will wrestle Milo of Croton, and you will lose. And you will be rewarded handsomely."

Leon took a breath, but Nicomedes raised a finger, stopping his words.

"Your family will be moved into the city a month after the games conclude. You will want for nothing for the rest of your life, nor will they. Your wife will spend her days as a lady of leisure, lunching in the square with other women of means. Your son will be educated at the finest schools. He will have his choice of profession. Anything he can dream, he will be. And you will never lift another bale of hay or plow another field. I swear all of this to you, by the gods."

Leon remained silent.

"Comfort yourself with the knowledge that you have absolutely no say in the matter," Nicomedes continued. "The choice has been made for you. And rather than a wilted olive branch and the drunken cheers of an unwashed mob, you will instead have wealth beyond anything you could have dreamed of in your former life. And that, my boy, is what winning really is." Nicomedes gripped the edge of the table and pulled himself to his feet. "I'll show myself out."

The old man shuffled to the door and pulled it open. Leon stared at the table, his eyes far away.

"Do get some sleep, Leon, and sleep well," Nicomedes said. "You have a match to lose. And a world to gain."

With that he pulled the door closed behind him.

Leon sat there for a while, head lowered to his chest. He closed his eyes, raised his arms, and gripped the back of his head as if in pain.

Damien hadn't understood any of it, what it meant, or why his father sat at the table as he did now. Finally he emerged from his hiding place behind the wall.

"Papa?"

"Damien, I told you to go to bed."

"Who was that man?"

Leon opened his arms, and Damien ran to him.

His papa wrapped them around him, squeezing him tightly. Damien never felt as safe as he did when he was in his father's embrace.

"That man is very important to this family, son. And to the city, for that matter. I never would have been bestowed such a great honor if not for him. We should pray for him and his good health."

"What did he mean when he said you had to lose?" Damien asked.

His eyes watering, Leon reached out and gently tugged Damien's earlobe, something he did when assuring him things would be okay.

"He was teasing me, Damien. I'm not going to lose. Now. To bed."

"Yes, Papa."

Before he left, he gave his father one last look. Leon's hands were clasped tightly in prayer, his eyes squeezed shut, his lips moving silently.

Damien was afraid but didn't know why.

## 30

*Logging Trail, New Mexico Territory; November 1855*

Damien and Josie rode at dawn, stomachs empty, eyes warily sweeping the trail. Although they were sitting ducks on the logging road, there were no other options. The surrounding trees were too dense for the horses to navigate effectively. Damien could smell an ambush coming, and just before noon that ambush did come.

They had passed between two boulders on either side of the trail, the huge stones blocking a view of the path ahead. Damien almost told Josie he'd best scout the area to make sure there wasn't anything waiting for them on the other side. He almost did, but didn't. No sooner did they pass through the rocks than they heard Ned shouting.

"Reach for it, Attica!"

The Morgan and Trotter reared up as Ned, Spivey, and three other men emerged from the treeline, all brandishing rifles and pistols. Terrified, Josie wrestled for control of her horse. Damien raised his hands over his head, as did she.

"That's good, Attica," Ned said, a Colt revolver in each hand. "That's real good."

"Point them irons at *her*, not him," Spivey instructed the rest of the posse. They did as instructed, turning the barrels of their Springfield rifles toward Josie.

"Now then. Attica, you mind what I'm saying and mind it well," Ned said. "With one hand—that's *one* goddamn hand —unbuckle your gun belt and drop it to the ground. Slow, like. You so much as flinch for one o' those black-eyed Suzies, we'll smoke your lil friend here. We clear?"

Damien nodded.

"Need to hear you say it," Spivey said.

"We're clear," Damien replied.

"Do it now. *Slow*."

Damien kept his left hand high as he eased the right down to the buckle of the leather holster across his waist. He pulled it loose and let it slide off his hips, his six-shooters falling to the ground around the Morgan's feet.

"That's just fine, Attica," Ned continued. "You doin' fine. Now sumpin' tells me you got that Bowie knife of yours tucked back 'hind your britches there, pretty as you please. Why don'tcha slowly...*slowly* pull that sucker out and drop it on down next to yer peacemakers. Again, any funny business and it's goodbye little Miss Josie."

Damien used his right hand to reach behind his back, pulled the bowie out, and dropped it, still in its sheath. "Now what?" he asked.

"Now what is that we're taking you to Mr. Greeley," Spivey chimed in, one of his pistols aimed at Josie, the other at Damien. "The both of ya. He's gonna make an example out of you two—you can believe that. I wouldn't trade places with ya'll for all the gold in California, and that's the God's truth. Jesus Almighty, ya'll are well and truly fucked."

A dozen Steller's jays landed in the pine branches above

their heads, chattering loudly. Ned and Spivey rolled their eyes up to them.

"Them birds are big as fuckin' cats," Ned said.

Spivey leveled his gaze back at Damien, a malevolent grin on his face. "Guess they came to see the show."

"Yes," Damien replied. "I guess they did."

"Why don'tcha git on down from that pony there," Spivey continued. "Slow as molasses."

Damien did so, throwing a leg over the Morgan's saddle. He then dropped to the ground, hands raised.

"Put them hands on your head."

Damien did, looking to the men aiming their rifles at Josie. "Who are they?" he asked. "The three Musketeers, that is."

"The three what?" Spivey spat.

"Musketeers," Damien said. "Athos, Porthos, and Aramis. Am I right? I'm quite sure I am."

"The hell you goin' on about, Attica?" Ned said, his nose scrunched.

"It was an attempt at humor," Damien replied. "Three Musketeers? Alexandre Dumas? Anyone? No?"

The jays in the trees above hopped between branches, screeching.

Damien pointed up to them. "See? They think it's funny."

Josie couldn't contain her laughter. Ned charged forward, pistol pointed in Damien's face. "I'm gonna shoot 'im in that smart mouth of his, Spivey!"

"You ain't gonna do no such fuckin' thing!" Spivey barked back. "Greeley ain't payin' the same for no corpse! Put that gun down! Right now, goddamn it!"

Ned pressed the barrel into Damien's upper lip. "Greeley's gonna make you scream, Attica," he snarled. "And I'm gonna be there when he does. We'll see who's laughing then."

"Ned!" Spivey placed his weapon inches from his partner's skull. "You just back off, now," he said. "Boy's gettin' what's coming to him. And we'll be there to see it, just like you said."

Ned pulled his pistol away and spat on Damien's boots.

"No honor among thieves, it seems," Damien said. "I should have killed both of you when I had the chance."

"Guess so," Ned replied. "But you're *our* collar now. Same as you, little miss." Ned swung his gun back to Josie. "You come down offa there now, nice and easy like Attica did."

"Oh, she's not going anywhere," Damien said. "At least, not with the two of you. Neither am I, for that matter."

"How the hell you figger that?" Spivey asked.

"Sorry," Damien said. "Am I the only one who sees them?"

Ned and Spivey exchanged confused looks.

"See who?" Ned asked.

"Them," Damien replied, pointing in either direction with his thumbs.

Ned and Spivey looked to their left and right, as did Josie, who gasped. She hadn't seen them either, nor had she heard a sound.

The pack of coyotes had returned, this time with reinforcements, two dozen in all. Their ears were flat against their heads, lips pulled back in snarls. They stood among the pine trees, still as statues.

"Mary, Mother of God," Ned said.

"Oh, boys," Damien said, his eyes turning over to black. "She can't help you now."

The coyotes attacked as one, rushing the posse from all sides. There was a crackle of gunfire as the men tried to ward them off, a sharp whine coming from one of the animals they'd managed to hit. The coyotes' numbers, however, were too great.

Spivey was brought to the ground, arms and legs encased in teeth. Ned kicked and punched and soon too was brought low, the largest of the coyotes getting a mouthful of his jugular. The riflemen tried to run but were pursued by half the pack, leaving them no choice but to wage a doomed battle for their lives. Canine snarls and human screams filled the air.

Josie covered her eyes. The Morgan and the Trotter hadn't moved, nor did they seem the least bit concerned about the events before them. Damien picked up his gun belt, replaced it around his waist, and watched as the five men were ripped to pieces before his dark eyes.

Ned bled out first, his throat torn wide open. Spivey died next, the arteries in his neck shredded by fangs. The other three had managed to make it twenty yards down the trail, but were now being descended upon by the coyote pack's full force. The jays jabbered away in the trees as Damien cinched his belt tightly and picked up his bowie knife. He collected the unfired Colt revolvers off the deceased and stuffed them into his saddlebag.

"Keep your eyes closed, Josie. Won't be a minute."

Josie pressed her palms even harder against her face as she listened to the strangled screams of the three men down the trail. Then, silence.

What came next was a sound she remembered from growing up on the farm, something she'd heard when her pa had butchered the hogs every October.

It was a *crunching*, a blade separating bone. Not wanting to imagine what was happening outside her vision, she forced herself not to look, not to lower her hands and open her eyes. Then Damien whistled.

"Is that...is that 'Camptown Ladies' you're whistling?" Josie asked.

"It is," Damien said. "Does it give offense? I'm not much of a whistler."

"I just don't see how you can whistle at a time like this," she replied.

"I whistle when I labor," Damien said. "Makes it seem less like work. Bennett used to do it. Picked it up from him, I suppose."

"I don't have anything against whistling. Just the circumstances being what they are was my meanin'."

"Be done in a jiff," Damien assured her. "I'll let you know when it's safe to look."

There was more crunching, then twisting, then a loud snap that made her jump in the saddle. Unable to bear it any longer, Josie dropped her hands and opened her eyes.

Damien was walking down the trail with his back to her, Spivey's severed head in his left hand, Ned's in his right, each dangling by a handful of hair. Josie squeezed her eyes shut again, deeply regretting having opened them in the first place.

"I looked!" she shouted.

"Why in heck did you do that?" Damien called back.

"I dunno! I was curious, I guess."

"Curiosity killed the cat, as they say."

"Who says that?"

"It's an expression."

"Why'd you cut off their heads?"

Damien considered this. "If we leave 'em like they are, it looks like what it is," he replied. "Which is a group of men felled by a pack of wild animals. But if I stick these two idiots' heads on sticks on either side of the trail, other operators coming up the path here will say 'That right there is the work of Damien Attica.' I have my reputation to consider. Make sense?"

"Not really," Josie answered.

"Be just one more minute. Promise."

---

Damien finished his work, and they rode down the trail, the coyotes congregating around the three riflemen, all dead and in various states of mutilation. Josie kept her eyes forward, willing herself not to take in the sight of their bodies or the heads of Ned and Spivey, both of which Damien had jammed onto tree branches on either side of the trail and were already attracting flies. Josie felt faint, unsure if this was one of her bad dreams.

"Aw, hell," Damien said, dismounting the Morgan.

His hands and forearms were covered in dark-red gore, a result of the recent butchering. Damien stepped through the pack to a coyote lying on its side, shot through the shoulder. It panted rapidly, tongue hanging from its slack jaw. Damien reached out a blood-soaked hand and rested it on the animal's flank.

Damien's lips moved wordlessly, the other coyotes shoulder to shoulder as their fallen mate breathed its last. Damien stood and the pack moved in, howling with grief.

"Shame," he said, mounting the Morgan.

A jaybird descended from the branches and landed on the horn of the horse's saddle, cocking its head and letting out a shrill cry.

"No argument here," Damien told the bird. "Onward we go."

"Damien..." Josie said.

He turned around to find her face drained of color. "Josie. You all right?"

"No. I'm not. Not at all. What the hell is all this?" She took a deep breath, her next words so quiet he barely heard them. "Is this some sorta witchcraft? Is it?"

"Witchcraft?" Damien asked. "As in, 'Double, double, toil, and trouble?' That sort of thing? That's just a play."

"None a' this is natural," she continued. "And there's nothin' you can say that'll convince me otherwise. These animals are touched, and something tells me you are too."

"Touched by what?" Damien asked.

"The Devil."

Damien laughed. "Josie, you surprise me. Truly. I didn't take you for the superstitious type."

"Not a superstitious bone in my body, Mr. Attica. I'm sayin' prairie coyotes don't pack up and kill for man. They *fear* man, least they're s'posed to. And wild birds don't sit on a saddle horn like that great big jay like it was a pet. There's somethin' about you, Damien Attica, somethin' not of God's creation. And I needed to say that out loud, plain and simple. Now we can move on along."

"You feel better?" Damien asked.

"A bit."

"Good."

Damien gently tugged the Morgan's reins and started back down the logging trail. The jaybird stayed perched on the saddle horn, content to hitch a ride.

The coyotes fell into step behind them, tails wagging, tongues hanging out of their bloodied maws. They circled around the horses, looking up at Josie with their yellow eyes, now docile as lap dogs.

"Damien..."

"Yes, ma'am?"

"They seem to be coming with."

"Sure they are."

"How's that?"

"I said sure they are," Damien repeated. "One of their sisters was just killed by Isaac Greeley. Maybe not directly at his hands, but by events that he put into place. Now they have a bone to pick with him, same as us."

The jaybird squawked, and he scolded it, telling it to hush and they were moving as fast as they could.

Josie shook her head. "You have a way of putting things that makes sense of all of this."

"Didn't say it makes sense. It just is. Heard that once when I was a boy."

They rode on, the coyotes at their sides, jaybirds above flying from branch to branch.

## 31

*Athens, Greece; the Month of Hekatombaion, 437 BC*

Olympic Stadium reeked with the odor of thousands of men. The sun blazed over the third day of the games, the sacrificial blood of slaughtered livestock trickling through sewers coated with large black flies. Damien elbowed his way through the crowd, down toward the arena. He was determined to be as close as possible when his father's arm was raised in victory.

His mother remained on the stadium steps outside, as women weren't allowed in the arena. Damien envied her as he struggled to breathe in the punishing humidity, the air pungent with fetid skin. At last he found a seat on the edge of a stone bench near the front.

A man selling roasted dates on a stick passed, and Damien's stomach clenched. He wouldn't dare spend his coin on a treat for himself, not after watching his father starve himself for two weeks to make weight for the match and knowing his mother was outside without a seat. Pushing his hunger down, he sat as straight and tall as he could, taking in the ring that had been laid out in the arena.

Someone tapped him on the shoulder. It was Nicomedes, flanked by two servants. "And what may I ask do you think you're doing, boy?" the man asked.

"I'm sorry, sir," Damien said, standing. "Is this your seat?"

Nicomedes laughed. "No, son. My seat is up there." He pointed to one of the balconies directly over the arena's stage. "So is yours, Damien of Attica. Come with me."

The old man offered his hand and Damien took it. He was led away from the crowd to a private hallway, empty of other people and blessedly free of their overwhelming stench.

"See? This is better, isn't it?" Nicomedes asked, plucking an olive from one of the servant's trays and popping it into his mouth. "Come this way."

After ascending a stone staircase, they arrived at an arched entryway walled off by curtains. Two other servants pulled them back, revealing wooden tables laden with trays of fish, bread, cheese, olives, and roasted meat.

"Yes, much better," Nicomedes said.

Damien chose a seat closest to the balcony's edge. It was lushly upholstered, softer than his bed. He eyeballed the feast surrounding him and swallowed hard, his mouth watering.

Nicomedes put his hands on the railing and peered down at the crowd. "I find a good match is enjoyed so much more when one has a full belly," he said.

Damien's eyes widened.

"Well? What are you waiting for? Eat, boy!"

Damien jumped out of his chair and ran to the table. He didn't know what to grab first but eventually settled on a chicken leg drizzled in honey. It was still as hot as if it had just been pulled from the fire. He sank his teeth into it, the

juices scorching his lips. He didn't care, slurping the drip-
pings from his fingers and stuffing the meat into his mouth.
The servants fanned the food with palm fronds to keep the
flies at bay, their eyes lowered to the floor.

Holding out a silver chalice, Nicodemes chuckled. A
servant with a pitcher of wine stepped forward to fill it and
bowed. Damien found room in his mouth to cram in a
wedge of sheep's cheese and began the work of chewing it
all down to something he could manage to swallow.

"Get used to this, young man," Nicomedes said. "Your
life will be soon be filled with everything your heart wants.
Good food and wine. A home with servants. In a few years
you'll have a wife. And many women besides. All the things
money can buy."

Damien had moved on to a tray of roasted lamb chops,
relishing the hot fat that ringed the meat, a delicacy for a
boy whose mother used it to make candles on the farm.

"It's starting, boy. Come sit."

Damien obeyed, holding the chop in a greasy fist. He
gazed down into the arena, at the insects swarming over the
heads of the unwashed men below, and bit off another
chunk of meat.

A tunic-clad man carrying a horn under his arm walked
to the center of the ring. He put the instrument to his lips,
sounded it, and the crowd went silent.

"We assemble today as tribute to Zeus, mightiest of all
the gods!" he announced to the crowd. "We submit in
homage a contest between two men, who battle for glory in
his honor!"

The Announcer pointed to his left.

"Milo of Croton!"

The crowd broke into cheers as Milo strode into the
arena, nude but for the laurel wreath nestled on his scalp.

He faced the masses, his muscles gleaming with sweat in the afternoon heat. Drinking in the adulation, Milo clapped his hands and slapped his shoulders.

The announcer held up a hand, and the cheering died down. "Leon, of Attica!"

The crowd erupted as Leon walked in, also wearing nothing other than his laurel crown. He flexed his arms and pounded his chest, then bowed to the ten-story-tall statue of Zeus that towered over the arena's stage. Damien rushed to the balcony, cupping his hands to his mouth and shouting as loud as he could.

"Papa! Papa!"

Of course the arena was too loud for Leon to hear him, not that he would have looked to the balcony in search of his face. Assuming Damien was down on the floor with the rest of the mob, he shielded his eyes from the sun as he peered into it, looking for him.

"Papa! Up here! Papa!"

"He can't hear you, my boy," Nicomedes said, draining his cup. "But he knows you're watching."

Something in Nicomedes's tone made Damien look at him. The old man wore a strange smile, as if he were harboring a secret.

"No matter what happens down there," the old man said, "your father is a great man who loves you very, very much. You and your mother. What he does today he does for you."

Two boys ran into the ring, each carrying baskets filled with gypsum powder. They set one before Milo and then Leon, bowed to the statue of Zeus, and scurried off.

The two wrestlers dipped their giant hands into the powder and shoveled it over their backs and necks. It clung to the sweat on their skin, and they were soon transformed into living statues. They dumped the last of it over their heads and rubbed it over their faces and into their hair. They then faced each other. The announcer gestured to the center of the ring, and Leon and Milo took their positions. The two men glowered at each other, awaiting the signal to start the contest.

"Improvise, adapt, and overcome," the announcer intoned, and then sounded the horn to start the match.

The crowd went wild as Leon and Milo charged at each other, their arms immediately tying up, each man fighting for control. They grappled like this for a few seconds. When Milo took a step forward, the slightest bit off balance, Leon swooped one of his long arms behind his knees, snatched them up, and the two men went to the ground.

The roar in the stadium was deafening as the wrestlers writhed before the statue of Zeus in the noonday sun. Damien was stunned to hear his father's name chanted below.

"*Le-on! Le-on!*"

Damien joined them, pumping his fist in the air.

"*Le-on! Le-on!*"

Nicomedes didn't join him in his cheers. He only observed, stroking his chin.

Leon lost control of Milo, who made it back to standing. Nicomedes cheered, pounding the edge of the balcony with satisfaction.

The old man's joy dissipated when Leon reached out and again snatched Milo behind a knee, bringing him back down. He grabbed his thigh, jamming his other hand under the smaller man's armpit, then rose to his feet, lifting Milo of Croton off the ground. Leon spared a second to look up at the statue of Zeus before using his whole weight to slam Milo into the dirt and fall squarely on top of him.

The announcer's reappearance sent the stadium into a frenzy. The match could be over, right there and then, if Milo yielded. As Leon gripped his opponent's legs with one arm and pressed against his chest with the other, it appeared there could be no other outcome.

Milo flailed his arms, desperately trying to maneuver out of his position. Leon grabbed one and wrapped it across his opponent's chest, effectively tying him down with his own limbs.

"Do you yield?" the announcer shouted.

Milo, face creased in pain, slapped his palm on the ground.

Nicomedes hurled his goblet of wine against the wall as the stadium erupted in cheers. Damien didn't know where to look: down at his father, who was helping the bested Milo back to his feet, or to Nicomedes, who paced the balcony, his fists balled in rage.

"The victor and your Olympic champion, Leon of Attica!" the announcer shouted, raising Leon's arm in the air.

Damien waved his arms over his head, hoping to catch his father's eye, when he was spun around, Nicomedes's red face inches from his.

"You. *Out!*"

When Damien didn't move, Nicomedes's skin went another shade darker as he pointed to the balcony's exit.

"Get him out of here! Now! Before I have you all whipped!"

The servants rushed forward, pulling Damien away from Nicomedes and dragging him toward the curtains. Damien didn't put up a fight as they unceremoniously led him down the stairs and back through the private hallway, the crowd growing louder with each step. Once they reached the general commons, they pushed Damien back into the heat and stink.

Outside, he searched the steps for his mother. Upon seeing Euthalia, he ran toward her. She in turn broke from the circle of women she'd been standing with and ran up the steps.

"For whom do they cheer, Damien?" she called out. "Tell me!"

Mother and son reunited, gripping each other's hands.

"Papa," Damien said, breathless. "They cheer for Papa. He is champion of the world."

## 32

*Logging Trail, New Mexico Territory; November 1855*

"Oh, Lord," Josie said. "Stop."

"Call it out, Josie," Damien replied.

"Up ahead. See that pine there, split by lightning? Just to the left?"

It was fletching, white hen feathers on the end of an arrow shaft. They were positioned at such an angle that the arrowhead was either stuck in an animal of some kind or a man. Damien was betting on the latter.

"Stay here, Josie. I'll take a look."

Damien got down off the Morgan, withdrawing a pistol in his right hand and holding the bowie knife in his left. Josie raised her rifle high and swept the barrel over the woods ahead.

The coyote pack crept along in the treeline, organized for a kill. Even the jaybirds above took Damien's cue, going silent.

"It's a man," Josie whispered. "I see his hat."

The situation became clear as he approached the split pine. Four armed men were dead: three pierced by arrows;

the fourth by a tomahawk blade to the spine, just below his neck. One hadn't expired fast enough for whoever had put an arrow in him and had been bludgeoned to death. Something about the method of execution and the ornate handle of the tomahawk struck Damien as familiar. When he understood what had happened, he holstered his pistol.

"Injuns!" Josie hissed.

"Not Injuns," Damien said in his full voice. "*Injun*. You can lower that rifle."

"The hell I will!" Josie said.

"Igashu!" Damien called out. "I know it's you! Come out and show yourself!"

Grinning, Igashu emerged from behind a thicket of trees, a heavy war club in his hand.

"I *tricked* you," Igashu said, laughing. "You were tricked."

Damien could only shake his head. "Couldn't help yourself, could you, friend?" he asked.

Igashu shrugged and opened his arms. They embraced, slapping each other on the back.

"Should I give you two a moment alone for this touching reunion between long-lost sweethearts?" Josie asked from atop the Trotter.

"I'm being rude and I apologize," Damien said. "Josie, this is Igashu. He's a Navajo from the pueblo southeast of Santa Fe."

"How do you do, sir?" Josie said. "Pleasure to meet you."

One of the men with an arrow in his chest groaned. Raising the war club high, Igashu stalked over to him. Josie barely had time to turn her head away before the Navajo brought it swiftly against the side of the man's head, caving in the skull. He hovered over his body, waiting to see if he would move again.

"Don't think he's getting up from that one, friend."

Igashu pointed up the trail. "Greeley," he said.

"Yeah, I know it," Damien replied.

"Three miles," Igashu continued. "No other path. Many men. Many guns. Cannon."

"A regular fortress is what it is," Damien said.

"Yes. *Fortress*. Good word."

"If that's true, we'll be dead long before we ever get to him," Josie said.

"Couldn't agree more," Damien replied. "We try to take him head on, they'll have killed themselves a woman, a Navajo, and a white man some used to call 'Sergeant.' They'll have a couple dozen coyote pelts too. Make blankets out of 'em for the winter."

Damien put his fingers in his mouth and whistled sharply. The coyotes came running, tongues and tails wagging.

Igashu yanked his tomahawk out of the dead man's back and brandished it at them. Shaking his head, Damien reached out and gripped his friend's arm. He crouched to the ground and the coyotes sniffed and licked his hands.

Igashu pointed at Damien. "Chindi," he said firmly. "Chindi."

"What's he sayin'?" Josie asked. "Chin-what?"

"Chindi," Damien replied. "Little nickname his people gave me."

"What's it mean?"

"Oh, hard to specify its exact translation. Closest thing to our tongue would be 'wise one,' I suppose. 'Wise man.' Something like that."

Igashu glared at Damien from among the coyotes.

"I don't think that's what it means, by the looks of him," Josie said.

"Sure it does," Damien said, heading to the Morgan.

Igashu whistled, and his Paint came galloping down the hill, hidden until now. A few moments later, the trio rode forward up the trail, the coyotes bringing up the rear.

## 33

*Outside Athens, Greece; the Month of Hekatombaion; 437 BC*

Neither Damien nor Euthalia understood Leon's silence as he maneuvered their cart through the streets, away from the stadium. He'd just proven himself the world's greatest wrestler but appeared as though he had lost the match. Euthalia brushed the chalk out of her husband's hair as the mule pulled their wagon through the dirt.

"You should be happy," she said.

"I'm just tired, dearest, is all," Leon replied. "Very tired."

"Papa bested Milo of Croton in less than a minute, Mama!" Damien called out from the back. "The crowd chanted his name!"

"See there? You've made yourself a hero to your son," Euthalia said, wiping powder out of her husband's ear. "Now your wife wants to see a smile on that handsome face of yours, and by the gods you will give her one."

Leon did as asked.

"There! Much better!" Euthalia grabbed his wrist and pulled his arm high in the air.

"Leon of Attica, champion of the world!" she yelled.

"Leon of Attica!" Damien repeated, standing in the back of the cart. Passersby pointed as they rode through the city. Soon they were cheering, Leon's name again filling the air.

---

That next morning, Euthalia was on her hands and knees scrubbing the floor when the sound of an approaching horse brought her to her feet. She struggled to a standing position and opened the door, revealing a primly dressed young man, who bowed to her.

"Greetings, dear lady. I am Solon of Athens," he said. "Blessings to you and the gods who watch over this house."

"And to you," Euthalia said.

"I come at the behest of the good Nicomedes. I am his servant and carry a message for your husband, the exalted Leon of Attica."

"He's working in the field. Please come in."

Solon again bowed and walked inside the family room.

"One moment," Euthalia said, and looked to the open back door. In the distance she saw Leon leading their horse through the manure as Damien followed, steadying the plow.

"Leon! You have a visitor!"

A minute or two later, father and son entered to find Solon standing at attention. "Greetings, Leon of Attica. It is my honor to be in your most esteemed presence. I am Solon of Athens. Blessings to you and the gods who watch over this house."

"And to you," Leon said.

Damien noticed his father seemed ill at ease.

"I come with word from my master, Nicomedes," Solon continued. "He wishes to celebrate your wondrous victory with a sacrifice of his fatted calf in the Olympian Temple. He requests your presence tomorrow just after sunup, if that is agreeable."

"Dear, how wonderful!" Euthalia said. "And may Damien join, too?"

"No," Leon said. "I will go alone."

"You will attend then?" Solon asked.

"Of course," Leon replied. "Give your master my thanks and our family's best wishes."

"I will give him your message, great Leon, champion of Athens," Solon said, bowing. "Master will be most pleased."

Euthalia opened the door for the servant. The family watched from the doorway as he mounted a horse fitted with an ornate dress saddle, no doubt one from Nicomedes's legendary stables.

When Solon disappeared around the bend at the end of the road, Damien tugged at his father's sleeve. "Papa, why can't I go with you?" he asked.

"Because there is much to do here," Leon said. "Summer will be over soon."

He hurried out the back door. Concerned, Euthalia and Damien stared after him. As he stepped outside, his next words came in a shout.

"Back to work, boy!"

Damien ran after him, leaving Euthalia to watch as they headed back to the fields. Something was wrong with her husband. She resumed her scrubbing, worried thoughts racing through her head.

The next morning, she had breakfast ready before dawn: a spread of bread and olives and cheese. Leon walked through the family room, cinching the belt on his tunic, his eyes roaming over the food.

"Dearest, you shouldn't have."

"Nonsense," she said. "I will not have you ride to Athens on an empty stomach. Not today of all days."

"Lower your voice, Euthalia. You'll wake Damien."

She pulled out a chair and pointed to the seat. Giving in, Leon sat. He tore off a piece of bread and took a bite, his gaze far away.

Euthalia sat across from him. "Leon."

"Hmm?"

"*Leon.*"

Her tone snapped him out of his trance. "I'm sorry, dearest. What is it?"

"I ask the same of you," Euthalia replied. "You've been moping since yesterday. Why? I don't understand. Neither does Damien. You are an Olympic champion. You will be handed an olive branch before a statue of Zeus—may he be blessed. And yet there is no smile, no joy in that face of yours. Tell me why. Right now."

Leon set down his bread and rubbed his temples. "Nicomedes came here two weeks ago while you and Damien slept. He sat in that chair as you are now and asked me to throw the match."

"Throw the match?" she asked. "What does that mean?"

"Lose."

"Leon! You should have told me! Why on earth would he ask such a thing?"

"So he could bet against me," he continued. "The odds of Milo besting me were a thousand to one, maybe more.

My losing would have made many men very rich...as it would have our family. We stood to gain a fortune."

"Not at the expense of your honor! Not Leon of Attica! Not ever!" Euthalia shouted. Damien's footsteps padded down the hall.

"No, dearest. And that is why I refused," Leon said, reaching out and taking his wife's hands. "I never would disgrace this family before the gods. You know that."

Damien rubbed the sleep out of his eyes and squinted in the predawn darkness. "Mama, why are you yelling?"

Leon shook his head at Euthalia.

"It was nothing, sweetheart," she told her son. "I'm just so excited for Papa's big day today. See? I set out something to eat. Sit with us."

Damien did so, picking an olive out of a bowl as Leon pushed back from the table. "I will see you both later this afternoon," he said. "Damien, we already are behind with our chores. I want the hay stacked as I showed you yesterday. All of it, by the time I get home."

"Yes, Papa."

"Good boy."

Euthalia followed Leon as he went outside.

"Tell him nothing of what I told you," Leon said, hitching the family's donkey to a cart. "He is too young to understand such things."

"I won't," Euthalia replied, her face creased with concern.

"I will be back soon." Leon yanked on the donkey's bridle. It lurched forward, and the cart's wheels began to turn.

Euthalia waited until he had rounded the bend at the end of the road before going back inside to their son.

Leon didn't return that afternoon. Not long after sunset, Euthalia panicked.

Damien did his best to soothe her, assure her he would be home in the morning. The cart's front right wheel had been coming loose of late, and they hadn't had time to fix it. Surely it had finally broken down, and Leon was at a farm somewhere near Athens repairing it. Euthalia made Damien promise they would walk the road to Athens in the morning to meet him halfway. Damien didn't see the sense in the plan, but refusing the idea would have made her even more hysterical than she was, so he agreed.

They sat at the table waiting for the sun to rise. When it finally did, Euthalia tied up a bundle of bread and olives for their journey. Damien had just pulled on his sandals when he heard the familiar creaking of a wooden cart's wheels outside.

"He's here! Thank the gods!" Euthalia cried, running for the door. She threw it open, but when she saw what was coming up the path, she screamed.

Damien's blood rushed to his head as he ran after her. Euthalia already was halfway to the cart, which wasn't yoked to their donkey but to the horse Solon of Athens had arrived on the day prior. The new rider was a serious man who didn't look at either of them.

The rider reached back and pulled up a tarp, allowing mother and son to view Leon's corpse resting on a bed of straw. Euthalia gripped the edges of the cart, her ear-splitting shrieks echoing across the fields.

"*Leon!*" she screamed, climbing on top of her husband's body. "*Leon!*"

Damien went numb as he took in the absolute stillness

of his father's corpse. Leon was naked from the waist up, large gashes in the flesh between his ribs. Damien could see inside the chest, at the waxy crimson organs exposed by the edge of a blade. Dark coagulated blood caked his father's pale torso, which now coated Euthalia's hands as they violently shook her husband, as though Leon were merely in a deep sleep and slow to wake.

The rider dismounted and walked to the back of the cart. He gripped the body by the ankles and dragged him off the hay and onto the ground. When Leon's head hit it with a loud crack, Euthalia collapsed into the dirt.

---

They buried him on the farm, under a cypress tree.

Euthalia retreated into herself, spending many days afterward sitting at the table, staring out the window. Damien did his best to keep up with the chores but didn't possess the strength or know-how to properly tend to everything. When it came time for the fall harvest, fully half of the wheat was left to rot. What could be salvaged was sold, the rest disappearing under a layer of frost and eventually a foot of snow.

Euthalia and Damien shuttered the farm for the winter, Leon's body beneath the frozen ground.

She started coughing not long after that first snowfall. By the time the second one came, she was bedridden, spitting dark fluids into a bucket Damien faithfully changed beside her bed. Soon his mother was delirious with fever, calling out Leon's name as Damien pressed linens soaked in snow across her forehead. She held on for many weeks like this, even showing signs of improvement as spring began its thaw.

One evening, as Damien sat by her bed, Euthalia reached out to him. He took her hand in his, the skin hot to the touch in a house that was cold, even with a fire glowing in the hearth.

"Damien," she managed, "I'm going to sleep now."

"Okay, Mama," Damien replied, kissing her forehead. "Good night."

He pulled the thin blanket up to her chin and put himself to bed. He slept unusually well that night and awoke to realize he hadn't heard his mother's cough, a constant in the house for the past three months. He walked down the short hallway to her room to check to see if she was awake.

Euthalia's arm dangled off the side of the bed, her lips parted, eyes open and unblinking. It was the second dead body Damien had ever seen, although it wouldn't be his last.

---

The ground was frozen, so Damien built a pyre, the way his father had shown him the winter of his grandfather's passing years earlier. Although he had been much younger then, he remembered everything, remembered how much wood had to be burned before the body was reduced to ashes. He swore he would do right by his father's memory and send his mother back to the gods.

Damien lit the fires as the moon rose. He had split the last of their wood to build the altar on which she now rested, her skin already turning black with putrescence. Damien pulled his tunic over his face as the winds picked up and the pyre exploded into a fireball, orange and red sparks swirling around him. As they did, a sadness he'd never known before consumed him, and he wept.

He was alone now, an orphan. He stood his ground as the flames burned his mother's body to cinders, never once looking away. The fire lasted through half the night, and only when he was sure the job was done did he allow himself to leave and go back into the house.

He slept much of the next day, awaking to the same empty feeling in the center of his chest, a hollowness that never would quite leave him. He stepped outside into the afternoon light, ash now falling instead of snow.

Damien used a branch to sift through the pieces of bone. He saw the cypress tree across the field, reached down, and filled his hands with her remains. He then sprinkled them around its roots. He wanted to say something, a prayer maybe, but no words came to mind. Instead he walked back to the house and paused along the way to bring the ax used to chop the wood that had cremated his mother back inside. The blade had cracked with overuse, and now he would have to fix it.

He placed the ax on the table where the family had sat that last morning they'd all been together. The crack went nearly clean through and was sure to break the next time it was swung. His father hadn't taught him how to forge steel before he had died, leaving Damien with no clue how to repair it. When he picked it up, it easily snapped in two.

Damien sat like this for a while, dejected. The ax had broken in such a way that one half resembled a hunting blade, thick and blunt at the bottom, pointed and razor sharp at the top. He turned it over in his hands for a while, watching the edge glint in the sun.

That night he made himself a bindle of what little food was left in the house. He wrapped the broken ax blade in his father's spare tunic, which hadn't been removed from its drawer since his passing. The next morning Damien cinched it all with rope and threw it over his back, setting out into the chilly spring air and down the road, looking over his shoulder once more at the small stone farmhouse where he had been born and raised.

He knew he would never see it again.

## 34

*Logging Trail, New Mexico Territory; November 1855*

The trio spent a cold night camped a safe distance from the trail, not daring to make a fire. At sundown the coyotes had left their side, off on a hunt. Igashu chewed on the end of his unlit pipe while Josie tended to the horses, loosening their bridles and walking behind them as they combed the forest floor for sustenance. Damien was content to read his book by the moonlight, pausing occasionally to take a spoonful of cold beans.

"What'cha reading?" Josie asked.

"Book by a Mr. Walt Whitman," Damien replied.

"What's it about?"

"A man brought down by drink."

"There's plenty of those," Josie said.

"Yes, ma'am. There sure are. Beans?" Damien offered.

"Not hungry."

Damien squinted in the darkness at Igashu and slapped his book closed. "Igashu. Beans?"

Igashu shook his head.

"Friend, you've been chewing on that pipe with a

mournful expression since sundown. You want a smoke that bad, head on out a distance and spark a flame. You're making me anxious for a puff, and I don't even smoke."

Igashu pulled the pipe from his lips and responded in Navajo, his tone curt.

"That's not on me. You're here of your own volition," Damien retorted.

"How'd you two meet anyway?" Josie interjected. "You never said."

"That's a book in itself," Damien replied. "Let's just say Igashu and I traveled in the same circles. Or, to put it more succinctly, we found ourselves after the same men. Rather than compete, we joined forces, as it suited our mutual interests."

"Didn't mean to pry," Josie said. "Just curious."

Damien nodded. "We're an odd pair. I know it."

A quiet descended on the camp for a while, Damien reading, Josie leading the horses through the trees in search of better forage. Igashu had just wrapped himself in a thick blanket for bed when the horses bolted back through the camp, nearly trampling them. Josie was close behind, running backward and frantically waving her hands.

"Back! Back, you!" she shouted.

Damien leapt to his feet, whipping the Colts out of their holsters, ready for anything. Igashu came his side, tomahawk in hand.

"How many?" Damien asked.

"Just him!" Josie shouted. The thing she pointed to was barely visible, its features outlined by the moonlight.

The black bear crept forward, ears low, pupils dilated. It settled on Damien, who holstered his weapons. "Stay back, you two. Just stand still," he instructed, then walked toward the bear, hands at his sides.

"Be careful!" Josie hollered.

Agitated, Igashu shouted in Navajo.

"I'm all right. Just stay there," Damien said.

When he was a few feet away, the bear sat down on its haunches and bowed its head. Damien placed a hand on its back and gently stroked its thick fur.

"I'll be damned," Josie said. "I will just be damned. What's that word again? Chin something?"

"Chindi," Igashu said.

"Right. That. I'm starting to understand its meaning."

"Aw, he just wants to come with is all," Damien said.

The bear lumbered into the camp on Damien's heel. Josie and Igashu both took a protective step back.

"Oh, he won't hurt you. He's friendly," Damien assured them. "Least he is to us."

The bear went to Damien's horse blanket and flopped across it on its belly.

"Guess I'll go get those horses back," Damien said.

"No, you stay here with your new pet," Josie replied.

"I told you. He's friendly."

"You two are a coupla kissin' cousins, to that I will attest," she said. "His feelings for me and your friend here is what I'm not so sure about. Come on, Igashu. Let's try to corral those ponies."

Igashu followed her, not taking his eyes off the bear. Damien got to the ground and lay his head against the beast as though it were a giant pillow.

"Don't take it personal," he said, reaching over his head and scratching its fur. "You'll all be thick as thieves come morning."

Josie and Igashu returned a short while later, horses in tow. They settled in for the night, the bear snoring loudly.

"Never thought I'd say this, but I prefer sleeping among coyotes," Josie said.

———

Josie opened her eyes. What she awoke to made her think she might still be asleep and dreaming. Igashu was also awake, his neck craned up to the trees. Damien was lying against the bear, reading his book.

Every branch of every tree as far as she could see was filled with birds. Crows, jays, sparrows, grackles, owls, hawks. Even a vulture had found a perch. They chirped and crowed and chattered, the branches bending under their collective weight.

"Let me finish this paragraph and we'll get a move on," Damien said. "Not like I haven't read this a thousand times of course."

"Jesus me," Josie said. "Look at 'em!"

"Guess they figured we needed reinforcements," Damien said matter-of-factly. "Can't say I disagree."

Just as he closed the book, the whine of canines echoed across the mountain and the bear's ears went back, a growl rising in its throat.

"You hush up," Damien said. "They're with us."

The coyotes reappeared among the pines, now joined in equal numbers by gray wolves, animals twice their size.

"Regular army is what we are now, by golly," Josie said.

"Takes an army to fight an army," said Damien. "Something tells me Isaac Greeley and I are going to remake each other's acquaintance today. Best get to it then."

———

The black bear took the lead through the forest, the birds above causing a downdraft with their wings, the thousands-strong flock fluttering from tree to tree.

"Maybe we should get back to the trail," Josie offered.

"These animals know these woods better than we do," he replied. "Seems there's a back way to Fort Greeley."

"Fort Greeley?" Josie asked. "That what you're calling it?"

"That man puts his name on everything. What else would it be called?"

"You got me there, Mr. Attica."

They rode on until the early afternoon. At one point the animals slowed, as did the birds, twittering and screeching above.

"We're close," Damien said. "See where those trees start to thin there?"

Igashu spoke a few words in Navajo and Damien nodded.

"Igashu wants to scout ahead. If it's the fort, he'll give us the signal."

"What's the signal?" Josie asked.

"Bird call."

Josie gestured above her head. "And you're going to hear this bird call how, exactly?"

"Good point," Damien said.

He looked up into the trees and put a finger to his lips. The birds fell silent.

"Thing is maybe one day I'll have grandkids," Josie said, "and I'll tell them about all this and they'll send me to the nuthouse."

Igashu rode ahead, pulling his ax out of the saddle ties and disappearing among the trees. Damien and Josie sat silently with the birds. Minutes passed, and then they heard the perfect replica of an owl hoot.

"That's Igashu," Damien said, and eased the Morgan forward.

As they approached, Igashu lay flat on his stomach, overlooking a ridge. Damien and Josie dismounted their horses and crouched beside him. Igashu pointed to the valley below.

At least a hundred men were laboring at Fort Greeley. Pine trees stripped of their bark had been erected in a circle around the camp, forming a wall between the men and the surrounding forest. Heavy cannons pointed outward, gunpowder kegs and musket balls stacked nearby. A two-story log cabin stood on the highest point, overseeing all.

"Who the hell does he think he is?" Josie said. "Santa Anna himself?"

As if on cue, the front door to the cabin opened and Isaac Greeley walked out onto his porch, a glass of whiskey in hand.

"Speak of the Devil," Josie continued. "Looks to be havin' himself a fine time."

"Most of these men were in the Sixth Mounted Company," Damien said.

"How you figure?"

"'Cause I was its sergeant."

"Hold on a second," Josie said. "You *know* these men?"

"Some of 'em, yeah," Damien replied, and pointed them out to her. "That's Petey Ailes by the fire. Lost most of his teeth in a bar fight outside Mexico City. That tall drink of water not far from Greeley is Billy McGonnigal. They snatched his hide right off the boat from Ireland. Didn't even make it to the end of the dock, so he says. War made him crazy. I'll kill him first. He'll consider it a favor, I expect."

"Kill him first?" Josie asked. "You think you're just gonna ride down there and get to shootin'?"

"No. You'll go down first, hollering up a storm. Create a diversion," Damien told her.

"The hell I will!"

"Thought you said you were here to back my play."

"Back your play, yes. Court suicide, no."

Damien shook his head. "Don't worry. They aren't going to kill you. First woman they've seen in months, they'll be too dumbfounded to shoot." Damien took Josie's hand in his. "Just speak from your heart. Give 'em a what for."

Josie surveyed the valley of soldiers and cannons. "I'm scared, Damien, and ashamed to find myself admitting it."

"Josie, wanting to turn away from this out of self-preservation isn't fear. It's wisdom."

"It's cowardly."

"You're no coward, Josephina Llewelyn," Damien assured her. "You're a good person who never wanted any part of this violence. That's what I'm here for. All I need from you is to ride on down there. You'll be just fine; you have my word. Do it for your pa."

"And what will you and Igashu be doing?" Josie pointed to the bear, the wolves, the coyotes, and the thousands of birds in the forest, all of which were watching patiently. "And all them, for that matter?"

Damien smiled, his green eyes sparkling in the afternoon light. "You'll find out when it happens."

## 35

*Athens, Greece; the Month of Hekatombaion; 437 BC*

A benevolent grocer took pity on the young boy in the street clutching a tunic. The white-haired man came from around his stall of fruits and vegetables and got to one knee. He put his hand on the boy's shoulder and pointed to a magnificent home at the top of a hill overlooking the city.

"That's Master Nicomedes's house up there, boy," he said.

"Thank you," Damien replied.

"Are you looking for work? Is that it?"

"Yes, sir."

"You have any experience with horses? Mucking stalls? Baling hay?"

"Yes, sir."

"Master Nicomedes has the finest horses in all of Greece," the grocer said. "They'll find a use for you, I'm sure."

"Thank you, sir."

Damien continued down the city street.

"And boy!"

He turned back to the grocer.

"Use the back entrance, not the front. Back's for servants."

"Thank you, sir."

"Go with the gods, child."

"And you, sir," Damien said, and hurried up the road.

---

It took the rest of the day for Damien to reach Nicomedes's estate, a sprawling piece of property overlooking a valley of manicured grass. Upon arriving at the stone gate, he was greeted by a tall broad-shouldered man with a dagger on his hip. He glared down at Damien and waved his hand as if to say, *Leave*.

"I'm looking for work, sir. Where is the servants' entrance?"

"Be gone with you," the man said.

"I've mucked stalls and baled hay for many a master. Where are the stables, sir?"

The big man pointed down a hill. Torchlight illuminated the gateway to acres of land designed to keep horses, surrounded by a wooden fence.

"Thank you, sir."

Unlike the main house, the stables were unguarded. Damien crawled through the slats in the wooden gate and walked the path to the stalls, practicing the story he had concocted on his long journey to Athens.

A woman wrapped in a shawl brushed a white stallion's mane. Damien went to her.

"Excuse me," he said.

The woman turned to him, clearly startled. Her skin was

a deep brown from days in the sun, her cheeks bearing the heavy scars of ritualistic mutilation.

"Never come upon someone like that, child!" she scolded him in a thick Syrian accent.

"I apologize," Damien said. "Are you who I should speak to about working in the master's stables?"

"And who are you, child?" the woman asked.

"Eryx of Croton," Damien lied. "And what is your name, good lady?"

"I am Rasha. Who sent you here?"

"I was summoned by Master Nicomedes," Damien continued. "I am to work as his stable boy."

"I've never heard of you," Rasha said, crouching and giving Damien a once-over. Now that she was closer, he saw her left eye was clouded and blind.

"I am the son of Milo," Damien said. "Our family is poor and in need of bread. The good Master Nicomedes has shown mercy on us."

"You are Milo's son."

"Yes, lady."

"The wrestler. The...*loser*."

"Yes, lady."

"And your family is starving? Is this true?"

"Yes, lady."

"Don't call me 'lady.' I am a slave to this house."

Rasha dropped her brush in a bucket of water and slapped the horse on its rear, sending it back into the stables. She plucked a small bindle of valerian root out of her cleavage, stuck it in her lip, and chewed it over while glaring up at the big house on the hill.

"That your family should starve is monstrous," she finally said.

"We won't now that I am here to serve the master," Damien replied.

"Yes. The Master," she said, spitting into the mud. "He who must be served."

Clutching his father's tunic to his chest, Damien pointed up to the house. "Is that where he lives? Up there?"

"Of course, child."

"Where does he sleep?"

"Where does he sleep?" Rasha repeated.

"I mean in that great big house. I've never seen one so big."

"In my country that house is called a village," Rasha said. "It is disgraceful to have so much when many have so little." She pointed to the eastern wing of the compound, which faced the sea. "He sleeps there. So he can rise with the sun."

"And where will I sleep?" Damien asked.

"In the stables. In the hay. Come."

Damien sat in the corner of an empty stall, chewing a crust of salt bread in the darkness, grateful for Rasha's charity. He'd run out of food two days earlier.

She appeared at the stall's door with a torch in her hand, surprised to find him awake. "We rise before dawn. Sleep, child."

"I will."

"In the morning I will take you to Solon. He's the bastard who really runs this place. You will answer to him, not to me. I am just a slave."

"Yes, you said," Damien replied.

"Good night."

"Good night."

Rasha continued down the stalls, horses neighing at her footfalls. Damien stood and peered around the door.

"Rasha?"

Her good eye met his, the torchlight illuminating her scars.

"Yes?"

"Thank you for the bread, lady."

"You're welcome, boy. Now sleep."

When he was sure she was gone, Damien went back for his father's tunic. He unwrapped it and removed the ax blade.

There was enough moonlight for him to find the path up to the main house. He tiptoed up the staircase that led to the eastern wing, the blade secured in his tunic's belt. He dared not make a sound.

The thud of footsteps sent him over the wall, clinging to its edge. The passing guard took no notice of the boy's hands gripping the stone. When Damien was sure the guard had left he pulled himself along the exterior, then up toward the balcony jutting out of the top floor. He arrived wheezing from the effort, fingertips scraped and raw.

Sea breeze blew the curtains surrounding Nicomedes's bedchamber outward, revealing the master, asleep next to a slave girl with scars much like Rasha's. Damien gave a cautious look over the balcony, straining to see any sign of a guard. Spotting no one, he climbed through the window.

His heart was beating so hard and fast he was afraid it would wake Nicomedes. Still, the old man didn't stir, even when Damien climbed onto his bed, raised the ax blade, and slammed it into his chest with every ounce of strength he could muster.

The slave girl screamed as Damien yanked it back out,

dark blood rushing out of the deep gash left behind. Nicomedes gasped, the wound sucking and gurgling as he struggled to take a breath, footsteps and shouting filling the hallways outside the bedchamber door. Damien was dimly aware of it crashing open as he lifted the blade one last time, burying it in Nicomedes's throat, the master's cries ceasing as his vocal cords were cleaved in two. A moment later, Damien was in a large man's grip, then another's, and was tackled to the floor.

---

The trial barely lasted a full morning. Damien sat stone-faced as men in expensive chitons waved their arms and argued over the fate of the murderous child.

Damien's advocate, a slight man with a surprisingly powerful voice, was passionate in his belief that he should be shown mercy, as it was his father's recent murder that had brought him to commit such an unthinkable act. The prosecution argued that suggesting the good Nicomedes was somehow responsible for Leon of Attica's death was preposterous, not to mention slanderous. They went on like this for some time until the head of the court council raised his hand, signaling he had heard enough.

The court ruled that the child would not be executed, would not even be imprisoned. It was rare to have a boy of Damien's tender age charged with murder, and as such, finding any precedent as to what a just punishment might be would prove impossible and a waste of the court's valuable time. Therefore Damien was sentenced to banishment. He would be removed from the city walls, and the Attica farm would be razed, the lands returned to the Athenian government.

"It is so ordered," the councilman intoned, bringing down his gavel.

Several large men led Damien from the court to the city's gates. When they arrived, he was given a hard shove over the line demarcating the city from the rest of the world, sending him to the ground. He picked himself up, bleeding scrapes on both his knees.

"Do not return, upon pain of death," one of the court officers said.

He then walked back into Athens, leaving Damien to his banishment.

## 36

*Fort Greeley, New Mexico Territory; November 1855*

Billy McGonnigal ascended the steps to the cabin with a bottle of whiskey in hand. Greeley sat in a rocking chair, looking out over his valley. McGonnigal uncorked the bottle and refilled his employer's glass.

"Thank you kindly," Greeley said.

"Pleasure, sir," McGonnigal replied in his thick brogue.

"Love the smell of the ponderosas in fall. What about you, Lieutenant?"

"They smell just fine, sir."

"Your men comfortable? How do they find the food?"

"The men were last bivouacked in a canyon just north of Juarez, sir. Little piece of misery, that was. They're happy as fleas in a doghouse to be here, they are. The vittles are as fine as we've ever had."

"Good to hear," Greeley said, sipping his whiskey.

"And if I may, sir... Attica's a deserter. We have as much resolve to see him meet justice as you do."

Greeley drained his glass and set it on the porch with a

smile. "Oh, I doubt that, Lieutenant. Though I do appreciate your enthusiasm for the task."

Greeley stood up and walked among the platoon of soldiers, nodding appreciatively as they went about their work. Something on the hillside caught his attention, and he shaded his eyes, trying to make it out.

It was a woman riding a horse, headed straight for them. And she was carrying a rifle.

"McGonnigal," he called back.

"Sir?" the soldier replied, jogging up to his side. When Greeley pointed to the rider, McGonnigal withdrew his sidearm. "Look lively, lads!"

Josie rode the Trotter down the mountain, the wind whipping through her hair. She held the reins in her left hand, the rifle in her right. The soldiers congregated behind their lieutenant, unsure what to make of her. Pete Ailes raised his rifle and took aim.

"The fuck ya doin', Peter?" McGonnigal shouted.

"She's got a rifle, sir!"

"I can bloody see that, ya tub of guts. Put the fuckin' rifle down."

"Easy boys," Greeley said calmly. "Let her come."

Josie rode into the valley, stopping the horse twenty yards from the soldiers. "Isaac Greeley!" she shouted.

Greeley made his way through the men and emerged at the front, his hand raised. "Present, Miss Llewelyn. Welcome to my humble abode. I only wish I had known you were coming. As you can see, we weren't expecting visitors."

"You killed my father, you dastardly son of a bitch," Josie spat. "I pray you rot in hell!"

"You tell him, sweetheart!" Pete Ailes called out, and the other men laughed. Josie raised her rifle, took aim, and shot Pete in the chest.

He crumpled to the ground, dead. The other soldiers scattered for cover. McGonnigal fired a shot at the Trotter, hitting its flank. The animal reared up, throwing Josie off its back. She hit the ground hard, the breath knocked out of her.

"Cease fire!" Greeley commanded.

The wounded Trotter fled as Josie crawled toward her rifle. When she reached it, a snakeskin boot stepped on her hand.

"Just couldn't stay away, eh?" Greeley said. "I'm flattered. And might I presume Mr. Attica is within the vicinity as well?" He knelt and leaned into Josie's face. "You forget yourself, Miss Llewelyn. Don't you know the only thing between you and certain death these many months has been my benevolence? That all that prevents these barbarians from taking your honor by force is my command? Do you?"

McGonnigal and another soldier dragged her to her feet.

"McGonnigal. Your sidearm."

"Sir." McGonnigal handed Greeley his pistol.

Greeley took a step back and pressed the barrel to Josie's right temple, his eyes searching the hills.

"Attica!" he shouted. "Do you hear me?"

Silence.

"I give you three counts to make your presence known! To face death like a man! Or this woman dies in your stead!"

More silence.

"One! Two!" Greeley cocked the pistol. "Three!"

"He ain't here, you gutless son of a bitch," Josie said.

"Such filthy mouths on you prairie types." Greeley lowered the weapon. "Take her inside."

Josie struggled mightily as McGonnigal wrapped his arms around her and wrestled her toward the cabin.

"Get your goddamn hands off me!" she shouted.

"Permission to strike her, sir?" McGonnigal asked Greeley.

"Go ahead."

McGonnigal twisted Josie around and grabbed her by the throat. "You mind your tongue in this here platoon. You hear me, girlie?" he snarled, then pulled back his free hand into a fist.

Suddenly the birds ascended from the trees, thousands of them, all at once.

McGonnigal and the other soldiers craned their necks, the flock deafening. The birds swirled into one great, black cloud, then fell, diving right for them.

They descended as one, so fast Greeley and his men barely had time to react. Josie broke free of McGonnigal's grip and ran for the hills as the birds tore through the platoon, their beaks and claws ripping into the men's skin, hair, and clothes.

She ran for a thin line of smoke at the top of the hill, the screams of birds and soldiers melding behind her. When she reached the top, she found Igashu stoking a small fire.

"*T'aa shoodi,*" he said, handing over Damien's copy of *Franklin Evans,* half the book now kindling. Josie took over, tearing out pages and feeding the tinder.

Igashu untied a quiver of arrows from the Paint's saddle, the tips thickly coated with resin. He chose one and dipped its point into the flames.

---

The birds ascended back into the clouds, leaving the field full of bloodied, bewildered men. Greeley shoved wounded soldiers out of his way, scurrying for the cover of his cabin. McGonnigal managed to stand, his uniform in tatters.

Then a shot rang out from high in the hills.

"Back in formation!" McGonnigal yelled. "Quickly now!"

The battered soldiers reassembled their firing lines, muskets fanning into position.

"Shot came from up there somewheres!" a soldier named Misko offered.

"Anyone hit?" McGonnigal asked.

"Ailes is down!" Misko said.

"*She* shot him, ya fuckin' gobdaw," McGonnigal replied, and another shot rang out across the valley.

The men's heads swiveled, searching for the source of the gunfire. Panic set in and they broke ranks.

"Hell's bells, we best get to cover!" Misko hollered.

"Quiet! All of you!" McGonnigal ordered. "Shut yer traps! Attica's a crack shot. That ain't him."

The men quieted down and listened.

McGonnigal heard it first, a sound not unlike sand pouring off a shovel. He turned his head to find two leaks in a large barrel of black gunpowder hanging off a wagon a few feet from the platoon, the substance forming a neat pyramid of explosives on the ground below it. The wagon itself was filled with boxes of the dynamite sticks they had used to blast through an acre of mountain rock.

"Oh, my holy God," McGonnigal said.

A Navajo warrior emerged from the treeline and let out a mighty war cry. They all looked to him, then up to the flaming arrow that had just launched off his bow. The arrow traveled through the air in a perfect arc and landed dead center in the pile of gunpowder, igniting well over fifty pounds of US Army–issued TNT.

It exploded into a ball of fire, washing over the soldiers

in a wave and engulfing them in flames. The men dropped and rolled. Everything was consumed, men and grass alike.

Misko stood amid the chaos, ripping off his flaming clothes. Once naked, he pointed up the hillside that led into the valley. The name he shouted froze the blood in McGonnigal's veins.

"*Atticaaaa!*"

Eyes black as midnight, Damien charged into the hellfire. The Morgan's reins were clenched between his teeth, Colt revolvers blazing from each hand. He dropped man after man until the pistols fired dry, then leapt off the horse and landed in a crouch.

Uniform ablaze, McGonnigal raised his rifle. Before he could fire, Damien's bowie was hurtling through the air before landing in the center of the Irishman's forehead. McGonnigal hit the ground already dead, his fresh corpse overtaken by fire.

Damien yanked his blade out of McGonnigal's skull and wiped it clean on the lieutenant's smoldering coat. He ignored the embers catching on his own trousers as he surveyed the bedlam with profound satisfaction.

Soldier after soldier hit the ground aflame. One chose the quicker way, putting a rifle barrel in his mouth and blowing the back of his head out. Their screams were like music to Damien's ears, a symphony of agony he had composed.

*I am singing my song,* he thought.

## 37

*Outside Athens, Greece; the Month of Hekatombaion; 437 BC*

Damien walked into the wilderness with the idea that if he could get to the beach, he would be okay. On a fishing trip a year earlier, his father had built a lean-to out of palm fronds against a rocky cliff. They had made a fire and roasted fish and slept in the warm sand. All he had to do was get to the sea.

The landscape veered south, rocks and scrub brush poking through the soles of his thin sandals. He hadn't eaten since his release from the city jail, and by the look of his surroundings, he wouldn't anytime soon. Hungry as he was, he was grateful for the solitude. Jail had been a chaotic and frightening affair, the stocks populated by madmen.

He spent the first night under a tree, having dug himself a bed out of the earth. He felt safe there, invisible to the world. He rose with the sun and walked until his legs grew weak.

Damien didn't quite trust his eyes when he came upon campfire, smoke wafting out of a grove of trees. As he got closer, the orange glow of the flames outlined other humans around it; then he inhaled the smell of meat.

Cautiously he approached the camp. As he got closer, he spotted two men sitting on logs on either side of the flames, roasting hunks of animal flesh off tree branches.

"Hello," Damien said, his voice cracking. When they didn't look up from their meal, he announced himself again, louder this time. "Hello. My name is Damien. Of Attica."

The men raised their heads. They were heavily bearded and wore animal pelts for clothing. Their hair was long and matted, the taller one's bleached yellow by the sun. The skin not covered by animal hide had been baked into dark, wrinkled leather.

"What's a boy your age doing all the way out here?" the taller one asked. "Or am I dreaming?"

"Maybe he's a satyr," said the shorter one. "Show me those hooves, boy."

Damien slipped his foot out of his sandal.

"He's no satyr, for God's sake," said the taller man. "He's a boy. What's your name again, child?"

"Damien. Of Attica."

"I'm Otus. This here is Tiro."

"Hello," Damien said.

"You out hunting with your father?" Otus asked.

Damien swallowed the lump in his throat and shook his head.

"You out here all by yourself?" Otus continued.

"Yes."

"How is that?" Tiro chimed in. "Athens is nearly a two-day walk from here. You lost?"

"I am banished," Damien replied.

Otus's and Tiro's faces broke into smiles.

"So are we!" Otus shouted.

"He's starving, the poor thing. Look at him," Tiro said.

"You hungry, boy? You want some meat?"

"Please," Damien replied.

"Come then," Tiro said. "Sit."

Damien took a place around the fire. A recently slaughtered deer hung by its neck from a tree, its guts in a flyblown pile. Animal bones littered the camp, skulls and antlers and gnawed-over rib cages. Tiro handed Damien a hunk of meat at the end of a stick.

"Take it, boy. Careful. It's hot."

Damien stuffed the meat into his mouth all at once, making Otus laugh.

"Just like my first days in exile," he snorted, taking a bite of his own food. "I'd have eaten the ass out of a dead donkey had I found one, gods as my witness."

"Both of us have been where you are, Damien," Tiro said, wiping grease out of his beard. "You're among friends now. Eat your fill. There's plenty more."

Damien ate deer meat until he couldn't take another bite. Eventually his eyes grew heavy and he nodded off. Tiro took the stick from his hand and dropped it into the flames.

"Bedtime for you, boy," he said. "We sleep by the fire, most nights. Lay yourself down, eh? Rest your weary head."

Damien did as told, stretching out on the ground a few feet from the campfire. He fell asleep moments later.

---

He woke up in the darkness, barely able to breathe. He was being suffocated under the weight of something, his half-sleeping mind unable to remember where he was. He twisted his head to the hanging deer carcass in the dim light of the campfire. Next came Tiro's voice, inches from his ear.

"Don't be scared, boy. It only hurts like this the first time."

Damien kicked himself out from underneath Tiro. The two men stared at him across the fire, naked.

"Fight if you like, Damien," Tiro said. "I fought too. But if you don't, I promise I can be gentle."

"I thought I was first," Otus said.

"You thought wrong," Tiro replied.

"Over here, boy. Come now."

Damien sprinted from the camp. Tiro panted as he chased him through the brush and tackled him to the ground. Otus soon joined, and the men dragged Damien back to the fire, where they threw him face first into the dirt and pinned him down with their bodies.

Damien cried out as his tunic was ripped off, the men's hands groping at his kicking legs. Tiro managed to pull them apart; Damien reached for a bone by the fire and gripped it tightly. When Tiro's engorged manhood brushed his thigh, he sent it back overhead as hard as he could.

Shrieking, Tiro leapt to his feet and staggered through the camp. The jawbone of a small deer jutted out of his right eye.

Tiro collapsed to his knees, his fingers fluttering around the bone, his left eye turned inward toward the wound.

Otus charged Damien, teeth bared in a snarl.

Damien waited until the man was almost on top of him then stepped to the right. Otus flailed forward and Damien grabbed his wrist, punching up through the man's elbow, the bone snapping in half and puncturing through the flesh. Otus screamed, blood running in thin rivers out of the compound fracture.

Damien jerked Tiro's head back by the hair and pulled his face upward. He yanked the deer bone out of the right eye and jammed it into the left, then grabbed him around the neck.

He and Tiro grappled as Damien twisted his head around as far as he could. When the man's neck snapped, he released his dead body into the dirt.

He wrenched the bone out of the dead man's eye socket and went back for Otus, who was now limping away from the camp, clutching his ruined arm. Damien jammed the sharp end of the bone in the flesh behind Otus's right knee, bringing him down.

Otus reached back and got Damien in a headlock, and they rolled in the dirt. Damien twisted around and secured the man's left ear between his teeth, biting hard and tearing it off his head. Otus released him and Damien went for the largest stone ringing the campfire. He picked it up and brought it down on top of Otus's skull, splitting it.

A dog barked just outside the camp and Damien picked up the deer bone, clutching it tightly.

He held it out in front of him, blood dripping down his face.

"I'll kill you too!" Damien screamed.

A large mastiff emerged from the darkness, barking. Its master materialized from the shadows, dressed in a hooded robe. He pulled it down to reveal a bone-thin face and hair shaved to the scalp. His eyes were dark yellow, the color of the sun just before it slid into the sea.

The hooded man snapped his fingers and the mastiff heeled, now silent.

"Greetings, child," the man said. "My name is Scylax. I come in the name of the great, wise Orpheus—may he be blessed. I am sorry I did not arrive sooner."

Scylax observed what was left of the camp and at the

naked corpses of Tiro and Otus. Damien stepped back, deer bone raised in a fist.

"I mean you no harm," Sclylax continued. "I reside at the Orphic Temple and have been asked to take you there, if you wish to do so. You *are* Damien of Attica, murderer of the villain Nicomedes, are you not?"

Damien nodded.

"Very well then," Scylax said, extending a hand. "Free yourself from exile and follow me."

Damien fainted.

---

"That's the last thing I remember," Damien said.

Praxis and Ignatia sat back in their chairs as Damien set the deer bone on the desk.

"Very good, Damien," Ignatia said. "It's what we needed to hear."

"So I can stay?" Damien asked.

Master Praxis and Ignatia exchanged an uneasy look.

"Damien, Master Praxis and I have taught you everything that we can," Ignatia continued. "You will now be instructed by another master."

"'Now' meaning...when?" Damien asked.

"Tonight," Master Praxis said. "Your teacher awaits you in the Great Round Room inside the temple. Go to him."

Damien was surprised to find tears in his teachers' eyes.

"Goodbye, Damien," Ignatia said.

---

Having never been in the temple after sundown, he struggled to navigate its winding torch-lit halls to the Great

Round Room. When he found it, the doors were propped wide open. Sitting on the stage atop the stone wheel was Scylax, with what looked like an insect crawling over the back of his hand.

"Hello," the monk said without looking at him.

Damien walked down the aisle. He stopped just short of the wheel and bowed respectfully.

"Sit as I do," Scylax instructed.

Damien climbed onto the wheel and folded his legs underneath him. What appeared to be a giant spider wound its way over his teacher's hands. It wasn't a spider, though, as spiders didn't have long tails with a needle-sharp stinger at the end.

"Do you know what this is?" Scylax asked.

"No, Master."

"It is a scorpion. Fascinating creature. Would you like to know the most interesting thing about it?"

"Yes, Master."

"Should it find itself on the losing side of a battle, it will kill itself rather than allow the opponent to emerge victorious."

"Is that true, Master?" Damien asked.

"So they say," Scylax said, and offered the scorpion to Damien.

The boy cupped his hands and received it, his skin prickling as the arachnid's legs poked his flesh.

"You have remembered the night of our first meeting," Scylax continued. "Otherwise you would not be here."

"Why haven't I seen you since then, Master?" Damien asked.

"Because I am a creature of the darkness. Now you too will sleep by day and live by night. As I do." Scylax pointed to the scorpion. "As it does. Do you understand?"

"Yes, Master."

"Look at me, Damien." Damien did so. "When you killed Nicomedes. When you killed those men in the forest. Tell me. How did it make you *feel*?" Scylax asked.

"I...I don't know," Damien mumbled.

"I can't hear you."

"I said I don't know, Master."

"That is a lie," Scylax said. "You know *exactly* how it made you feel. When you plunged a dagger into the old man's heart. When you took the eyes of the pedophile and broke his neck. When you split the other's skull. When they lay there, dead, at your hands." Scylax's yellow eyes bore into Damien's. "*How. Did it make. You feel?*"

Damien swallowed hard, summoned his courage, and looked back into Master Scylax's unblinking gaze. "Good, Master," he whispered. "It felt good."

"That is the truth," Scylax said. "And now our work begins."

## 38

*Fort Greeley, New Mexico Territory; November 1855*

With ruthless efficiency, the wolves and coyotes hunted down the soldiers who had managed to flee. The black bear, less adept at chasing down prey, settled on easier pickings: men immolated and near death. He chose the fattest of the group, ripping open the man's belly with his claws and vigorously tucking into the exposed entrails.

The grass fires were now merely smoldering around Fort Greeley, the balcony burning. Damien stepped over bodies to get to the Morgan. He opened the saddlebag and removed the piano pliers he had acquired at Bennett's Trading Post weeks earlier.

"Told you these would come in handy one day, Bennett," Damien said.

He ascended the steps to the cabin, the porch and roof lighting up like a match as the cinders leapt to it from the grass. He then grabbed the latch of the cabin's front door and pushed it open.

Greeley fired from a derringer pistol, hitting Damien in the right side of his chest. Damien returned fire with his six-shooter, the bullet piercing Greeley's gut. Dropping his weapon, the older man staggered back and fell into a chair.

"Damn it, Greeley," Damien said, placing a hand over his wound. "You just sit there now."

Greeley regarded the bullet hole above his navel in disbelief. Damien stumbled to a seat situated across from him and collapsed onto it. The hole in his chest leaked blood down his ribs. Wincing in pain, he pressed it.

Greeley wiped his mouth with a shaky hand and looked Damien squarely in the eyes. "You know what this godforsaken place would be without my influence?" he asked. "Without my money? It would be Sodom and Gomorrah. Overrun with savages. It would be nothing. *Nothing.*"

"Not nothing," Damien replied. "Just Mexico."

Damien reached into his back pocket, removed the piano pliers, and held them up so Greeley could see them.

"I was going to crucify you, Greeley," Damien said. "That was the plan anyway. Was gonna gather some of this wood you have here and build a cross, then nail you to it. Make a little sign that said GREELEY and hang it over your head, since you like to put your name on everything. I had it all figured in my head, like. Didn't work out that way. How plans go sometimes. 'Such is life,' as Bennett would say." Damien coughed, and swallowed blood. "That church of yours talks about Heaven and hell and Jesus this and Jesus that. Thought maybe you'd like to die like he did, big Christian that you are," he continued. "Thing of it is, Greeley, is that Jesus isn't just some character in a book. He isn't a work of fiction like Franklin Evans, say, or the Ghost of Christmas Past. He was a real person. Name was Joshua bar Joseph. 'Bar' translates to 'son of.' Meaning he was Joshua, son of Joseph. Read that in a book somewhere. He lived in a desert a lot like this one. A good man. When you got up on that pulpit and spoke his name, you defiled his memory."

Damien planted his hand on the chair, and pushed himself to standing.

"You won't speak it again."

He staggered over to Greeley, grabbed him by the throat, and squeezed until the man's lips parted in a gasp for breath.

Damien inserted the pliers and slid them around inside Greeley's foaming mouth, struggling to find purchase. Greeley slapped and clawed, but Damien was relentless. When he achieved the grip he was looking for, his eyes went over black like a lunar eclipse.

Damien ripped Isaac Greeley's tongue out with a loud snap, then tossed the organ onto the floor like the discarded trimmings of a Sunday roast. Greeley let out a strangled howl as blood shot out in a geyser from the back of his throat, Damien pressing his palm over his mouth and sealing it shut with his last bit of strength. He held him like this as the fluid backed up into his lungs. Only when he fully aspirated did he release him, watching the last, convulsing breaths leave his body.

Greeley tipped over out of the chair and onto the floor, dead.

"It is finished," Damien said, and walked out the door.

The cabin collapsed into flames as his boot stepped off the porch. He walked a short distance away from it, then collapsed himself.

A thundercloud formed overhead, and he rested his gaze on it, content. Then the skies opened, extinguishing what fire was left in the valley.

Birds landed in the surrounding grass and hopped over to him. He smiled as they chirped and sang, their curious heads cocking left and right as they looked over his bloodied body.

"Damien!"

It was Josie.

She fell to her knees at his side. Igashu was there too, taking his hand.

"No!" Josie cried. "No!"

"Josie, none of that now."

"Greeley do this? Where is he?"

"Greeley's dead."

"We're gonna get you fixed up, you hear me? You hang on."

"Josie..."

Igashu gently opened Damien's shirt and exposed the gunshot wound. He'd lost a great deal of blood, too much. Josie started to cry.

"Josie, I told you I wouldn't be riding back down this mountain. Meant what I said. You just leave me be. Go on home."

Josie wiped her eyes. "I don't have a home to go back to."

"Then you make a new one," Damien said. "And you forget about me and everything you saw here."

"I can't do that."

"Sure you can. People do it all the time. If people couldn't forget, how could they go on? They do it and so can you."

Damien raised his hand. Igashu grasped it. "*Yá'át'ééh,*" Damien said.

Igashu's eyes brimmed with tears. "*Yá'át'ééh,*" he replied.

Damien looked to Josie, his last breath rattling in his chest. "I'll be right back," he told her, then died.

Igashu threw his head back and let out an anguished cry. Josie wept as the birds soared above their heads, filling the valley with their songs. Igashu reached down and gently closed Damien's lifeless green eyes. He took Josie's hand and they prayed, the clouds parting and revealing the high desert sun. What neither of them knew—what they couldn't possibly know—was that the friend they were praying for already had fallen halfway into hell.

## 39

*Hades, Banks of Acheron*

Damien fell.

His clothes burned away and, not long after, his hair. The skin on his throat opened like a flower, the veins within dry and withered.

He slept, the warm ash-filled air lulling him into dreams about battles in a desert he already was starting to forget. When he stirred, he was still falling, with no ground below, consumed by a void.

He awoke to find himself on a riverbank. He sat up, the ground beneath him ash. An ancient figure with fine white hair cascading down its shoulders watched him with an eyeless face.

Damien stood, staring back into the hollows of its skull. "Who are you?"

"I am Charon," said the figure. "Can you pay?"

Damien looked down at his body, naked but for the tattered remains of a blood-red smock. "I have nothing," he replied.

Charon opened its mouth, lifting a black oily tongue.

"It's usually here," Charon said. "Check."

Damien lifted his tongue and touched it. "I don't understand what I'm looking for."

"A coin," Charon said. "Do you not have one?"

"No. I have nothing. As I said."

"Then I can't take you," Charon said, disappointment in its voice.

"Take me where?"

Charon turned away, to the river behind it.

"Take me where? Tell me. I beg you."

Silent, Charon kept its back to him. Damien asked again and again, but no answer came.

So Damien walked.

He kept the river to his right, having chosen a white rock on the horizon as his destination. But no matter how many steps he took, the rock never grew closer. It sat there, at the edge of everything, maddeningly within reach. Some days Damien walked and some days he ran. After a hundred years had passed, he crawled.

Every day was the same.

One day, a day indistinguishable from the thousands before it, a sound came. It was the first he had heard since his conversation on the riverbank with the thing that called itself Charon. At first he wasn't sure if his mind was playing tricks on him, but it persisted, and the farther he crawled, the closer it got.

It was a slow, steady clap.

Before him was the rock, white as snow. Sitting upon it was a demon, and before her was a pool of clear liquid, the first Damien had seen since the river. All he wanted in the world was a drink from it. He would have done anything to have one.

The demon stopped clapping and laughed in such a way that Damien's brain felt as though it were detaching from the inside of his skull.

"Chindi! Oh, my Chindi!" the demon cried. "You were marvelous! *Marvelous*! I had no idea you would be so entertaining!"

Damien pulled himself to the water's edge and stared at his reflection. Like Charon, he had no eyes, and he could see his own larynx through the gash in his throat. He didn't look at all like what he'd expected. He looked like a living corpse.

"This time we're going to try something different," the demon said. "A little...*twist*. It will make things a bit more difficult for you, but I think you're up to it. In fact, I *know* you are."

Damien cupped his hand in the water, groaning with relief upon realizing it wasn't a mirage. He'd seen many of those on his hundred-year journey and didn't think his sanity could bear another one.

"Uh-uh-uh!" the demon scolded him. "You have something to say first."

"I...do?" Damien asked, his voice a rasp.

The demon tapped at the space just beneath her throat.

Damien yanked a golden chain off his neck. He opened the small cylinder at the end of the necklace, and a slip of parchment fell into his hand. He unfurled it and read the words to the demon, his voice breaking after decades of silence.

"I am but mortal flesh, a child of the gods," he said. "Take pity on me, and allow me to drink from the sacred water."

"Yes, yes, yes. Drink. Drink, chindi! Drink," the demon said, laughing.

"Why do you call me that?" Damien asked.

"Because it amuses me. Now. *Drink.*"

Damien fell back to his knees and did as the demon commanded.

## 40

*Field; Strasbourg, France; March 1945*

Hours before dawn, Sergeant Mike Etheridge used binoculars anyway, sweeping the grassy field for any sign of Clementine. He heard her voice first, the lyrical French accent high and bright.

"Michael!"

"Here!" he called out in the darkness.

Clementine's strawberry-blond hair emerged from the shrubbery, haloed in moonlight. They ran to each other and embraced. Her kiss tasted of stale cigarettes.

"*Mon amour,*" she squealed.

His hat fell off his head and tumbled to the ground as he lifted her off her feet. Others were with her, sticks and leaves crunching beneath their boots.

It was a man, thin and bearded, and a petite white woman. When she spoke unaccented American English, his mouth fell open.

"This him?" the woman asked.

"Yes," Clementine said.

The woman walked up to him and gave him a once-over. She wore a tan military-issued jacket and what he immediately recognized as a parachute pack.

Mike's eyes met hers, bright and green and glinting in the low light of the moon.

"You know how to fly that thing?" she said, eyebrow raised.

Mike turned around to his biplane, the dark-blue paint making it nearly invisible in the night.

"Well, yeah," he said. "'Of course."

"Good," she said, and pointed to the bearded man. "Iggy, where's Benny?"

Iggy, the thin bearded man, pulled what appeared to be a rucksack off his shoulders. The woman took it and cradled it in her arms. Mike could now see it wasn't a rucksack. It was a flamethrower.

"All right, then, Benny," the woman whispered to the weapon, as if addressing a pet. "You ready?"

Clementine gripped Mike's elbow and pulled him around to her. "Get her as far in as you can," she said.

"Get her *where*?" Mike asked.

"Germany," Clementine said, as if it were the most obvious answer in the world.

A thunderhead rumbled in the distance. Mike pulled Clementine back to him, kissed her, and they all ran for the plane.

Mike hopped into the bucket, the plane's body sagging with the weight of the second passenger. She clapped a hand on his shoulder.

"Let's go," he said.

Clementine gripped the propeller and spun it. "Contact!" she yelled, the plane's engine sputtering. "*Bonne chance!*"

Mike steered the biplane right, away from the group and into the dark borders of the grassy field. He felt under his seat and brought up two pairs of aviator goggles. He strapped one around his scalp and held the other pair over his shoulder. The woman snatched them out of his hand.

"High as you can go," she said over the propeller's hum.

Mike gave a thumbs-up. He climbed out of the field, into the stars above. When they leveled out, his passenger exhaled loudly.

"Everything all right there, gal?" he asked.

"Everything's grand," the woman said. "I'm right where I need to be."

A flock of godwits appeared to his right and left, climbing to altitude with the plane. They squawked, tucking their long sticklike legs up into their wings.

"Looks like we've got some visitors," Mike said.

"Yeah," the woman replied from the back. "Guess we do."

He pulled back on the controls, bringing the plane up to five then ten then twenty thousand feet. The birds kept pace, stretching their wings and cruising alongside.

"Let me know when we get there," the woman said. Mike turned around in his seat as she pulled the goggles down over her eyes and closed them behind the glass.

Mike steered the biplane, keeping a wary eye for roving German Luftwaffe. The godwits chirped among themselves, and after a while, the woman snored.

Mike shook his head. Now he had seen everything.

The German border soon loomed below, dimly lit by farmhouse campfires. Mike flew until the hair stood up on the back of his neck. He had flown into Nazi territory far enough.

"Hey," he said. "Girlie."

The woman sat forward, rubbing her eyes under the goggles.

"That's *Lieutenant* to you, Sergeant," the woman said. "Not 'gal.' Not 'girlie.'"

"Say what?" Mike said.

The woman draped her arm over his shoulder, the silver bar on her uniform signifying her rank brushing his cheek.

"*Lieutenant*," she repeated.

"Lieutenant," Mike said, eyeballing it. "Yes ma'am."

"Better. I'll get out here."

He heard the gasoline slosh in the flamethrower's tank as the woman stood in her seat. The godwits twittered and drifted within feet of the biplane's wings, bobbing along in the propeller's downdraft.

"Ask you something, ma'am?" Mike said.

"Go ahead," she said.

"Who *are* you?" Mike asked.

The woman lifted a boot out and dangled it over the ground thousands of feet below.

"Lieutenant, like I said," the woman shouted over the roar of the wind. "Attica."

Mike looked back over his shoulder. She was perched on the edge of the biplane, like a bird about to take flight.

"But you can call me Dee, Sergeant," she continued. "Everybody does."

Dee winked, clutched the flamethrower to her chest, and dove headfirst out of the plane. The godwits slapped their wings against their flanks and dove alongside her. Mike watched as Dee rocketed down into Germany, the blue pilot light within the flamethrower flickering in the night sky until it disappeared along with her and the flock. Eventually her parachute bloomed open, white and round, like the moon above.

"I'll be damned," Mike said, and guided the plane back toward France.

# EPILOGUE

*Los Angeles, California; Present Day*

"And you will return in three...two...one."

Damien opened his eyes with a gasp.

"You're back, Damien," Angela said, reaching out and placing a hand on his knee. "You're back."

He pulled himself up in the chair, shirt soaked with sweat. He glanced at his watch. Almost six hours had passed.

The hypnotherapist stood, cracking her neck and rolling her shoulders, a yellow legal pad filled with scribbling dangling from her hand.

"Great work today," she said, tapping the screen of her phone, stopping the session's recording. "Just great. Really."

Damien wiped his face and steadied himself. He glanced at the top page of the legal pad, words written across it in the long, broad strokes of his therapist's handwriting, illuminated in the pulsating green-blue light.

*00:10   IMMEDIATELY   AGITATED.   1:15   HELL/DE-MON/POOL OF MEMORY RECCURENCE. BALAZARUS (ARMY?) 2:20 IGASHU/BENNETT/ISAAC RECURRENCE.*

*2:00/4:10 GREECE?? ("ANCIENT TIME") DREAM WITHIN A DREAM?? 3:15 NUNNERY/ JOSIE. 5:30-45 FEMALE?*

"Let me get you some water," she said, heading for the kitchen down the hallway.

Damien slid down into his chair, letting the traffic sounds outside bring him into the here and now.

---

*New York City; Present Day*

FBI Agent Aja Arkadia seated herself across from Julie, who was curled up in the corner of her couch, her mother at her side. Aja set her phone on the coffee table and tapped the "record" button on the screen.

"Special Agent Arkadia interview of Julie Hastings. Valerie Hastings, Julie's mother, is also present. Time is ten-thirty a.m.; Tuesday, May seventh."

Julie leaned back in her chair, rubbing her sweaty palms on her jeans.

"I know this is really hard," Aja said.

Julie gripped her mother's hand.

"We need to go over what happened yesterday. In as much detail as you can remember."

"Okay," Julie said, then burst into tears.

Aja had a tissue at the ready and handed it across to her as Julie's mother put her arm around her.

"I'm sorry," Julie said, accepting it.

"Don't be," Aja said.

Julie wiped her eyes and pulled herself up on the couch.

"You said this man's name was John Anderson."

Julie nodded. "Yes."

"And why was this man meeting with Mr. Griggs?"

"Andy...Mr. Griggs...wanted someone to write his auto-biography."

"Okay. And John Anderson was who he hired?"

"Yeah. Well, it was like an interview."

"Describe to me what he looked like."

"I already went over all that with the police."

"Yes, of course. A lot of my questions will overlap what you told the NYPD detectives. We're from different agencies, though. I have to ask my questions too."

"Sorry. That was rude."

"You're not rude at all," Aja said. "You're traumatized."

Julie took a shaky breath.

"Was he white? Black? Hispanic?"

"White. Well, maybe Italian. Or...I don't know."

"Olive skin? Not white, white?"

"Yeah. Sort of like your skin a little actually. You have really nice skin, by the way."

Aja smiled. "Thanks. How tall was he?"

"Maybe six feet. Just under six feet maybe."

"What color were his eyes?"

Julie's forehead creased.

"You don't remember?"

"No, I remember. They were...like yours."

"Like my eyes?" Aja asked.

"Yeah. Like...*just* like yours."

"So they were green?"

"Yeah, but...I mean you literally have the same eyes."

"Same shape?"

"Uh-huh."

"Same relative size?"

"Yeah. It's weird. Sorry."

"Don't be sorry," Aja said. "It'll help the forensic artist."

They talked for another half hour, until Aja heard Julie

begin to fade. She left her card and told the women they would meet again.

---

Aja drove to Pearl and Fifth in her rental car, an SUV she was having trouble navigating in bumper-to-bumper Manhattan traffic. She should have argued for the compact-size car she had requested but hadn't had the energy for it, a decision she now regretted.

She turned on her hazards and stepped out, flashing her badge to the street cop guarding the yellow tape surrounding the crime scene. He lifted the tape for her, and she ducked underneath it, holding up her badge as she made her way through a small army of investigators.

Less than twenty-four hours had passed since Andrew Griggs had been unceremoniously tossed out of his office window and onto the street fifty-two stories below. A tent had been erected over the bloodstains, one Aja now entered, careful to step around the evidence, and addressed the blood tech who was cataloguing the crime scene.

"Was it the fall that killed him?" Aja asked with a straight face.

"Asthma attack," the tech replied without missing a beat.

Aja ducked back out of the tent and looked straight up. She saw the dark void created by the missing glass, the only square on the high-rise not reflecting the Manhattan skyline across from it.

"John Anderson," she said. "You do get around, don't you?"

Gary Foyet, a probationary agent in his late twenties not long out of the academy, approached Aja, a clipboard thick with data printouts in hand.

"Agent Arkadia? Ma'am?"

"Whatcha got, Gary?"

After Aja took the clipboard, Gary pointed out high-lighted strings of numbers. "Phone records show up the same as last time, ma'am. Nothing traceable."

"Well that's wonderful," she said.

"Used a burner. Most big-box retailers carry them. You buy the phone with cash, activate it with a card over the phone. All handled out of some call center in India."

"I know what a burner is, Gary."

"Right. Sorry."

"And his emails?"

"He used a VPN, also like last time. No way to trace his IP."

"Gary?"

"Ma'am?"

"Did you eat something with onions for lunch?"

"I had a hot dog, ma'am."

"Go buy yourself some gum before we get back in the car."

"Yes, ma'am."

Aja straightened in her seat as Supervisory Special Agent Kevin Boxall twirled a pen, thinking.

"What are the other names?" he asked.

"Sir, he's also operated under the aliases Brian Jones, Steve Smith, Greg Johnson, Bill Brown, Jim Williams, and Bob Wilson," Aja replied.

"And now John...?"

"Anderson."

"Common names. Generic. Unmemorable," Boxall said.

"Exactly, sir."

"How did he kill the other six?"

"Stabbing, shooting, bludgeoning, electrocuting, burning, hanging, and now defenestration, sir," Aja replied.

"Defense...what?"

"*Defenestration*. It means throwing someone out of a window."

Boxall smiled. "This is your baby, isn't it, Agent Arkadia?"

"Sir?"

"This case. Keeps you up nights, doesn't it?"

"Yes, sir. It does."

"Can I see the sketch again?"

"Yes, sir."

Aja handed a manila envelope across to Boxall, who pulled out an eight-by-ten color rendering. A slim, handsome man with olive skin and bright-green eyes looked back at him.

"Green eyes," Boxall said. "That's been consistent?"

"Every witness, sir. First thing most of them say when describing him."

"Your eyes are similarly striking, you know. Can I even say that anymore? Well, I just did."

"It's been remarked, sir. Many times."

"And he's not white-white. Hispanic maybe? What's your thinking?"

"Hard to say, sir."

Boxall slid the rendering across to Aja. "And you want to release this to the public."

"Sir, I think we're there. Past there, frankly. He's a serial killer."

"And the murders are all over the place, geographically speaking," Boxall said.

"Yes, sir. A Klansman in Decatur, a pedophile soccer coach in Tucson, a district attorney in Seattle disbarred on corruption charges, an abortion-clinic bombing suspect in Wichita, a corporate lobbyist in DC, a serial rapist in Pittsburgh, and now Andrew Griggs."

"A Wall Street banker," Boxall replied.

"Bureau's been trying to make a fraud case against him for the last ten years," Aja said. "Nothing stuck. He was slick."

"So this guy—John Anderson or whoever he is—goes after *assholes*, for all intents and purposes. Right?"

"They were human beings, sir," she replied. "Murder is murder."

Boxall twirled his pen for a while. "I'll take releasing the sketch under advisement. This is all good work, Agent Arkadia."

"Thank you, sir."

---

Aja stared at her phone in the federal building's courtyard as people streamed through the revolving front doors and into the fading daylight. She always felt melancholy at this time of day, when the light outside turned blue just before sunset.

A pigeon fluttered down off a street lamp and landed at her feet while she scrolled through the transcript of that morning's interview with Julie.

*What color were his eyes? You don't remember?*
*No, I remember. They were...like yours.*
*Like my eyes?*

*Yeah. Like...just like yours.*
*So they were green?*
*Yeah, but...I mean you literally have the same eyes.*
*Same shape?*
*Uh-huh.*
*Same relative size?*
*Yeah. It's weird. Sorry.*

The pigeon flapped its wings, commanding her attention. Aja looked down at it and raised an eyebrow.

*Yes?* Aja asked.

*Forgive me for saying so,* the pigeon replied, *but did you really think you were the only one?*

———

Damien pulled out his phone and checked the time. It was just after 3:00 a.m., and he was wide-awake. He sat on his couch, staring at the glittering Los Angeles skyline, waiting for the mountain lion to arrive.

He had opened every window in the house. If she were going to show up, she would have already. He told himself he'd go back to bed and try to fall asleep again at three-thirty. He again checked the time.

Three-fifteen.

Damien eyed the large plastic bag on his coffee table. It contained a purchase made at the hardware store on his way home from the hypnotherapist's office. The wooden handle was sticking out, and he stood from the couch and grabbed it. He pulled off the plastic and dropped it to the floor.

It was the biggest sledgehammer the store had carried. He hefted its weight then cocked it over his shoulder like a batter at home plate. He swung, grinning at the satisfying *whoosh* it made as it sliced through the air.

An ophthalmologist in Denver named Richard Rumbold had been in the news lately. Rumbold had embarked on a private hunting safari in Zimbabwe, during which he had shot and killed a fourteen-year-old black rhino. The University of Oxford biologists who had been tracking the endangered animal for most of her adult life had named her Gerta, and her death had caused an international outcry. As Rumbold had a legal permit for the hunt, he wasn't expected to face criminal charges.

Damien hadn't had his eyes checked out in years, so he made an appointment with Dr. Rumbold under the name Jack Stone for the following Tuesday afternoon. He would begin his drive from Los Angeles on Monday morning to ensure he'd make it on time.

He again swung the sledgehammer. The grip felt good in his hands.

Damien headed down the hall to his bedroom, where in no time at all he fell into a deep sleep.

His dreams were bad.

# ACKNOWLEDGMENTS

My sweet wife Heather, who unfailingly puts aside her library book long enough to read my pages and ensure I'm not making a fool of myself.

And my great friend Mike Loeffelholz, who is kind enough to read my stuff after his kids have gone to bed and offer me his thoughts and encouragement, often via text message at two o'clock in the morning. Every writer needs a friend like Mike.

# ABOUT THE AUTHOR

Sam Luna lives in a very small apartment in Los Angeles with his patient wife. He spends his free time hiking in Griffith Park and drinking too much iced tea. Much unlike the Orphic Assassin, he has fainted twice at the sight of blood. He invites you to visit his website samlunabooks.com where you can sign up to receive email updates.

Made in the USA
Middletown, DE
16 July 2022